# Amanda Goes to Las Vegas

# Amanda Goes to Las Vegas

## Revised Edition

A novel by Nancy Dick

**Works by Nancy Dick**

Copyright © 2011, 2015 by Nancy Dick

All rights reserved. No part of this book may be reproduced or transmitted in any form or by any means, electronic or mechanical, including photocopying, recording, or by any information storage and retrieval system, without permission in writing from the copyright owner.

Inset cover photo courtesy of iStock
a subsidiary of Getty Images

For more information: please email questions to
worksbynancydick@gmail.com

This is a work of fiction. Names, characters, places and incidents either are the product of the author's imagination or are used fictitiously, and any resemblance to any actual persons, living or dead, events, or locales is entirely coincidental.

ISBN—978-0-9961402-0-1

**PRINTED IN THE UNITED STATES OF AMERICA**

This book is dedicated to love, family and marriage—and to happily ever after.

# Chapter 1

The hot spring air brushed along Amanda's young skin. Her dark hair moved with every breeze. It was the same breeze that brushed against the walls of the house she lived in. And, it was the same breeze that moved back and forth making its way through the branches of the trees in the orchard that grew behind the house. She loved sitting on the porch steps during this time of year. She almost thought she could see little green sprouts in the farm field in front of her that would become autumn's corn crop. The last snow fall melted away a few months back. The world was alive again.

Monday would come awfully quick as once again the yellow school bus passed in front of the driveway in front of the farm for her to board to go to school. The school bus knew where to stop since there was a wrought iron arch over the driveway leading to the farm that said: Miller Farm. But, today was Saturday. Her school work had been done on Friday in the upstairs bedroom at the desk by the window overlooking the farm. She sat there for hours, in fact years, looking out at the farm she loved.

The farm belonged to her father, Thomas Miller, who was a well known local farmer. The farm was located about an hour's drive from Indianapolis, IN. Her mother's name was Carolyn Miller, a housewife. She was needed at the farm to help raise her and her brother Tommy who was 10 years older than her. She missed him but, could hardly remember his face since she was barely seven years old when she last saw him. He ran away from the farm right out of high school to join the military. He never came back. And, to this day, her father was bitter about it since it was his dream for his only son to inherit the farm that had been in the family for many generations.

Secretly, her father wished for her to be his second son to help run the farm. She secretly wished she was born a male as well. She longed to please her father. She loved him so. And, she tried to help with the chores like a man....so, did her mother. But, her father had to rely on hired farmhands to do the bulk of the work since she had to take off for school.

She considered school to be like a full-time job since so much of her time was spent away from the farm. And, so much of her evenings were spent on schoolwork for her teachers. She never knew really why she had to go to school anyway if she was only going to be a farmer's wife which was her father's wish for her. He drummed it into her head ever since Tommy left the farm since it was dad's big dream for the farm's survival. How was the farm going to make it if something happened to dad she wondered? A tear fell down her right cheek as she brushed it away since she never wanted her father to know she worried too. After all, this was home.

And, she had loved her grandfather with her whole heart. His name was James Miller. He was a good farmer man who loved working the land as far back as Amanda could remember. He was buried in the family cemetery in the back of the farm that was a family tradition since they lived in such a rural setting. They had to keep the family farm in the family since Grandpa Jim was buried here. He belonged no other place but, with his family.

Now, the nearest city was a good 20 miles away. And, it had a feed store & hardware; a gas station; a supermarket; and a chatterbox restaurant that was popular with the locals. But, coming to this city was a huge event for her parents for their supplies because it at least was a city that they could count on once a month or so. Rarely did Amanda ever come to the city since her parents took care of family business when she was off at school during the day.

However, her mother always surprised her with a gift from the city sitting on her pillow.

Amanda's mother always bought Amanda a barrette for her hair. Her mother always got together to brush her only daughter's long hair and admire the new barrette in her hair. It was also a time for her mother to tell her daughter about growing up to be a lady. Amanda loved the attention her mother poured onto her. She didn't want to break her heart that she had already learned this in school. This was important to her mother. Amanda liked telling her mother how much they looked alike. "You think so dear" said Carolyn as she smiled into the bedroom mirror while she finished up brushing her daughter's hair.

Her mother had nothing in life but, dad and this farm with Tommy gone which her mother mourned like he had passed away since she never got to see him for years. Amanda was all she had. Now, Amanda was 18 years old and about to graduate from high school. She worried that even if she moved after graduation from here to a neighboring farm, would the loss of her here for her mother feel the same?

Her mother was growing old from working on the farm. The veins on her hands were raised like her dad from years of hard labor on the farm. Her skin was weathered some from years in the sun working the field—though her mother was a "sun hat freak" to protect herself from skin cancer from the sun. She tried anyway to be youthful. She wanted her husband to appreciate her youthfulness all the same as if she was the young girl he had fallen in love with years ago when she was just 18 years old and newly graduated from high school—which was the same school that Amanda now attended.

Amanda wondered if she would end up like her mother. She certainly wanted a faithful hard working man like her dad. But, where was such a person for her? She attended a small school. Everyone was dating and taken. Next year was the high school prom. Since she lived so rural, after high school graduation, the number of young unmarried men that she associated would be even less than it is now thought Amanda.

She wondered if she should ask her dad to be her prom date. He would smile from ear-to-ear to do that. But, she would be embarrassed to not have a real date—though pleased at the same time about herself to ask her dad she loved to tag along. It would be a memory either way that would last a lifetime. Everyone remembers their high school prom forever thought Amanda. But, for now, she could afford to enjoy the day and quit worrying about the future.

Amanda attended parochial school that was located about 30 minutes outside of Indianapolis,

IN. Her teachers were nuns that lived in the convent next to the school. Her class had about 80 students. She loved the Catholic Church. She was baptized there. Her mother was raised a Catholic and dad intended to respect his wife's religious ways. But, he was born into the Baptist Church— and so were his father and his father before.

So, she and Tommy had to attend both churches on Sunday which both parents saw no conflict in both religious traditions since the Miller's family regularly invited both the Baptist ministers and the Roman Catholic priests to Sunday supper on the family farm. Carolyn's good cooking was well known to the locals. And, no one ever left the Miller farm empty handed from Carolyn's kitchen. The memory of eating supper in Tom and Carolyn's kitchen left a lasting memory as they loaded up the back of the family truck with gifts from the farm for their guests to take home.

If it wasn't a basket of tomatoes from the family's personal garden behind the house, then it was a box of apples from the orchard for fresh eating or cooking. In the late autumn, there was always an extra bag of ears of corn from the farm fields for the Reverends to take home for good eating. Everyone there knew that there was nothing that compared for good taste than home grown food because of the extra freshness. So, it was an absolute pleasure for guests to come to dinner at the Miller Farm. It was well known to the locals.

Carolyn grew tomatoes that she enjoyed watching them grow from yellow blossoms into bright red tomatoes for eating. She also grew beets; both green and yellow onions; carrots; cabbage; and potatoes. She also grew watermelons and cantaloupe with black plastic under the fruit to keep them from rotting from sitting directly in the soil as they ripened in the sun. And, she also had a strawberry patch that began as white blossoms which grew into bright red strawberries for eating. Carolyn grew giant yellow sunflowers next to her garden that was known to attract bees to help pollinate her garden. Carolyn liked the uniqueness of these flowers since they liked to move the head of the flower toward the sun which was amazing in itself to see to her.

Behind Carolyn's garden was the apple orchard always filled with pink blossoms in the spring that turned into bright red apples sprinkled with sweet spots that made the mouth water in anticipation of eating such an apple during autumn harvest. The sweet spots were a sign for the Millers of the extra sweetness of their fruit from the orchard. Grandpa Jim always went on when he was alive that he wanted to be buried next to these apple trees so he could look at then when he was in heaven with Jesus. He loved them so.

Amanda's parents though very kind to her, when it came to dinner guests at the family farm, they were from the "children shouldn't be heard" crowd. Therefore, it was a time for Amanda to retreat quickly after eating, to her bedroom to do her schoolwork while adults talked Bible together and how God had blessed them with the farm.

It was Amanda's time anyway to read her own Bible. And, she did manage to impress everyone at the table with a Bible quote or two—which made her father smile though saying nothing. He sat at the head of the table as he deserved from his hard work.

Her mother always told Amanda that she would have "her time" when she was a wife and mother to express herself at the dinner table. Amanda knew what she was talking about. Her mother helped to bring in the crops just like dad in all kinds of weather just like dad when they were short handed. Amanda mostly went to school in comparison.

They had a bright red and white trimmed barn which was the traditional colors for barns in the area. However, this barn protected the family tractor from the elements of snow and rain—and the hot sun in the summer. It was the traditional green and yellow John Deere tractor that you could see for miles away since it was so bright in color.

Dad needed the tractor to work the brown soil covered here and there with snow in the late spring to plant his corn seeds from the feed store in rows. The soil had sat all winter fermenting the fertilizer worked into the soil in the autumn season before they had a hard freeze that froze the ground solid from ice and snow until the spring thaw.

So now, we are another weekend closer to Amanda's high school graduation. She would be 18 years old then. Her parents had expectations of her to help save the farm and the family's traditions. But, how? And, who would she end up being married to that it would help out the situation? She hoped he was handsome and a nice man. At that, she smiled to herself.

She thought she would take a walk to her grandfather's grave to talk to him about things as she was prone to do. She had beliefs that he could hear her. The Catholic Church had taught her that she could pray to the angels and saints in heaven who would help her. Amanda had patron saints that she loved for that reason. But, certainly God loved her Grandpa Jim as a saint in heaven with Him, too.

Amanda cried as she walked to her grandfather's headstone. She carried a pink rose in her right hand that she had pinched off from the rosebush that grew in front of the house in honor of St. Theresa of the Little Flower. Her belief was that those who prayed to the saint had pink roses from the heaven as a sign of prayers answered. St. Theresa was a favorite saint of her mother. She laid the single rose at the foot of her grandfather's headstone.

Amanda sat in front of the headstone. She touched the embossed letters that said her grandfather's name. She felt the coolness of the marble under her fingers. Her father himself had carried the headstone to the gravesite in his black pickup truck to honor his much cherished father's life.

Amanda began her conversation: "It's me again, grandpa. It's Amanda, your granddaughter. I hope you are happy in heaven with God and all. I do. And, I don't mean to disturb your day in heaven and all. But, your granddaughter here on earth has only a short time to go before graduating from high school. Mom and dad want me to marry someone that will live on the farm to help it survive and stay in the family. I probably will marry and leave the farm. I don't even have a boyfriend. The only boys I know mostly are from the high school which is a long drive from here. And, these boys have girlfriends already. And, mom and dad are getting older each year. Tommy is gone as you know. And, what will happen here if I have to move away or anything happens to dad? What am I going to do, grandpa?"

"My grades are good at school. I try hard to please mom and dad. I do. I miss my brother, Tommy. I wish he never had left the farm. We wouldn't be suffering so much, now. He could have married and lived on the farm here forever like dad wanted from him with his wife and kids—hopefully many sons who would be farmhands for the farm. Now, there is only me to help, who is unlikely to bring a husband here who is a farmer to do this for the family since he is likely to be running his own father's farm as his father needed to pass on the farm as you did for your son. What will I do, grandpa? I know that you will know the answer for me. Will you talk to Jesus in heaven for me?" Amanda sat in front of the headstone and cried with her hands in front of her face covering her eyes.

Then, Amanda smiled slightly drying her tears with her shirt to hide them from her parents. "Look, grandpa" said Amanda pointing to the apple orchard. "The apple trees in the orchard are in bloom. They are budding now. The winter was hard this year with many feet of snow. The roads barely got plowed for the school bus to get through with one lane of width to pass through on the road. But,

I made it, anyway. And, some of the trees have light pink flowers that soon will turn into the apples you loved to look at growing. You can't walk through the orchard anymore like you did—except in thoughts from heaven. But, soon as you know, the tree branches will grow heavy with bright red apples with yellow blushes and sweet spots that you said was 'God's freckles for apples' " said Amanda.

"Remember me to Jesus" said Amanda to her grandfather. With that, she headed back to the house to open up the screen door on the front porch. She could see from the kitchen window her mother preparing dinner from the family garden. Her family only bought dairy like eggs, butter, and milk and meat from the supermarket. The family had a freezer plugged in that they kept on the enclosed back porch in the back of the house. There was no heat on that porch so things stayed very cold there in the winter. And, there were windows all the way around on the porch so that her mother could open the windows to ventilate and cool the freezer when it wanted to sweat as it was prone to have little beads of moisture on the outside door as it strained to keep everything cool on hot summer days that rarely but, still happened when the temperature ranged as high as 100 degrees. That was the days of making homemade lemonade to drink which was about the only fruit her mother bought at the store since citrus fruit can't grow outdoors in the Midwest because of the colder winters. Otherwise, her mother would probably try to grow that, too. Her mother tried to grow every vegetable known to man that could grow in that region that the family could possibly like to eat. And, she was good at growing cantaloupes and miniature watermelons, too. And, she did love her strawberry patch with the miniature white blossoms in the spring that grew into sweet strawberries that she pinched off to slice into the family's breakfast bowl to eat at the dusk together on the front porch. Her mother was quite "fun" with her food all the time.

She even grew her own pumpkins to put on the porch for Halloween. The farm house was too rural for neighborhood kids to come by for trick-or-treating. But, that never stopped her mother. And, she did manage to make her own pumpkin pies from the pulp of the Halloween pumpkins. And she did save her pumpkins for the revival hoedown in the barn. And, from the apples grown on the farm, she knew how to make her own apple juice and apple cupcakes—which was made of yellow cake batter with miniature pieces of apple folded in here and there. Dad opened up a long table along one side of the barn. Here, he cooked hot dogs and hamburgers with buns and condiments on the table for people to put donations in a jar to help the Baptist Church that her father grew up in. That would take place in the beginning of every October. And then, the driveway was filled with many pick-up trucks and farmers' cars on the Miller farm as local farmers visited wearing cowboy hats and kerchiefs around their neck while their wives wore square dance dresses to celebrate the annual church revival.

After that came the minister's sermon about loving God and thanking God for the farmers' harvest and many "Amens" from the audience. Then, the promenade began with the men on one side of the barn in a row and the women on the other side of the barn in anticipation of grabbing their dance partner in a moment of glee and barn stomping square dancing together. And, Amanda always knew that once they bowed to each other, the dancing would go on into the night. And even the Reverend would smile and dance with his wife which was rare since Baptist folks aren't generally prone to like dancing for religious reasons her grandfather had said. But, this was different. Everyone was celebrating God and all. He had done good. And, the Reverend would drive away with a good tithe from the folk to help his church he wouldn't otherwise have.

And, to the delight of Amanda, the local farmers brought out their fiddles and guitars for "pickin' and grinnin' " as they liked to call it. And, even Amanda was allowed to sing a tune or two in front of the crowd. And, she had sung a tune or two in both the Catholic and Baptist church on Sunday as long as it was for God. Then, it was OK with her parents with Amanda singing in front of an audience. She loved her music so. Her father didn't know that it was truly a great love of hers to sing for the audience and God. Her eyes turned bright blue in happiness when she sang. And, she liked her father and mother smiling proudly at their only daughter's singing.

But, then it was back to farm chores the next day. And, before that, her mother would come to Amanda's bedroom to say how proud she was of her. She would brush her only daughter's hair. And, she would take the barrettes carefully from the vanity's drawer that had roses carved into the wood handles to put in Amanda's hair. Outside, Amanda could hear the trees' leaves rustling in the breeze. She knew in the sun the next day she would see a bouquet of reds, greens, yellows, browns, and oranges in the branches before they all fell to the ground before the first winter snow. And, she could also hear the sun dried tan colored corn husks rustling in the wind waiting on her father to plow under the last of them into the ground for general composting and fertilizing the soil before the first big snow fall where the soil can no longer be worked.

Amanda counted the days now before high school graduation since it was so close. She looked at her picture of St. Mary, the mother of Perpetual Help and The Sacred Heart of Jesus. They were the Holy Family as she was taught. She hoped they would help her in her time of need. She knew how to say the rosary—and well. And, she knew how to use her Holy Water as she was taught in the Catholic Church. And, she loved her Baptist Church as well since it belonged to her family with her grandfather teaching her to love God as he was taught. She loved her grandfather. Therefore, she trusted and believed everything he taught her especially about God. He was her grandfather after all. He loved her: "I love you, grandpa" said Amanda. "I sang today for Jesus. I hope you like it from heaven" said Amanda softly. And with that, she went to sleep knowing she would have to wake up early to the sound of her mother's cooking in the kitchen. Her school bag, with her school assignments were already at the front door. So she wouldn't forget them. Too long a drive to return home to get them. Her mother would pack a lunch for her to take to school with her. Amanda believed it was OK for women to work. But, secretly she was glad to have her mother full-time to herself and her father. They needed her. And, their memories would last a lifetime for her to take to her own family's traditions.

Someday wasn't very far away now. Amanda looked forward to this day but, feared it mightily as well. How could she have as wonderful a family as her parents have been? She would have to pray to God to help her. That's for sure. He would help her.

# Chapter 2

Amanda pinned her graduation corsage to her dress. Her prom dress was white with sequins at the bosom. Her parents wouldn't let her show much bosom with the Catholic nuns and priests there. After all, they said that they give up their marital sex and relationships to devote their life to God. Father Louis who was the head pastor was the chaperon at the school gym. The school hired a band from Indianapolis, IN to play songs to dance by.

Amanda got a boy to agree to pretend to have a date with her there. He really had a steady girlfriend named Gloria who was a stacked blonde he adored and planned to marry right after graduation. But, he was a "good ol' Joe" of a friend to Amanda. In fact, his name was Joe. He would have some dances with her at the prom if she asked.

But, her date was a farm hand named John who tagged along who was in his 20s who looked youngish. So, he would pass alright. He was tall with sandy brown hair and blue eyes. His arms had real strength to them, so, she wasn't quite sure whether he was trying to dance or bailing hay on the farm since he danced so mechanically.

Her father laughed a lot silently. Amanda could see his chest go up and down watching it all. But, finally her real date which was her father had the last dance with her before the lights dimmed for the last time. In the end, Amanda was glad for her dates because as the classmates gathered to make out to celebrate graduation, she knew she wasn't ready for that yet. And, she didn't know when she would be. But, she knew the point of her life wasn't "make out city" but, for a real family for herself out of the deal.

But, her father had a ball tonight watching the nuns which he wanted to talk about to his wife when he got home. Sister Catherine, for one thing, accepted a date from a male classmate to be nice since he didn't have one. Her father took a photo of her with her corsage pinned to her habit near her left shoulder.

This must have been an experience for her. She was quite a pretty nun with big brown eyes and a big smile to go with it. All nuns looked pretty in Amanda's opinion anyway. But, she was especially so since she was such a young nun who was only in her 20s. She danced the night away to each song played by the band with her date. She joked how handsome her date was. She said how beautiful her corsage was. She accepted a goodnight kiss on her left cheek from her date. And, she shook hands in front of the classmates before she retired within the convent doors. She said that she would press the corsage for a memory—and thanked her date for the invite.

In the meantime, within the school gym, Roger constantly paraded himself in front of the nuns taking off his tie to ask if they would write him up for not wearing his tie since it was the school uniform for him. Three weeks from this day was graduation day. The nuns took it in good humor. They obliged him with a complimentary demerit to his delight. He held it to his chest like it was gold.

Then, the nuns told Roger to get out of the gym. Then, they as quickly changed their mind. They called after him. "Roger, Roger" they said.

"Roger and out" said Roger as he stormed out of the gym. They thought that he had left the prom. They were horrified as they sat in the bleachers.

He was really only outside to have a smoke. He as quickly returned with a handful of pink carnations that he had stashed in the car. He gave one pink carnation to each nun. He truly loved the nuns who were his schoolteachers.

He got on one knee and serenaded a love song to the nuns. He told them that he loved them and would miss them. And, he threw them a kiss. He said that they were his "favorite girls."

The nuns smiled at Roger. They knew in their heart, he was an absolute favorite child of theirs in the classroom. The nuns thought that he was very romantic. And, they talked among themselves what a fine husband he would be someday. They threw back kisses at Roger from the bleachers which Amanda could tell he liked very much by how big he smiled. He was a success with the nuns that day.

And her father was allowed to take a group photo of the nuns posing together with their flowers. Nuns were "big love people." That's for sure. They loved their children that they taught as their own.


Amanda and her father with John headed back home after the prom. "You were the prettiest one there by a long shot" said Amanda's father.

"Thanks dad" said Amanda. She appreciated the compliment considering the fact that she didn't even have a real date for her own prom. But, she knew her mother would appreciate these high school prom photos. Her mother would put them in her scrapbook for a keepsake of her only daughter. Amanda thought her mother would probably cry that her only daughter was growing up so quickly.

This time, both her parents were sitting in the audience of the school gym. One by one, the high school graduates were called to the podium to accept their diploma. Her parents were taking Amanda to a real restaurant after to celebrate the occasion. Some of the local farming families with her parents had planned a surprise party later in the day at the farm with gifts for Amanda. They had watched her grow up before their eyes.

They wanted to thank her for being there all those years for them with singing for their special occasions that were sacred to them such as weddings and anniversaries and such since there was no one else to do that for them being they lived so rural. And, they wouldn't of have wanted anyone else, anyway. That's for sure. They loved their little Amanda Miller. And, they wanted to express their affection.

Back at the farm, Amanda's parents laughed with Amanda as everyone danced into the night.

Amanda accepted requests to sing one last time for all they knew. She opened presents one after another. Her father gave her a jewelry box made by him with pink roses carved on the top. And, her mother gave her a set of custom-made guitar picks that said "Amanda Miller" on each one that she was thrilled to have. She cried when she opened them and hugged her mother to thank her.

She had 15 graduation gifts. Her thank you cards that she would give to her family that was really the neighboring farmers she had loved while growing up included the following gifts as she had showed her parents:

1. Aunt Helen—a black hand-knitted sweater with brown flowers.
2. Uncle Carl, husband of Aunt Helen—a small black suitcase.
3. Aunt Mary—a black hand-knitted scarf with black sequins.
4. Uncle Mike, her husband—a pin with gold roses that had real gold in it which made him proud.
5. Aunt Rita—a black handmade shirt and jacket for work.
6. Uncle Melvin, her husband—a handmade keychain that said "Home is where the heart is." And, on the other side, it said "Remember home always." It was shaped like a house made of wood. There were hand painted black letters with a red heart painted on it also that he drew himself.
7. Aunt Jenny—a recipe book with all the basics.
8. Uncle Willie—a wood rosary with the scent of real roses to honor
St. Theresa.
9. Aunt Carol—a handmade black cloth purse that could be used as a shoulder bag.
10. Uncle Gregory—a handmade wind chime made of pastel shades of pink, green, and blue to put in the window to reflect the light into the room.
11. Aunt Marie—a handmade black shawl to put over her shoulders.

12. Uncle John—a framed photo of the Miller Farm.
And,
13. old Uncle Anthony—who lived by himself since his wife died—a birthstone ring she had worn of a real pearl that he wanted Amanda to at least have as a memory of his wife since she loved Amanda so.

But, she got no word from Tommy, her brother yet. She worried. A few days later, a package came wrapped in brown paper that said from Thomas Miller to Amanda Miller. Inside the package was a framed photo of himself "in uniform standing in front of a jet he flew himself" he said. He said that he missed her and her parents and the farm. But, he said that he couldn't come back home yet. "The country needed him" he said.

"And, he had a job to do" he said.

Amanda put the framed photo to her chest. She now had a memory of what her brother looked like. Her eyes watered up as she said under her breath. "I love you, brother. And, I miss you, too. It has been such a long time since I've seen you. Our mom and dad have been waiting to see you for such a long time" said Amanda. The family had stayed in touch with him through the years.

He said that he had a graduation present for her. She saw a small gift wrapped with blue paper and a silver bow on top. She opened it to find a music book of Church hymns with a dedication written inside that said:

To my only sister, Amanda
Congratulations on your graduation from high school.
Love, your brother, Tommy

She ran into the house to show her mother what she had gotten in the mail from Tommy. She knew that her mother would probably cry to see a photo of her only son looking so adult and being so far away from home.

# Chapter 3

Amanda slept and slept after graduation. She didn't know what to do with herself. She had no job. She had no boyfriend or prospects of one. And living so rural, she didn't really know where to find one.

Tommy, her brother, wasn't coming back home to run the farm any time soon. He sometimes was even in another country for the military.

And, on top of it, her high school classmates were long gone as far as she was concerned. She would never see them again—at least not at school anymore. That part of her life was over.

She would try to run the farm. But, she knew her father wouldn't let her. He wanted her to get married like her mother like an adult woman. "Great" she thought. She didn't even have a car of her own. "So, how in the heck was she going to get out of here" she thought to herself. And, where would she go in the first place?

And, what was going to happen to the farm and her parents and herself? thought Amanda. She wouldn't be able to bear it if she caused her family to lose the farm that belonged to her Grandpa Jim. "He was buried here for Christ sake" thought Amanda. "Who else could possibly own it but, her family?" said Amanda.

She had to do something she thought. But, what? She had said that over and over again. I had better pray really hard. "I am so afraid God. Please help me" said Amanda.

Her mother served supper as usual in silence. Her parents gave knowing glances at each other. Amanda knew they had words together.

Amanda retreated to the glider on the front porch in the dark by herself for hours. Then, she walked in the dark with a flashlight to sit in the cornfield among the stalks of corn in neat rows that her father had planted for late autumn harvest. She walked in the dark to the apple orchard. She touched the branches of the trees touching each tree like she was holding them in her arms. "I have to save you, you know...This is my father's life work—and my grandfather" said Amanda. Amanda cried so hard that it felt it lasted for hours. She returned to her room to sit in the dark in the rocker by the window looking out at the farm. "I love you, farm. I love you. I love you. And, if I leave you to save you doesn't mean that I don't love you," said Amanda. It sounded silly to say, but, it was what was in Amanda's heart as she knew.

Her father always had an instinct about his only daughter. In the morning, Tom, the farmer by profession and family tradition determined to help his daughter since he could see her suffering. Her hair wasn't combed. She barely ate. And, she slept almost non-stop when she wasn't wandering around the farm at God knows what hours or sitting by herself in the dark.

"What am I to do to help you, kid?" said Tom to his daughter, Amanda. "You can't stay like this forever, you know. The farm will eventually perish this way. I'm not going to stay young forever, you know. Your mother worries about you and cries into the night. She isn't sleeping well. She is going to get sick on me this way. She can't keep on this way. And neither can you," continued Tom.

"Let's put our heads together to help this family and my only daughter. OK?" said Tom, the father now. He kissed his daughter on the forehead and put his arms around her as they sat on the glider together looking at the stars. Without the city lights around, the sky was pitch black. And, the stars seemed to be out tonight by the thousands like row after row of endless stars among the soft light of the moon with a single cloud that had decided to embrace the moon in the night. Her father was her favorite man on earth she thought as they sat there. I doubt that I will ever find a man half as good as this man to marry, but, God gave me a good father at least thought Amanda.

Finally, Amanda spoke to her father: "Dad, can you buy me a car, so I can get a job? I've been thinking that I won't be able to find a husband, a good farmer boy and hopefully with brothers who are farmers sitting here."

"Sounds like a plan. Let's do that. Tomorrow, we will go out to buy Amanda a car. Let me tell your mother" said Amanda's dad. And, so with that they shook hands to "seal the deal" as was a family tradition.

"I want you up by 6 AM tomorrow. No more sleeping in until noon for my daughter. Right?" said Tom Miller. "Right" said Amanda. And, for the first time since graduation Amanda brushed her hair; put out some fresh clean clothes to go into the city; and most importantly set the alarm clock. An outing to the big city was always a special event for the Millers anyway since they so rarely got to travel into the city. It was one of the reasons that Amanda thought that they were so close. The three of them had to stick together as family. It was all they had. And, Amanda was secretly glad that God blessed her to be born into such a family.

It was a lot of hard work to live like this instead of being just a city kid. But, who would pass up a chance to live on a farm if they really knew all the love there was to share with a farm life? The love of the farm was so much part of her heart. If she could she would hug every tree on the farm and kiss every cornstalk that her father grew and every star that shined above her family's farm so faithfully.

Around her life was nothing but, endless farm after farm down the country roads. It was a miracle that the neighboring farmers had stayed so close to the Millers. It was probably, in part, a desire to reach out to each other because of their aloneness—regardless of how precious and special their life was to have inherited their livelihood from birth. But, it was also mighty lonely and downright dangerous at times to not at least be friendly enough to create a family among the farmers in times of need with bitter cold weather and all—and struggles to tame the farm field enough to get a good yield.

Farmers were good at helping each other even if they hadn't seen each other for a good long time between. In the winter, it was hunkering down to get through the blowing snow. In the warm weather, it was all work and a labor of love for the farm and family of the past, now, and the future.

Tomorrow, Amanda and her father were getting a car. She doubted that she would get a new one. Anything that drove down the road would be "great" thought Amanda. It would be her first car that she ever had. She couldn't take her father's only pickup truck. He needed that for the farm and to get into the city for himself and her mother. She was glad to have such a good father.

Her father drove Amanda to Indianapolis, IN to a used car lot. She had a drivers' license since she was 16 years old from drivers ed from high school. So, she was ready to go. Her father had let her drive on the farm from time to time already.

She had chosen a used car that was dark blue. She didn't know its make and model. She just knew that it was hers. She saw her dad give the man $450.00 for it. It had sat on the lot for two years. So, if she wanted it, it was hers. "Anything to get rid of it" said the car dealer.

Amanda thought that she had died and went to heaven. She drove the car. It worked. So, it was good enough. She was comfortable behind the wheel. In fact, it was rather "zippy" thought Amanda.

Her dad told her to sit inside the pickup truck while he finalized the deal with the used car dealer. He was good with things like this. "And, she wasn't" he thought.

A few minutes later, he handed her the keys and the title in her name. "Congratulations, kid. You are the proud owner of your first car" her father said. She shook his hand as was the family tradition. "I will take care of it well" promised Amanda to her dad.

"Drive in front of me. I want to make sure it drives OK first before you drive it on the road by yourself" said Amanda's dad. She said "OK." And, so they did.

She kissed her father's cheek before starting the motor of the car and belting in. And, then slowly and carefully, Amanda drove home to show her mother her new car. "Even if it was 'used', it was new to her" thought Amanda.

She pulled into the driveway at home. Her mother must have heard them. She came running out the door. "Well, I'll be. It looks like a fine vehicle to me, daughter" said Amanda's mother.

"It sure is. And, dad bought it just for me. He is going to look under the hood before I drive it by myself" said Amanda to her mother proudly.

"Good idea. But, first, let's have lunch. I have it warming on the stove. I knew somehow that you would be home soon. Your dad is a good shopper that way" said Amanda's mother. "He sure is" agreed Amanda. And, suddenly, Amanda found her appetite back. She even asked for seconds. Her parents were glad to find their old Amanda, their little girl back.

Dad worked into the night looking under the hood of Amanda's car. He was happy enough to give her the keys back to her car. "Drive carefully, kid," he said to her before she retired for the night. Her dad kissed her on the forehead and hugged her goodnight.

That evening she walked to visit her Grandpa Jim to tell him what happened.

The next day, she woke up bright and early at sunrise. She ate breakfast. She kissed her mother and father's cheek.

And, she headed to the nearest city to find a job.

# Chapter 4

"What a feeling of joy and sorrow to leave the farm this way" thought Amanda. It was nice of her mother to pack her a lunch to take with her in a small red and white cooler. She had it sitting on the floor of the car on the passenger side. She had kissed her parents on the cheek goodbye. They both wished her "good luck."

"Bright sunny day, anyway" thought Amanda as she drove down the country road heading for the nearest city where her father bought his supplies from the feed store and some basic food at the supermarket that couldn't be grown on the family farm.

It sure was a "long ride" she thought when you are driving by yourself. "God" she thought. She was glad that she had a relationship with God. She didn't know how she would make it otherwise.

The first thing in town, she headed for the one and only restaurant. At the counter, the waitress asked what Amanda wanted to order. She blurted out what came first from her mind. "Coffee, please" she said. She thought that sounded so adult-like. She was frightened just saying that. She wasn't used to being out and about. "Sugar or cream" said the waitress. Amanda didn't know what to say.

"Well—I don't have all day. It's not rocket science, kid. Sugar or cream" said the waitress.

"Both" said Amanda.

"Good choice" said the waitress.

Amanda handed the waitress a dollar and a quarter for the coffee. She sat down at the table overlooking the feed store where her father often had taken her as a kid. She decided that was going to be the first place that she would apply for a job now that she was such an adult and all.

Coffee drank. Amanda left the car in the restaurant parking lot. She headed to the feed store across the street. The clerk who turned out to be the owner named Ralph said to her as she approached the counter: "Can I help you?"

"Yes. I would like to put in a job application" she said.

"What makes you think that there is a job to put in an application about?" said Ralph.

"I" said Amanda upset and fighting back the tears. "I'll just go. I'm sorry to have bothered you, sir" said Amanda again crying inside. She was visibly upset. Her body shook from fear of this man and what was happening.

"What makes you think that you bothered me?" said Ralph.

"I—" said Amanda. "I—" said Amanda.

"Listen, kid. Do you want a job or not?" said Ralph.

"What can you do?" said Ralph.

"I—never had a job before. So, I really don't know. I..." said Amanda startled with her voice trembling.

"Here kid" said Ralph handing her a broom.

"Can you sweep this floor?" said Ralph.

"I think I can" said Amanda holding the broom in her hand.

"You think you can or you can. Which one is it?" said Ralph. With that remark, Amanda began sweeping the floor vigorously.

Seeing Amanda trying to sweep the floor, Ralph said: "That's enough, kid."

"Now, kid" said Ralph.

"I give you $10.00. I am a customer. What I am buying costs $5.66. How much change do you give me?" said Ralph.

Amanda said right off: "Four dollars and 34 cents in change."

Ralph checked it out on a scratch pad. "OK" said Ralph.

"Now, a customer gives you $20.00. What he is buying costs $17.22. How much money does he get back?" said Ralph.

"Two dollars and 78 cents in change" said Amanda again right off.

Once again, Ralph checked it out on a scratch pad. "OK" said Ralph.

"You see these bags under the counter. That is where you get the bags with the feed stores name on it in various sizes to put the customers' purchase in. Got that?" said Ralph.

Amanda nodded.

"Now, can you say when you see a customer: Howdy, how can I help you?" said Ralph.

Amanda repeated Ralph's words: "Howdy, how can I help you?"

"Perfect" said Ralph.

"Congratulations," said Ralph grabbing Amanda's hand to shake. "You are hired. It pays minimum wage. The hours are 7:30 AM to 5 PM with an hour's lunch" said Ralph.

Amanda started walking out the store. Ralph called out after her to say: "One final thing, wear jeans to work here and a clean shirt."

"See you tomorrow. I look forward to working with you, kid" said Ralph. Ralph waved goodbye. Amanda waved back.

Amanda was so happy. She couldn't believe what had happened to her. And, the very same feed store her dad had come so often when she was growing up.

Ralph opened the door to the store: "Oh, by the way, kid. You get a 10% discount on anything you purchase from the store as an employee. See you tomorrow."

"Thank you" called out Amanda to Ralph.

"No, thank you for applying for a job at my store. It took guts, kid" said Ralph.

"And, I could use a helping hand. I never had thought about hiring someone until you showed up" said Ralph.

"Oh" said Amanda standing outside the store about now.

"In that case. I'll see you bright and early at 7 am tomorrow" said Amanda shaking Ralph's hand while smiling at him straight in the face being a little more brave than she had been.

"Great" said Ralph closing the door to the feed store after she began walking across the street away from his store.

Amanda walked across the street to the restaurant. She walked to the counter. "You again, kid. It seems that you can't get enough of our coffee" said the waitress.

"Seems so" said Amanda. The waitress remembered Amanda's order. So, she gave her what she had ordered here before.

"I just got hired today at the feed store across the street" said Amanda.

"Well, congratulations. Hey...The coffee is on me then for this time. My name is Stella by the way.—And your name is?" said the waitress.

"Amanda" said Amanda.

"Well, happy to make your acquaintance" said Stella.

"I suppose that we will be seeing a lot more of you" said Stella to Amanda.

"I suppose that you will" said Amanda to Stella. And, with that, Amanda walked to the very exact table she sat before. Amanda was so happy. She hoped her parents would be happy, too.

Amanda determined to bring her parents back a gift to celebrate her being hired. She decided that while sitting there sipping her coffee as she eyed the supermarket across the street.

Finishing up her coffee, she walked across the street to the supermarket. There, she saw a yellow and green John Deere Christmas ornament that looked like it had been sitting there on the rack for ages. The cardboard that encased the ornament was faded from the sunlight. But, the tractor reminded her of her dad's very own tractor.

She asked the clerk: "How much?"

"It's not Christmas, kid" said the clerk.

"I know that" said Amanda.

"But, how much for it?" said Amanda.

"For you, kid, $2.00 plus tax" said the clerk.

"I didn't even remember that it was there" said the clerk with her right hand at her waist about now.

"I just got hired at the feed store. I start tomorrow" said Amanda to the clerk.

"Well congratulations" said the clerk.

"In that case, just keep the ornament if it means that much to you" said the clerk.

"Thank you" said Amanda as the clerk wrapped the ornament in white tissue. And then she put it in a bag. And then, she handed it to Amanda.

"It's for my dad" said Amanda.

"Well, wish him Merry Christmas for me, then" said the clerk.

"Thanks. I will." said Amanda missing the comment. After all, she was a "wide-eyed kid."

Amanda headed to the barrettes to get one for her mother. Her mother never had a barrette before. Her mother only got one for her kid and not herself. So now, her mother would have one for the first time in her life.

She could wear it to Church on Sunday. She found a gold embossed barrette that had a rose that was pale pink with small light green leaves on it. Her mother loved her flower garden that she grew herself. It reminded her of her mother's garden.

"How much?" she said to the clerk.

"Two dollars plus tax" said the clerk surprised to see Amanda again.

Amanda gave her the money. The clerk again wrapped the barrette in white tissue. She put it in a bag.

"It's for my mother" said Amanda.

"Oh" said the clerk smiling at Amanda.

Amanda waved goodbye to the clerk. The clerk waved back. She headed back across the street to her car.

She headed home to tell her parents the "good news". She decided to travel back and forth for awhile to save on apartment rent. She would live at home for awhile with her parents on the farm.

Her parents couldn't have been happier. They thought it was the "perfect" place for their daughter to meet her future husband! A feed store where farmers shopped. What could be more perfect? And, it was better than moping on the farm. Plus, Amanda would have a paycheck to help take care of her own living expenses.

It was a good reason for her mother to bring out the good china for supper. Amanda's mother made her daughter her favorite meal: baked chicken with homemade stuffing with melted butter and hot sliced apples on the side spiced with cinnamon sprinkled on top.

Carolyn, Amanda's mother, read off the recipes.

## BAKED CHICKEN WITH HOMEMADE STUFFING

Ingredients

    1 fresh chicken
    1 package of spiced bread crumbs

2-3 stalks of celery, chopped
2 Tablespoons of butter (as needed to keep moist)
1 medium chopped onion
I can chicken broth (to keep stuffing moist)

## Directions

Preheat oven at 375°. Wash the fresh chicken with cool water and placed in roasting pan with a cover. Put in oven. Bake for 1½ hours or until fully cooked. During last 10 minutes or so, take off cover to brown chicken. While chicken is baking, chop celery and onions. Melt butter in frying pan over low heat until melted. Pour mixture over butter. Pour desired amount of bread crumbs over this. Can wait to put in bread crumbs until onions are translucent. Mix all 3 ingredients together. Can add more butter as needed one tablespoon at a time until onions are cooked. Can leave on top of stove until chicken is baked and ready to come out of oven. Or, you can pour mixture into a baking dish with a lid. And, then bake in the oven next to the chicken. Can spray the surface of baking dish with vegetable oil to keep surface from sticking. Pour chicken broth over mixture to moisten. Can dot the surface with butter pieces of one teaspoon each to keep mixture moist. Can remove lid for last 10 minutes or so of baking if want surface brown and crunchy. Remove chicken from oven. Slice desired portion for each serving. Scoop a serving of ½-1 cup of stuffing to serve next to chicken. Serve at once while hot.

In the meantime, while the chicken and stuffing is baking:

## COOKED SPICED APPLE SLICES

## Ingredients and directions

Peel and core 3 apples. Slice into slices. Boil until soft in water. Drain. Keep a lid on top of pan until ready to serve. Sprinkle on top with cinnamon. Serve next to chicken and stuffing on platter.

Tom, Amanda's father bowed his head to pray:



"Amen" said everyone after hearing Tom.

They were so happy to be together for this occasion.

They sat by candlelight like three adults. Amanda and her parents clinked together goblets filled with apple juice from the farm with crushed ice together just after saying grace with bowed heads thanking God for their blessings.

And, Amanda brought out her treasures she purchased for her parents after the dinner.

"What a sweet daughter" they said of Amanda together. They laughed together which they hadn't for a long time as family with Tommy gone and all. It weighed heavy on them. Now, there was hope they all thought.

Amanda could barely sleep that night: Imagine her first job.

"Six AM will come around really soon" thought Amanda. So, she made herself go to sleep so that she would be rested for work.

Her mother and father treated her like a "queen" in the morning. They placed all their dreams on their only daughter.

"If only Tommy had stayed on the farm, I wouldn't be in this situation" thought Amanda.

"Well, God" she thought.

And before you know it, Amanda was down the road with a trail of dust from the road following all the way to the feed store. Ralph was waiting for her when she came into the store. He had just brewed coffee for her. Mostly, they just talked all day long. They only had two customers all day long.

Ralph said that he wished he could attract more customers. It was such a small town. Maybe, Amanda had ideas to help. These were Ralph's hopes. Amanda and Ralph became best friends.

Amanda and Ralph went across the street to the restaurant for lunch. Ralph had a writing tablet to write down ideas. Ralph paid for the lunch which was hamburgers with French fries and a cola for both of them.

Ralph sat in the restaurant for more than an hour talking to Amanda. Ralph said that he had peak seasons such as autumn during the harvest and the spring during the planting season from neighboring farms. Otherwise, he suffered, he thought. Larger neighboring cities have taken away a lot of his business he thought. "If only he could attract them back" said Ralph to Amanda squeezing her hand from across the table at the restaurant.

In return to Ralph's comments, Amanda said that since the feed store doubled as a hardware, "we" really have all the supplies "we" need to revamp the store. "'We' could make it over so that it looks like such a swell place that nobody could resist coming here to shop" said Amanda.

So, Ralph made a list of possible things to do:

1. Paint the walls.
2. Paint the counters.
3. Paint the shelves.
4. Wash the front windows.
5. Put in flower boxes in the front of the store.
6. Put signs with specials in the front windows.
7. Put ads in local "penny saver" papers to remind locals about the store.
8. Put in a cooler with sodas for sale.
9. Have a rack by the counter with snacks to buy such a potato chips etc.
10. Put "impulse" items on the counter like gums and candy bars.
11. Re-arrange the items more attractively on the shelves.
12. Put ads in local church circulars.
13. Re-varnish the floors.
14. Paint the outside trim bright white.
15. Have a "grand opening" after through re-vamping the store.

"Well, that is a good start. I'm really glad, that I hired you. This could be a 'new start' for the store" said Ralph.

"I'm glad you hired me, too. It means a lot to my parents" said Amanda.

And, Amanda told Ralph the story about the Miller Farm and her brother Tommy.

Amanda loved working for Ralph. She never could do wrong by him. He was willing to try anything to help the store. It was worth a try to him. "The store hadn't gotten a 'facelift' for as long as he could remember it" said Ralph.

He had inherited the store from his father who had inherited it from his father which was the reason he owned it. Ralph was grateful for the company as well which he never intended to mention to Amanda because he was "all man" in Ralph's opinion. He needed to seem strong and manly in her company.

Ralph became good friends with the Millers all the same especially Tom, Amanda's father. Tom appreciated the 10% discount to help the family farm with what supplies they needed. It helped the family get through. And, he appreciated the transformation that took place on Amanda's life. She was a new woman because of the job her father noticed.

Tom came by Amanda's work to surprise her on one of his trips into town to "thank" Ralph in person and invite him to dinner at the Miller Farm. He gladly accepted.

After that, Ralph was a regular there which delighted Amanda to have her two favorite men get along so well. Ralph even got invited to her 19th birthday dinner at the farm which was a small gathering of local farmers who he could advertise along with Amanda about his feed store and hardware. "Please do come to the Tomlingson Feed Store & Hardware for all your farming needs. Amanda works there too" said Tom.

They opened up one large table with a white linen table cloth that they placed in the middle of the barn for good farm eating to celebrate her day. And, the local farmers came to play: "Happy Birthday" to Amanda wearing overalls to boot. Jacob played the fiddle. Travis and Lee played the guitar. They were always "pickin' and grinnin'" anyway after a long day of working in the fields on their farms. They were the Johnson brothers who owned the farm down the way. They lived together which is why they were such a success. Jacob was married with one son who was 3 years old. The other two brothers were engaged to be married but, the date of their marriage hadn't been set.

Everyone including Ralph sang "Happy Birthday" to Amanda. Secretly, Ralph was deeply in love with Amanda. But, he knew he would never tell her so because he was a good 30 years older than her. "And, who would take care of the feed store if he took her as a wife and moved to the farm?" he thought.

He stood there startled at how beautiful she looked to him with her dark chestnut hair; light complexion; and soft pink lips. He suddenly realized he longed to kiss her including this moment. Ralph did some mighty loud thinking to himself right then. He surprised even his own self, the strong emotions that he felt for Amanda.

In a half hour or so, he was on the road heading back home. His home was an apartment above the feed store and hardware. He lived there rent free which he was grateful for the break. Ralph owned the store which is why. But it had been a lonely existence before Amanda came along. It ran the length and width of the store. So, it was quite roomy.

And, there was a porch upstairs in the back of the apartment. It had an overhang that helped keep the rain and snow off the porch. Ralph liked to sit there after a hard days work. And, there was a table there with two chairs. He only ever used one chair since he never invited anyone upstairs. The two chairs were there from the days when his father lived in the apartment.

And, in the backyard, there was a small single car garage to put his car to keep it from the elements. He rarely used it because in town, he could walk to everything. But, he kept his car for such occasions as going to see Amanda at her family's farm. It was too far to walk there. "That's for sure" thought Ralph. No city bus to it either being so rural. The car was the only means of transportation there.

Ralph never took Amanda to the backyard. He was quite a farmer his own self. He could grow almost anything. So, he grew most of his own vegetables his own self to save money and better taste than the store. And, he enjoyed watching things grow.

It was just a small fenced in yard that was his. Well, it was small compared to a farm. He never had enough money to buy a "real" farm. But, he could pretend it was the Tomlingson Farm all the same because it was his.

Tomorrow, he would get up early to weed; water; and pour as much love as he could over his garden. He even had a small St. Mary's garden there with a garden bench where he loved to say his rosary. He worshipped the Virgin Mary as his patron saint and heavenly mother since he never knew his own mother. She had passed away during childbirth.

Ralph only had a photo of his mother that he kept on his wall to remind him of her love for her son that his dad said she had for Ralph. He asked "his" mother Mary to watch over his "earthly" mother in heaven for him until he joined her God willing to live in heaven at her side with his father. He always prayed that. His father had never dated after his wife passed away that way. He devoted himself to his only son and the store that kept a roof over their head. Ralph loved deeply his father. He never quite got over his dying. He missed him every day.

Now, Ralph asked his heavenly mother that he regarded as "his"—"Mother of Perpetual Help" to watch over his store and "his" Amanda that he loved in his heart as his wife. But, he knew there would never be more between them than what he had this moment. But, she comforted him all the same.

Ralph loved the flowers that he planted around the statue of St. Mary to honor her. She was "his" mother. So, she deserved it for bringing her son Jesus into Ralph's life as "his" savior.

"Thank you, Mary, my dear sweet mother" said Ralph.

And, after making the "sign of the cross" at the end of his morning rosary, he entered the back door of his store to make the morning coffee for Amanda. She would be there by 7 AM as usual.

It took two months to get the store into shape. It was the "prettiest" store in town thought Amanda. Even Ralph was surprised at the store's "new" look. And, surprisingly, he had an amazing amount of new customers as a result. He was the "talk of the town."

People gossiped that Ralph and Amanda were a couple. It couldn't be farther from the truth. Ralph would take her as his wife if he could. If only she and her family could accept him as the husband of Amanda.

But, he dare not risk what he had going for himself and lose the whole deal. He didn't think that he could cope at this point without Amanda. She had done so much for him and his store. She meant the world to him. He figured that she at least knew that much.

The "grand opening" sign got put outside the store. More customers flocked. Ralph was very pleased. Ralph told Tom, Amanda's father, what a wonderful asset she was to the store...

The autumn leaves were starting to turn. And, the autumn air was becoming brisk. Amanda became worried about the slick roads to and from work to home and back twice a day. "What to do?" thought Amanda.

She couldn't afford an apartment on her wages. And, she hadn't met anyone that she could marry as her father thought she would. In fact, she never got an offer for a date. Most of the farmers who came into the store were older men with wives already. And, they lived on farms far away from the store as a rule, too.

She was happy too, which made it worse. Ralph was great company. Secretly, she thought that she was in love with him. She looked at him with "adoring" eyes. Her heart raced whenever he stood near her or said her name.

But, her father would have a fit if they become a couple. He wasn't a young man. He wasn't a farmer. He had no brothers, either. "What would happen to the farm if she chose unwisely for a husband?" thought Amanda. Still, she loved Ralph "dearly" though she knew she could never say so which would break her parents' hearts, especially her father, if she did. That's for sure.

# Chapter 5

Amanda was very proud of Ralph. He was a new man at the store. He sang at work. The store had more than pulled itself together since the grand opening of the store. He had more customers than he ever hoped to have. Customers actually responded to his ads that Amanda had put out.

The new look of the store was a big plus. And, the flower boxes in the front of the store with salmon colored geraniums added a touch of class. Plus, Amanda herself stenciled on the glass of the store: The Tomlinson Feed Store & Hardware with the store hours below in gold letters. It was a proud moment. Things were going well.

Still life weighed heavy on her. The ride back to the farm was going to get really slow on country roads in the snow. If it blew over, she would get stranded. She could freeze to death literally in such a rural area with no one to help her out. Her father was smart enough to never brave the roads like that. Most farmers drove a skimobile to get out for safety purposes.

It was heading toward late October. The farm was absolutely gorgeous with the stands of trees on the edge of the farm with leaves of golden yellows with orange; browns; and greens. The apples have already been harvested from the trees. What hadn't been sold already were sitting on the enclosed porch in baskets with straw to keep the fruit in good condition for winter eating. The ears of corn have already been removed in their husks from the cornfield. The cornstalks have already turned from green to tan. They made a crackling sound in the wind. Soon, the cornstalks would be plowed under before the winter for compost preparing for yet another generation of cornfields in the spring. It was nature at its best braving season after season to live out its life cycle before the next generation took over.

She loved the farm during this time of the year. The air was just nippy enough to put your sweater on to keep the chill away. It made for pleasant walks to the back of the farm field to talk to Grandpa Jim. She liked walking everywhere on the farm as it is. She didn't know what she would do when she no longer lived on the farm and was a married lady.

But, now, her thoughts turned to Tommy. She wondered if he had plans to ever return back to the family farm. It would make a big difference to her life if he was returning in any immediate future. It would certainly take the pressure off of her to find a suitable spouse to fit what dad had in mind for her, and the future of the family farm. It was a reasonable request but, more easy to think of it, than actually to do it.

She had been at the store while working looking high and low for the right guy to marry. Never once did she get asked out on a date by anyone. There were plenty of farmers that came into the store all right all sweaty from working their heads off. And, most were all business about their farm. Plus, most were older married men who had wives for years. And, the few stray younger men that wandered in the store were already married since they were about the business of getting mated up from high school on. So, they didn't waste any time finding the right girl to help them to continue the generations of farm life that they craved.

But, something sat gnawing in the pit of her stomach. She knew that she wouldn't be able to handle the country roads to and from the store to the farm throughout the winter. There would be too much snow and ice on the roads that could potentially make her drive on the roads a good 2 or 3 times longer than she was doing now. It would likely be dark by the time she got home. In the warm weather, it was a relatively short ride for her to manage. She needed a place that she could stay in the city just for the winter until the weather cleared. She knew that she didn't make enough money at the feed store to rent an apartment so that she would be close to her work. She would talk about it to Ralph tomorrow.

Amanda felt uneasiness in the pit of her stomach as she neared Ralph. She wished that all answers were easy. She wished that she made more money to afford an apartment in the city. But, she knew that she couldn't ask Ralph for a raise. He was just getting on his feet at the store. She knew that he really appreciated everything she had done.

Ralph was as usual near the coffeemaker with 2 cups of coffee: one for himself and one for her made exactly the way she liked it. She never used sugar in her coffee. She only used cream in her coffee. She loved coffee that was light tan in color. It tasted creamy to her that way.

She knew that this was the best time to approach the subject before the customers poured into the store. With the facelift the store recently went through, it really buzzed with business. People here liked being friendly if they knew you were trying to take care of their needs. The store was actually "the talk of the town." And, Amanda was tickled to see these good things happen to Ralph. He was a good man. He deserved good things.

Amanda drank her coffee in silence for about a minute she guessed. It seemed like an eternity to her. Finally, she decided to speak.

"Ralph, you know that I love working here" said Amanda.

"Do you have another job?" said Ralph.

"Because if you do, I don't want to hold you back. And, I love working here with you as well" said Ralph.

"No. It's nothing like that" said Amanda.

"Things have been working out really well with my working here and living on the farm. But, soon the winter snows will close off the roads. I won't even get through at times. And, I don't know what to do. I thought that you would have the answers. I count on your advise" said Amanda.

"Well, that certainly is a problem," said Ralph.

"I would let you stay upstairs in the apartment. I would in a heartbeat. But, it's small. There really is no room" said Ralph.

He knew that there was plenty of room but, he doubted that he could keep his hands off of her if they were alone in private quarters. He didn't want to tell her how much in love with her he was.

"Well, whatever you've got to do, I will respect" said Ralph.

"I will keep my eye out for a vacant apartment in town in your price range" said Ralph.

"OK" said Amanda.

"So, let's open the store for business. We have customers already outside waiting," said Amanda.

Ralph nodded and smiled. She loved his smile.

Some weeks passed. Amanda didn't sleep well at night. Ralph could tell.

"Listen" said Ralph.

"Perhaps the only answer is your relocating to Indianapolis at least for now" said Ralph.

"You mean Indianapolis, IN…" said Amanda. Tears rolled down her cheeks. She did nothing to hide them from Ralph.

"How will you make it without me?" said Amanda looking around the store. It was a huge place for one man to have to take care of himself.

"I don't know" said Ralph.

"But, there are buses there to get around in the winter. And, there are a lot of apartment houses and jobs there. At least it will be an answer for now. And, maybe when the spring comes, you can come back to work for me again. Maybe by then, we will have a solution about your living quarters because I haven't found a place for you to stay in town here" said Ralph.

"And I don't mind temporarily sleeping downstairs in the store on a cot. But, you know that I have a bad back. And, I don't want you to have to sleep in the store. It wouldn't be proper. And, if we stayed upstairs together, the people would just talk. It is a small town and all, you know. That wouldn't be proper, either" said Ralph.

Amanda tearfully nodded. She couldn't stop crying. She asked if she could just go home so she could tell her parents. Ralph agreed.

Better to get going. He had to hold down the fort here. So, he couldn't really go. Otherwise, he would if the truth be known. He wanted to close the store right this minute. What was life without Amanda? The store would seem empty without her. And, so would his life. But, he had to do what was best for Amanda. He had to keep her safe. That was the important thing now.

Amanda called off coming in the next day to the store. She told him that she was packing up her things at home. She didn't know if she was leaving the car at the farm or taking it to the city with her.

Ralph felt lost without her, already. He told her to come in when she could.

"I want to get you something for a going away present" said Ralph trying to help Amanda through this time. He could hear her crying on the phone.

"Please, don't cry, Amanda. We'll stay in touch. This is not goodbye. It is just for now. Just let me know if you are coming by the store or whether I should come to the farm. I don't want you leaving without seeing you. Agreed?" said Ralph.

"Agreed" said Amanda.

"And, no more crying now" said Ralph his heart breaking. How could he let her go? She was his love.

"We'll stay in touch. I promise" said Amanda. And, she hung up the phone.

Tom decided that Ralph should come by the farm for dinner. He thought that it would be too hard for Amanda to return to the store when she had to leave like that. Amanda agreed. And, Ralph deserved a good home cooked meal. She knew that her parents would fill the back of their truck with many goodies from the farm for Ralph to take home with him. This would be a big help to Ralph who lived by himself.

Amanda would worry less that he was eating well if her parents were watching over him while she was gone. In fact, she asked them to do that. And, they agreed because they didn't like the idea that such a nice man lived by himself. At least her parents had each other. So, they were glad to accept the responsibility. They loved Ralph. And, he loved them. And, that took a load off Amanda's mind.

You would have thought it was the Holidays the way that the dinner table was set with the best china and linens. You could smell the sweetness in the air of the homemade apple pie in the oven baking. It mingled in the air with the scent of round steak with vegetables cooking in the electric skillet on the kitchen counter. Carolyn loved her round steak recipe that basically had all the beef stew vegetables to it that cooked up together moist and soft. In fact, she called it her "round steak beef stew" recipe.

ROUND STEAK BEEF STEW

Ingredients

Round steak
1 yellow onion, chopped
1 tablespoon of oil
6-12 carrots (peeled and cut into slices)
4-8 potatoes (cut in 4-6 pieces)
¼ cup of green frozen peas, optional
Water, enough to cover ingredients

## Directions

Brown the round steak on both sides with one tablespoon of oil in the electric skillet. After browned, add potatoes, carrots, and onions. Cover with water. Put lid on skillet. Allow ingredients to boil slightly for about 1½ hours or until the vegetables are fully cooked. Pierce potatoes and carrots with fork to see if soft and fully cooked. Add green peas the last 10 minutes or so of cooking for extra color and flavor. Cut meat into desired serving size. Serve vegetables as many as desired with a slit spoon. Can use juices for potatoes after mashed with fork to pour over potatoes as gravy.

Ralph looked more handsome than what she remembered. He was wearing a white shirt that she had never seen before with his usual jeans. His hair looked freshly cut. It showed off the waviness of his dark brown hair against his brown eyes that looked golden in the sun.

She never told him how much she loved looking at his eyes. She blushed at the thought of doing so. She secretly wished that she could. She was starting to believe that she was in love with him. Tommy, her brother, needed to write back soon with news of when he was returning to the family farm for good. It would set her free to be with Ralph which is what she was beginning to feel she wanted. She hated the idea of leaving Ralph.

Ralph came to dinner with a bouquet of flowers he said was for the dinner table. They really were for Amanda but, he didn't want to say. Under his arm was a smallish size package wrapped in brown paper.

Ralph wasn't a fancy man. But, he was a good man. Amanda knew that. He must have gotten the paper from the hardware at the store. He said that this was for later. So, he wasn't going to give it to her until after dinner.

Amanda nodded. She asked her mother for a vase for the flowers. Her mother had never seen so many kinds of flowers together at one time in a bouquet. Usually, her bouquets were one kind of flower cut from the garden.

So, this was really a special bouquet that deserved to be put in the center of the dinner table in the best vase the Millers had. Carolyn put the flowers in a heavy glass vase with a gold trim at the lip of the vase. The flowers seemed to go well with the look and feel of the vase. They were long stemmed yellow and white daisies, pink and white roses; yellow carnations; and white mums. Amanda's dad volunteered to take a photo of them with Amanda and Ralph together. They were that spectacular of a bouquet for Tom to want to do that. They had a regal look to them having such long stems sitting in a vase that could support the weight of them. And yet, they looked so soft and "country" to the eye since especially the daisies mingled between all the other flowers had all the original foliage that nature offered. Ralph was good with flowers. Tom told Ralph that he would see that Amanda and Ralph got a copy of the photo for a memory.

"That is awfully nice of you. I'll have to keep a photo of Amanda at the store so that no one ever forgets what Amanda has done for the store and me. I really appreciate having her" said Ralph.

"Well, we appreciate what the store meant to her, too" said Tom. And, Carolyn nodded.

Amanda's parents decided after dinner to make themselves scarce so that Amanda and Ralph could visit together for awhile. They decided to get an early rest. So, they went upstairs to their bedroom. They knew that Ralph had brought a present for Amanda.

Amanda went to the living room couch. Ralph followed Amanda with his present. He sat on the stuffed chair sitting next to the couch. Amanda took the package from Ralph's hand carefully opening it. Inside was a box that she opened to find a gold heart shaped locket on a gold chain. She opened it to find a miniature photo of Ralph.

"It's so you always have me with you" said Ralph touching Amanda's leg. Amanda took the heart shaped locket from the box. Ralph reached over to put it around Amanda's neck. She turned around facing Ralph, touching the heart with her hand. Amanda kissed Ralph's cheek to thank him for the thoughtful present.

"I'm glad you like it" said Ralph. And, returning affection, Ralph kissed Amanda's cheek. They both sat watching the sun set that blushed pink up against the blue sky until the sky turned black. It was so quiet Amanda thought she could hear Ralph breathe. She realized that she loved hearing him breathe.

Amanda decided to drive into Indianapolis with her dad. She drove her car into the barn to protect it from the elements. She found out that not all apartments there had a place to park. She didn't want to have to keep her car in a parking garage. And, besides there was the city bus there. And, her father could always bring the car there later with Ralph's help perhaps after she gets settled in if she needed it.

She knew a high school friend that now lived in Indianapolis. That made her father feel a whole lot better about her living there by herself. She was to meet her friend for lunch. They were to meet at the Circle by the fountain which her father was familiar where that was. They would have lunch at the Circle.

The Chocolate Cafe is where they decided to dine. They could see the people walking up the eloquent whitish steps toward the fountain splashing into a pool of water where coins were tossed generously for "good luck" for anyone and everyone feeling the need. Above towered multi-colored strands of tree lights in a configuration of the largest Christmas tree of its kind. It was a pride of Indianapolis.

It wasn't second nature for any of them to see such grandeur as this since they were used to manly things from nature being farm folk and all. The street and the sidewalk outside the restaurant encircled the fountain. Decorated poles lined the sidewalk with huge Christmas ornaments and gold tinsel.

All three of them sat at the table nearest the window to watch the snow that was now falling. It made everything seem even more festive and "Christmassy."

Amanda sat looking out at the scenery. "This is such an ornate and grand city" said Amanda.

Amanda couldn't believe how pretty everything was. She had never seen anything like it.

"It sure is" said Tom really pleased that everything seemed so nice for his daughter.

Amanda thought that she would love living here for now since it was so pretty. She pushed back the thought of missing the farm and the store where she worked with Ralph.

Right now, she had to live in the moment. Amanda's dad was listening intently to her high school friend. Tom already knew Sarah since he knew all of Amanda's friends in high school. He tried hard to be a good dad that way. Sarah was going on with Amanda's dad about her work in Indianapolis' bustling downtown. Amanda tuned in.

Amanda interrupted. "So, Sarah I love seeing you and all. It is quite beautiful here and different as can be from the farming community we grew up in and our high school days. But, you did say that you had news to tell me" said Amanda.

"Well Amanda, my roommate is moving out in about a week. And, I need someone to share my apartment. And, since we know each other, I was wondering if you would be interested in taking over the lease and going in half on the rent? It won't be ready for a week though. And, I know that isn't the most convenient" said Sarah.

"But, it is better than living alone in a city you don't know at all. And, if you would do this for me, since I don't like living with a stranger much, I think I could get my boss to hire you at my office as a 'receptionist slash secretary' since there is an opening coming up. It only pays minimum wage but, it should cover your rent with some left over. I know that this is short notice but, what do you say?" said Sarah.

Amanda looked at her father. "Dad?" said Amanda.

"Let's do it!" said Tom to Amanda.

"You know that you will be at home still for the week. We'll have to drive home. But, your mother will be happy to know that you will be in good hands with your good friend, Sarah" continued Tom to his daughter, Amanda.

"We thank you so much" said Tom to Sarah.

"And, let me pay for lunch for helping my daughter. It is the least I can do" continued Tom to Sarah, Amanda's high school friend and soon to be roommate.

"Well, she is helping me as well. But, I am glad to do it" said Sarah to Tom.

"Well" said dad on the way home driving Amanda and himself back to the family farm.

"I never expected things to turn out so well. I am so grateful to your friend, Sarah" said Tom to his daughter, Amanda.

Carolyn came running out the door when she saw Amanda. "Daughter, I am so glad to see you. But, what happened?" said Amanda's mother.

"Let's go inside. I want to tell you the good news" said Amanda to her mother. And, Amanda told her mother about her day at the Circle.

Then, Amanda called up Ralph with the news. Ralph didn't want Amanda to come back to the store. He thought it would be too hard for her to leave again. He agreed instead to close shop each night to come to the Miller farm for dinner as a cherished family member. He could spend the evenings walking on the farm together visiting each other. And, there was Tommy's room where Ralph could sleep. And, in the morning he could have breakfast with the Millers before heading off to work for this one special week.

Ralph showed up that week with a brown tattered suitcase. He looked uncomfortable. "It is all I have. I didn't want to buy a new suitcase for just the week. But, I have enough clothing to last the week by golly" said Ralph to Amanda.

He wouldn't let Amanda carry the suitcase up to Tommy's bedroom. "Just point the way" said

Ralph to Amanda. And, so they went to the bedroom on the opposite side of the hall across from Amanda's bedroom. Ralph could see the apple orchard's branches in a distance that looked almost black against the gray-blue autumn sky.

Ralph thought that he would be happy for the week. He didn't know about after as he looked out the window at the darkening sky. Ralph loved the seasons especially autumn because of all the colors and cool air.

He would look forward to his evening stroll on the farm with Amanda. He loved his alone time with Amanda. This would be a "special memory" thought Ralph. With that, he headed for the bathroom attached to the bedroom. He was grateful for the privacy as he bathed for dinner. He could already smell the food from the kitchen. It made his stomach growl.

Amanda decided to meet Sarah at the Circle in Indianapolis precisely one week after they had met there. Ralph's store was closed on Sundays. And, he wanted to come along to Indianapolis to say goodbye there. And, he wanted to meet Sarah and see her apartment.

Tom agreed that would be a good idea since he had meant so much to the family and was so much part of this. Amanda was thrilled as she said that her "two favorite men" were sending her off.

Once there, hugs passed around. Amanda and her caravan walked to her new apartment in walking distance to the Circle. It was a brown stone apartment. She would live on the second floor overlooking a busy street. She would have her own bedroom.

Everything was already there. The apartment came with furniture. The rest, Sarah had already supplied before Amanda came along. All she had to do is unpack her belongings from her suitcase.

Sarah planned to walk to and from the apartment to work with Amanda. "It will be like the old days when we hung around together in high school" said Sarah to Amanda and her dad with a smile in her voice.

Sensing this was a family event for Amanda, Sarah said: "I will leave you alone to say goodbye." With that, she left the room.

Amanda's dad was the first to hug Amanda and say goodbye. "Write and call us" said Tom to his daughter referring to himself and Amanda's mother.

"And often" added Tom.

"I will" promised Amanda to her father.

Then, Ralph pulled Amanda into his arms for the first time. Tom stared on in silence. Amanda began to cry. "Hey, this isn't goodbye. You'll be back to work at the store in no time" said Ralph as she brushed away her tears.

"Like your dad said: 'Write and call often'" said Ralph. And, with that he handed her a small piece of paper with his phone number and mailing address on it for that very purpose.

And, then he pulled out of his jacket pocket a 5x7 inch framed photo of himself standing in front of the store where she and Ralph worked together. Amanda glanced at the photo. She instantly loved what it was because it was a photo of him and something of their life together at the store.

"For you to remember what I look like" Ralph said. Amanda put it on the nightstand by her bed. She said that she would keep it next to her photos of her parents and Tommy, her brother when he was a kid.

Ralph and Tom left the apartment together. They walked in silence out of the apartment. After the pickup truck carrying them both was now on the country road heading back to the farm, Tom spoke for the first time.

"You're in love with my daughter, aren't you?" said Tom.

With what seemed like an eternity, Ralph said but one word: "Yes." And, they drove home the rest of the way in silence.

Ralph headed back to Tommy's room immediately after coming to the farm. He thanked Tom and Carolyn for allowing him to be their house guest. They loaded up his car with gifts of food from the farm. He got a bushel of apples; several bags of ears of corn; home canned vegetables from Carolyn's garden; apple jelly; and homemade breads. The entire back seat was filled with goodies. It was enough really to help get him through the winter. Tom and Carolyn were determined to treat him as family.

And, they waved in the driveway as he drove away.

By himself on the road, he cried.

Ralph was quick to dry his tears before he got to town. It was not becoming of a storekeeper—especially in a small town where people talked. He had an image to maintain even though he was a very humble man.

He knew that he had to look put together. His customers counted on him to protect what they had going for them on the farm. And, he loved his business. But, about now he wished that he didn't have it so that he could run off to be with Amanda.

He had better call her to let her know that he returned home safely. He didn't know what was going to come out of his face. The phone rang.

"Hi, Amanda" said Ralph.

"Hi" said Amanda.

He really wanted to hear the sound of her voice. It hurt inside that he wouldn't see her for months.

"Hi, Amanda. It's Ralph. I just wanted to let you know that I got home safely. So, how's it going?" said Ralph.

"It's going just fine since I've only been here a few hours, you know" said Amanda.

"I miss you already" said Ralph.

"I miss you, too" said Amanda.

"Well, I'd better say goodbye now" said Ralph.

There was a long pause on the other end that seemed like an eternity. Ralph didn't know what to do. So, he hung up.

He thought that it was best to go to bed even though it was still light outside some. Maybe, it will take away some of the pain he was feeling inside.

# Chapter 6

It would have been scary to have lived in the big city and have to get around by yourself when you are only used to living where there is only a small population. In the big city, cars and buses were constantly traveling to and from. People were walking everywhere.

Amanda obediently followed Sarah to work and the lunch room at work. She already knew everyone there which was a big help. And, Sarah guided her through everything she needed to do for the job.

The same applied at the apartment. They cleaned the apartment together and cooked together. And, they even cried through love story movies together with a bowl of buttered popcorn that they ate together.

One day, on a really cold wintery day, Amanda and the co-workers decided on Friday night that they were going to go to a local watering hole for a few beers. Sarah said that they served sandwiches there, too. Amanda was always pre-occupied about eating a proper meal after living on a farm and all.

There, Amanda met Jerry. He was tall and lean. He had sandy blonde hair. And, his blue eyes sparkled when he smiled. He was sitting at the bar with a glass of beer in a frosted mug. Sarah nudged her forward. She whispered in her ear what to say. Amanda nodded. Then, she said: "Mind if I join you?"

"Sure. What are you drinking?" said Jerry.

"Whatever you are drinking" said Amanda thinking that was probably a safe thing to say.

With that, he reached into his pocket with a twenty. And, he handed it to the bartender. "Get her a beer and get me another. And oh, keep the change" said Jerry.

"So, what's a pretty lady like you doing in a place like this?" said Jerry.

"Oh, my roommate Sarah and the co-workers wanted to go out tonight here. It's close to work. And, I work there, too" said Amanda.

"Well, it's as good a place as any to be" said Jerry.

"So, you were born here in the city?" said Jerry.

"Gosh, no. I'm from north of here about an hour's drive away. My parents own a farm. I grew up there with my brother, Tommy. Sarah and I went to high school together. That's how I ended up working and living here. I needed a job and a place to live. And, Sarah was already here when the need arose. So, here I am" said Amanda.

"Quite a story" said Jerry putting out his hand.

"My name is Jerry by the way" said Jerry shaking Amanda's hand.

"And, your name is—" said Jerry.

"Amanda" said Amanda.

"Glad to make your acquaintance" said Jerry turning back toward the bar to sip his beer.

"I like to come here on Fridays sometimes to unwind. I work downtown near the Circle as a clerk for the government. It's a job. But, I like it—at least for now. I, too, come from a farm north of Indianapolis. I wanted to get away for awhile. I wanted to see the world some. This is as far as I got. I hope to travel someday" said Jerry.

"By the way, do you think your friends would mind if we took a walk together? Sometimes, it's awfully stuffy in here. And, I thought that maybe you would like to see some of the Christmas lights with me. It was snowing when I came in the door. We won't be long" said Jerry.

"Let me tell Sarah that I'm going. I'll be right back" said Amanda who began looking through the crowd at the bar for her roommate so that she could feel free to take off with Jerry for their "Christmas walk" together.

So then, Jerry and Amanda headed out the door like best friends. Amanda didn't quite remember what streets that they walked on. He strolled down the street holding her hand tightly so that she wouldn't fall on the snow and the ice.

"It's so close to Christmas, I thought that it would be nice. It is pretty. The snow is really falling. Nothing like it" said Jerry.

"The snow looks like little wet rainbows of pink, yellow, and blue-green" said Jerry. He caught a snowflake in his glove. He gently put it in hers. Then, he caught several other snowflakes to show her.

"They say that no two snowflakes are ever the same. I think that it is a miracle of God" said Jerry.

She looked up at him. He then put his arms around her to pull her close to him. And then, he pressed his lips on hers to kiss her.

"I'm sorry. I didn't mean to do that. It's just that you looked so pretty in the falling snow" said Jerry. With that, Amanda reached up to kiss him.

"Then, I'm taking it that it was OK with you. By golly, I have a girlfriend" said Jerry.

Just then, a man passed by on the sidewalk. Jerry introduced Amanda to the man. "This is my girlfriend" said Jerry smiling to the man with obvious delight in his voice.

"Well, congratulations" said the man as he passed by smiling back at Jerry through the thick snow drifts swirling around him as he made his way down the sidewalk.

And, Amanda laughed at Jerry's reactions. Jerry was a nice man thought Amanda. She was happy that she came with Sarah tonight.

Now, Jerry walked her back to the bar. Jerry volunteered to walk the girls to the apartment so that they were safe. Amanda was glad to meet Jerry. She would be a lot less lonely with Jerry around.

But, she felt guilty for leaving Ralph by himself at the feed store. He knew that he missed her. She missed him. But, she was here, now. And,

God only knew her future. And, she knew her father's plans for her.

Jerry knew the farm life. Maybe, he would be what she and her family needed. It was worth the try. He was handsome and gentlemanly. "And, he seems to really like me" said Amanda softly to herself as she retired for the night. This was her very first date that she ever had with a man. It was exciting to her.

She awoke in the morning to a car honking outside. It was Jerry. Amanda had slept in. He had managed to make a snowman that was smiling at Amanda from her bedroom window.

Jerry was waving at her to come on down. She dressed quickly. Then, she ran to Sarah's bedroom to tell her that she was going out with Jerry for awhile.

"Like the snowman that I made for you" said Jerry.

"I love it" said Amanda.

"But, isn't the face supposed to be facing toward the street?" said Amanda.

"Well, yes. But, then, it couldn't smile at you. Could it?" said Jerry. Amanda laughed, Jerry was great fun to be around. He was really sweet.

Jerry took Amanda to breakfast at a downtown restaurant. She had never had breakfast before where linens were on the table and candles.

The table was by the window. Amanda could feel the draft from the window. But, the snow sparkled in the sun. And, the hot chocolate served with the breakfast seemed to go well with the season. Amanda could see from the window the holiday decorations sway on the street lamp posts in the wind. Jerry and Amanda held hands across the table. Amanda felt blessed to have his company.

Once through eating breakfast, Jerry asked her if she wanted to walk awhile in the snow since it was falling and so beautiful looking like "white wet lace from the sky" to Jerry. They held hands as they walked. There were carolers in the Circle singing Christmas hymns.

He held her hand tight as she walked up the marble steps to the fountain at the Circle. He didn't want her to fall on the snow. The snow crunched under their feet. He then handed her a penny from his pocket to throw in the fountain for "good luck" for them both. She did. She watched it float to the bottom to rest on the tiled floor of the fountain among the other coins others had thrown in for "good luck." She secretly hoped everyone's wishes would come true. And, she secretly wished for Jerry and her wishes to come true, too.

Jerry held Amanda in his arms. He kissed her lips softly and moistly. Amanda kissed him back.

"I love kissing you," said Jerry.

"I love kissing you, too" said Amanda. They held hands together walking among the snowflakes around the fountain feeling the snow brush against their cheeks. They spent the better part of an hour visiting each other and walking against the background of the splashing sounds of the fountain's waterfalls into the pool below churning in constant motion. The snow seemed not to let up. It was determined to empty every last snowflake in thick drifts that made it difficult to see even when walking.

"There is nothing more Christmassy than snow" said Amanda to Jerry looking amazed at how much snow was falling all at once.

"That's true. It sure is beautiful—and Christmassy. Do you have a Christmas tree up yet in the apartment? I mean you probably would like one if you don't" said Jerry fidgeting.

"Well, I could like a Christmas tree. That's for sure" said Amanda.

Jerry said: "Come on."

"Where are we going?" said Amanda.

"You'll see" said Jerry.

They went back to the car. They drove to a lot where live Christmas trees were being sold. He walked around looking at them with Amanda. He said: "Pick one that you like."

Amanda smiled as she chose one with real cones still attached to the tree. The man selling the trees in the lot hit the trunk of the tree onto the snowy ground to help fluff out the tree branches for Amanda to get an idea what the tree really looked like. The tree had just come off the truck bailed in wire lying on top of each other as they traveled to the lot the man selling the trees indicated. He told Amanda that the tree is a white pine.

"It's a white pine" said Amanda looking very pleased as the snow fell softly on its branches as she stood there with Jerry admiring it.

Jerry held the tree by the trunk as he looked it over. "The trunk is straight. It has no bare spots. It's a real beauty" said Jerry.

Jerry paid the cashier. And, the man tied the Christmas tree on top of the car with a rope to keep the tree flat as Jerry requested while they traveled on the road. They headed back to the apartment.

Jerry pulled into a dollar store parking lot to get strands of Christmas tree lights. He told Amanda to run into the store while he stayed with the tree so that no one would take it.

"They can't take my Christmas tree. I just love it" said Amanda.

"They won't. I'll stay with the tree. Just run into the store so that we know for sure that we have Christmas lights for the tree when we get back to the apartment" said Jerry.

"OK. I'll be back in a minute" said Amanda.

"Hurry. But, don't hurry. It's starting to snow again. And, we're going to have to shake out all that snow from the tree before we go into the apartment and put the lights on" said Jerry.

"Alright. I'm on my way" said Amanda so happy to be doing a Christmas event with Jerry. She could only imagine the look on Sarah's face when she sees this tree. She only had a tabletop pre-decorated tree that you plug in. But, this was a real tree.

Amanda found four sets of Christmas lights that were miniature multi-colored sets. And, since Jerry had handed her $5.00 to shop, she decided to pick up a miniature Nativity set that had a manger and all the major figurines including the Baby Jesus for Christmas. Amanda thought that they were pretty. And, she couldn't imagine Christmas without a Nativity under the tree. And she had a little change if needed for the cashier in her coin purse.

Back in the car, Amanda showed Jerry what she bought. He started the motor the very second he saw her come out of the store, "I hope that you don't mind that I bought the Nativity for under the tree with the money you gave me" said Amanda.

"I couldn't imagine Christmas without a Nativity under the tree" said Jerry. With that, Amanda leaned over to kiss Jerry's cheek while he was driving to the apartment.

"Merry Christmas" said Jerry.

"Merry Christmas" said Amanda. The radio played Christmas hymns and the snow lightly fell.

Amanda could see some of the tree branches of the Christmas tree as they drove which she thought was good because at least she knew the tree was on top of the car still. The man at the Christmas tree lot had tied rope around the tree and into the inside of the car to hold it in place. The car windows had to stay partly open because of it. Some of the snow was coming inside the car while they drove toward the apartment. But, it was a gloriously beautiful Christmas day with her Christmas tree and snow and all. Even the melted gray slush in the parking lot that made her socks wet some inside her shoes didn't bother her today. She would change them for dry ones back in the apartment. It was officially Christmas now that she had her Christmas tree.

She glanced over at Jerry smiling at him. How she loved her dear Jerry. He made everything seem special to her. It could be the simplest thing like a snowflake. Most people wouldn't even pay any mind to a single snowflake.

But, Jerry had to have more than a nodding acquaintance with it. He treasured everything small and large that God had made. He told her: "If it is good enough for God to make it, it is good enough to appreciate the specialness of it. It had to be special since God made it. He had a reason for making all the things he made in nature so beautiful because He just made it the way He was."

Amanda could listen to Jerry talk for hours. He was a very philosophical man that saw the world from his own eyes that most would never know thought Amanda. That was why he was so special thought Amanda. She never wanted necessarily to tell him that because it would make him feel self-conscious. But, he came from a farmer family. And, these folks are tuned into nature as it is.

Sarah was at the apartment when Jerry and Amanda came to the door. She had just dressed. She just smiled when she saw the seven foot Christmas tree that Jerry was carrying into the apartment. Sarah just hugged Amanda. They loved the Christmas tree that Jerry was carrying and, they loved what was about to happen. An old fashioned Christmas tree decorating event was just what the apartment needed to start the Holiday season.

"It's a beauty" said Jerry as he strung the lights with vigor climbing up the ladder to reach the top of the tree. Then, Jerry plugged in the lights to make sure all the lights worked before putting on any ornaments.

The tree faced the street so that Amanda could see the tree as she walked up the walk to the apartment after work. Amanda said that she wanted the snowman that Jerry made for her to be able to see it from the street. With that Jerry kissed her lips and hugged Amanda while Sarah stood there smiling at the two.

"What do we have for ornaments?" said Jerry.

"We don't have any ornaments for the tree. Should we go out to get some? It's snowing awfully hard out right now" said Sarah.

"On the farm, we just make our own decorations. They're much better than store bought anyway" said Jerry.

"Let's pop some popcorn and make our own old fashioned garland" said Amanda.

So, they headed off to the kitchen to make a giant bowl of popcorn to put in the middle of the kitchen table. Then, Sarah brought out 3 needles and 3 spools of thread. And, she threaded each needle leaving the thread attached to the spool since she didn't know how much popcorn was going to be threaded on each strand of garland. So, the afternoon was spent piercing kernels of popcorn with the needles until there was enough popcorn to put on the tree for garland.

That being done, the tree definitely had an old fashioned charm to it from times long time passed. "But, what will we do for ornaments that will go well with the tree? We don't have any, you know" said Amanda.

"What do we have?" said Jerry.

"We have multi-colored glitter; some glue; scissors; and, some thread sitting in the kitchen drawer. But, that is about it" said Sarah.

"OK. Put that on the kitchen table while I run outside for a second" said Jerry. Jerry headed out the door while the girls filled the kitchen table with what they could find to help decorate the tree.

In a few minutes, Jerry carried into the apartment a white plastic bucket he got from his car. Inside it was filled with pine cones he found outside the apartment sitting under the trees outside. "We can decorate the cones with glitter and use thread to hang them on the tree for ornaments. They will go well with the pine cones already on the tree" said Jerry. The girls just smiled as the tree started getting all decked out like an old fashioned tree—all from things from nature.

They just touched glue to the pine cones here and there and sprinkled glitter over it. And, they weaved a single thread around each decorated pine cone to hang the ornament on the tree with. And, one by one, each went to the tree to hang their decorated pine cone to sparkle in the sun and dry. Nobody could take their eyes off the tree since it sparkled so.

"The tree is the most beautiful thing I've ever seen" said Amanda.

"It sure is" said Sarah.

"It's a beauty" said Jerry.

Amanda put a white pillow case under the tree to resemble snow. And, all three put the manger under the tree putting the Nativity figurines in the folds of the cloth to keep the figurines in place. "Now, it's perfect" said Amanda. They all agreed that it was the prettiest tree that they ever saw.

"Can't beat Jesus Christ any day of the week especially at Christmas" said Jerry. All three agreed Jesus meant the world to them.

## Chapter 7

Amanda was glad that Sarah had plans to be with her boyfriend this Christmas. And, Jerry was going home to the farm where he was raised to spend the Holidays with his folks. She never liked leaving her loved ones by themselves especially during the Holidays without her.

Now, that Sarah and Jerry had some place to go, she could relax a little more about going home to the farm with her parents she loved. So, she knew that they missed her being there all the time. But, she had to be here for now.

Tom, her father, would be here almost any time. Her suitcase was at the living room door to go down. She thought that she could almost smell her mother's pumpkin pie baking mingled with the scent of baked turkey and stuffing. Her mouth began watering with just the thought of this.

Down below was the parking place where her father would pull up. The apartment window was frosted inside on the glass. Amanda scraped off some of it with her fingernail so that she could see outside. Her fingertips on the glass could tell her how cold it was outside. From this, she knew that she would have to wear gloves outside to keep warm.

The snow was just beginning to fall. The roads were starting to ice up. She could tell because the sun glared so strongly off the ice that she could barely look at the road. She knew that winter roads like this were probably considered slick and hazardous as weather reports liked to call them. However, most people had to brave the roads anyway to get around.

She was starting to look anxious about her long ride home. She was glad that she wasn't driving. Her father was the good driver of the family.

"And, there he is" said Amanda as she saw her father pull up in the familiar family car. Out he came from the car to wave at her standing at her bedroom window. She waved back. She then grabbed her suitcase to take it down to the car.

In a moment, they were heading off once she exchanged a hug and a kiss. She had missed her father's hug so. She was anxious to hear her father's voice again. She was home again. She was a kid once again.

"Merry Christmas, dad" said Amanda.

"Merry Christmas, Amanda" said Tom to his daughter.

"Your mother is home cooking all day for your coming home. And, Ralph is already at the farm waiting on you. He looks like he is about to break a gut waiting on you" said Tom.

"Well, that's great" said Amanda.

"I thought that you would like it, too. We should be home in time for dinner" said Tom contently smiling that Amanda was coming home to be with him and her mother.

As Tom pulled up to the farm, Amanda couldn't help but, see how the snow falling made the house look like a Christmas card to her. The lights from the windows made the windows glow yellow from the distance. And, there was garland that glistened in the sun from the banister that led to the wreathe on the front door that had red Christmas balls on it that sparkled in the sun. The

Christmas tree that was standing in the living room window could be seen as they pulled up the drive.

She hadn't remembered her childhood home being quite so beautiful when she was growing up here. She didn't know if it was the fondness of her childhood memories here that made her so passionate to see this place with such love. Or, was it actually this beautiful to the eye to everyone?

But, hardly anyone ever came here to see her or her family unless they were family; a farm hand; or a neighboring farmer since they tended to pitch in together when in need. Like real family.

Perhaps that was why it was so beautiful because it had an innocence and charm to it of a place separate of the rest of the world. It was a farm after all thought Amanda. A very special place to help feed people since most people weren't able to provide for themselves what farmers do. Amanda took pride in what her family represented to people. They were good people.

Tom held his daughter's hand as she climbed up the snow covered stairs leading to the front door. The front door was open. Nobody was coming through the door anyway since it was so rural unless they were family or someone the family knew well. It was home.

The scent of pumpkin pie mingled with baked turkey and stuffing filled Amanda's nostrils. She smiled remembering her thought of her mother's cooking all the way from her apartment.

Ralph grabbed her around her waist to embrace her. He was somehow more masculine and sexy than she had remembered. She almost thought that she could hear his heart beat out of his chest as he held her near to him. She suddenly could feel his bulge under his jeans. She hadn't remembered that before. Maybe it was just her. But, she could feel something inside of her responding to him.

Tom stared on at the two of them grunting softly like a bull kicking the dirt about to stampede. Carolyn sensing this, grabbed her husband softly by the arm to help her in the kitchen.

"These two have a lot of catching up to do" said Carolyn. Tom contented himself with tasting of Carolyn's cooking in the kitchen. It was one of the things he liked best about her except his time in the bed with her. That thought made him blush with red running up and down his neck and cheeks. He was still madly in love with his wife even after all these years. Carolyn knew this too. This was the making of their long and happy marriage.

Ralph couldn't let go of Amanda's hand. He held it on his lap as he talked to her on the couch.

Somehow, he seemed more intense than what she remembered. She trusted Ralph and loved him, anyway. But, she didn't know why he was so different somehow than what she remembered. She would have to play it by ear.

It was the dead of winter after all. There was thick snow and ice everywhere. The roads were at times impassable. She had no place to live in town so that she could work at the feed store which is one of the reasons she was living in town in the big city with Sarah in the first place. Ralph, in part, sent her there.

Amanda was glad when her mother called her and Ralph to eat at the kitchen table. Tom bowed his head. Everyone held hands together.

Tom said:

Dear God. Thank you for this good food my lovely wife, Carolyn has cooked for us to share together with our loved ones today. Thank you for blessing us with this farm. Amen.

"Amen" said everyone at the table.

"Everything looks so good" said Ralph passing around the bowls for everyone to share this Christmas food.

"My wife is a good cook" said Tom. Carolyn smiled from ear-to-ear. It meant a lot to her that her husband appreciated her contribution to the family.

The snow was falling outside as the family gathered around the Christmas tree to share a cup of coffee and Carolyn's homemade pumpkin pie that was still hot from baking in the oven. The vanilla ice cream that rested on top of each piece was melting pools of white mush that sat around on the plate next to the pie and fork that rested near it.

Everyone was content with their belly being full and resting near the soft glow of the Christmas lights. No one wanted to talk. The snow pelting the windows of the farmhouse was a reminder of the bitter cold outside. All the while, they were safely warm inside enjoying the family's love that they shared together.

Ralph was glad to be part of the family. He wanted to always be welcomed here. Tom was a good customer of his at the feed store. He brought a lot of the local farmers to the store. He was good word of mouth advertisement.

Carolyn's cooking was above excellent. And, she treated him like the mother he never had. That meant a lot to him. And, he loved Amanda. He hoped that someday she would be able to return back to work at the feed store. She was good for business. She was a good employee.

That must be what he is missing he thought to himself. He had been there in the store working day after day by himself. Before that, he had Amanda there every day. That must be it. All the same, he was happy to be in her company, again.

The snow was piling up outside. Carolyn offered to show Ralph to his bedroom. He would use Tommy's bedroom which was just across the hall from Amanda if he needed anything. And, it had its own bathroom for privacy, thought Carolyn. Ralph grabbed his suitcase carrying it up the stairs following Carolyn.

"Well, I really appreciate the good cooking and you letting me stay overnight and all" said Ralph to Carolyn.

"You're family now. And, the roads are too slick to be traveling in the dark with the snow blowing across the fields like that—and on a holiday yet" said Carolyn to Ralph.

"Tomorrow, you'll have breakfast with us. We'll be opening presents together for Christmas" said Carolyn. With that, she opened the bedroom to Tommy's bedroom where Ralph carried in his suitcase secretly glad to end the day.

As much as he loved Carolyn and Tom, he was just getting used to them as family. So, he was always trying hard to please them with everything he did. His parents were dead. This was his first chance for family for himself. Ralph was glad to be by himself for awhile now that Carolyn had closed the door.

Barely had he stripped off his clothes and put on his pajama bottom when he heard a knock at the door of his bedroom. Startled, he opened the door to see Amanda standing there barefoot in a pastel blue nightgown and robe. Ralph grabbed his robe putting it on as he opened the door.

"I was just wondering if you needed anything before I retire for bed" said Amanda.

"No, your mother, Carolyn thought of everything as she always does" said Ralph with his hand on the doorknob feeling his hand all sweaty under it puzzled to even see Amanda in her nightgown much less in her own parents' home.

"OK, then" said Amanda as she started heading toward her bedroom. Then, with her hand on her bedroom doorknob, she looked back at Ralph.

"Anything else?" said Ralph.

"I was wondering if you would like to see my bedroom since we had talked so much about it at the feed store" said Amanda.

"You mean now?" said Ralph.

"Well, I don't know of any other time we will be here together like this. And, maybe tomorrow, I can show you around the farm" said Amanda.

"A gentleman should never refuse an invite from a beautiful woman" said Ralph softly to Amanda as he headed to Amanda's bedroom feeling suddenly filled once again with desire for Amanda. He wasn't used to being in close quarters with her for one thing.

Amanda led Ralph into her bedroom. She wanted to show him her shrine of the Virgin Mary where she had prayed for hours when growing up. Ralph just smiled. She opened her dresser drawer to show Ralph her barrette collection from Carolyn that she got for her daughter when she came into the big city where the feed store was located. Ralph just smiled as Amanda closed the drawer to the dresser. Then, she led Ralph to her desk next to the window where she looked out at the farm every day of her life.

By now, the moonlight shined within the window. Ralph could see the outline of Amanda's breasts under her nightgown as he saw her chest rise and fall with each breath. He stood there for a moment looking out over the farm in the moonlight.

Amanda looked more beautiful to him than what he remembered. Her hair glowed soft brown hues in the moonlight. He could see her eyes sparkle.

"The farm is really beautiful" said Ralph as he reached over to kiss Amanda's lips. She kissed him back. Startled at his own behavior, he headed toward the door. He hadn't meant to kiss her.

"You don't regard me as a woman" said Amanda to Ralph.

"No, it isn't that" said Ralph turning now to face Amanda.

"Then, you didn't like kissing me" said Amanda.

"No, it isn't that" said Ralph now holding Amanda around her waist. He looked down at her lips and lost control over himself. He couldn't remember how long or how many times he kissed her lips. He could feel the softness and warmth from her lips as she responded back to him.

He had lusted after her the whole time she was gone. Now, she was in his arms. He had to have her. He had to have her now. He was a man in love. She hoped that she wanted him back.

He opened his robe to reveal his chest. Amanda put her hands on his chest reaching down under his pajama bottom. It was all instinct now: pure total animal instinct.

He stepped out of his pajama bottom leaving them where he stood. He left his robe there, also. Amanda stood there while Ralph lifted her robe and nightgown above her head. He reached down to kiss her breasts. Then, he carried her in his arms to the bed lying on top of her determined to have her for his own forgetting where exactly he was.

All he knew is that he was with Amanda. That is all that mattered to him now. She must love him to let him have her. He kissed her into the night until he couldn't take it anymore. And finally, he gently at first put his hardness inside her to organism watching her arch her back as he came.

"I'd better get back to my own bed before your parents catch us in bed together in the morning" said Ralph. Amanda nodded getting one last kiss from Ralph before he closed the door.

The smell of the coffee perking traveled up the bedroom stairs along with bacon and eggs that followed that woke up Ralph from his sleep. He was hungrier than usual. Probably the good sex is what he thought. He showered quickly and put his jeans on. He found Amanda in the kitchen with Carolyn and Tom.

"Breakfast is nearly ready" said Carolyn.

"Good. I'm really famished" said Ralph.

"So, how did you like sleeping in Tommy's old bedroom?" said Tom.

"Just great. And, thank you" said Ralph exchanging glances with Amanda.

After breakfast, Carolyn asked the 3 of them to go into the living room while she washed the breakfast dishes. She didn't like dirty dishes in the sink. Amanda had already told Carolyn and Tom that she wanted to show Ralph around the farm while he was here. Tom was delighted. He always was delighted when anyone wanted to see his "pride and joy."

Carolyn being through with cleaning up, asked Amanda to come into the kitchen before they took off for their walk on the farm. "Amanda, I stripped your bed this morning to wash the bedding. I know what you did last night. You know how your father feels. He loves Ralph, mind you" said Carolyn.

"I couldn't help it" said Amanda.

"You love him" said Carolyn. Amanda nodded with tears running down her cheeks.

"Just don't tell your dad. It will kill him. He had dreams and expectations for you and this farm. We'll just have to figure something out is all. Just don't tell your dad" said Carolyn hugging her daughter. Amanda wiped away her tears with Carolyn's help.

Winter coats and hats on, everyone headed out the door to show off the farm to Ralph with Tom leading the way. Ralph was impressed with how large the farm was since he had never walked it on foot before. There was the acres of cornfields now plowed under with row after row furrowed under with snow and ice filling the crevices. A walk through the barn let Ralph see Tom's tractor where he proudly showed him where he stored it there to protect it from the elements until he used it once again to plow up the fields. Then, Amanda led the way to Grandpa Jim's gravesite to visit her much cherished relatives now that he was co-living with God in heaven. So, he couldn't visit his granddaughter on earth. Next, Carolyn led the way to the apple orchard to show Ralph the trees where she harvested the apples for her pies and other much loved recipes. Ralph liked the look of the black branches of the trees pointing to the heavens now sitting with snow resting at their feet. Tom had wrapped the trunks with burlap to try to keep the trees warm during the winter.

Ralph seemed exhausted from all the walking. His cheeks were bright red from the cold. They headed back to the farm house confident that they had impressed Ralph enough with the farm as much as they were. It meant a lot to them.

Ralph was actually in love with everything and anything they showed him because to him they were showering him with love. He had been without love for a long time. They gave him what he wanted. He kept coming back for more.

Back in the house, everyone huddled around a warm cup of coffee in the kitchen. The warmth of the coffee cup around their fingers warmed their hands. They welcomed the touch of it.

Carolyn offered to make a light lunch. In the warmth of the kitchen, it seemed like a good idea to everyone. Soup bowls were passed around while Carolyn made a quick tomato bisque.

## CAROLYN'S TOMATO BISQUE

### Ingredients

One small onion, minced (can add more a little bit at a time)
One tablespoon of melted butter (can add more little bit at a time)
One small to medium size can of un-spiced stewed tomatoes (can add more ¼ cup at a time)
Note: can chop the tomatoes in a bowl to create small tomato pieces if like smaller pieces of tomatoes.
Skim or whole milk (add ½ cup at a time until get to desired thickness of bisque)

### Directions

In frying pan, melt butter over low heat. Pour in minced onion into butter. Stir often to keep onion form burning and until translucent. Use low heat throughout cooking! Now, pour in milk, a 1/2 cup at a time. Mix all of the ingredients together. Now, gently mix in the stewed tomatoes 4 to 8 ounces at a time. Can use a whisk or a spoon to do so! How much milk is used depends on how milky you want the bisque! And, how much tomato you use depends on how tomatoey you want the bisque as well! It is best to add a little bit at a time to determine this! Make sure that tomatoes are mixed evenly into all of the mixture (and gently since that keeps the tomato pieces intact). Don't overcook the ingredients since you don't want to scald the ingredients (burn them). Never boil the bisque as you might with soup. Just bring to where all the ingredients are warmed instead. Can touch surface of bisque in pot carefully with finger to see if feels warm enough to touch to be ready to serve. Then, turn off the heat immediately moving the pot to a cool surface so that it doesn't continue to cook. Keep lid on the pot to keep warm until serving the bisque. Serve at once while warm.

Hot tea filled the teapot sitting in the center of the table covered with a towel to keep it warm. Crackers sat in the center of the table for everyone. Lunch was ready as far as Carolyn was concerned. Soup bowls were filled with steamy tomato bisque sitting next to soup spoons. Everyone's stomachs would be warmed in a moment or two from now. She was good at this kind of thing being a farmer's wife and all.

Everyone bowed their heads. And, Tom began to pray:

Thank you God for this wonderful warm lunch my wife Carolyn made us on this so cold, but beautiful day you gave us today to share together. Amen.

"Amen" said everyone.

Everyone was delighted to be together today. Everything smelled so good. And, the house was toasty warm, too.

"I thank you for that wonderful lunch, Carolyn. I was wondering if you would mind if I

116

took Amanda to the feed store today. I want to show it to her since she hasn't been there for awhile. And, I know she'd love to see it all decorated for the Holidays. And, I wanted to bring back some Christmas presents from the store for everyone if you wouldn't mind" said Ralph.

"It's OK with me if it's OK with Tom" said Carolyn looking at Tom's expression on his face.

"You want to go or stay, Amanda" said Tom.

"Well, it would be nice" said Amanda.

"Well, that settles it, then" said Tom pushing his chair from the table.

"Take good care of my little girl. And, call me when you get there so her mother doesn't worry. OK?" said Tom.

"OK" said Ralph helping Amanda put on her winter coat.

"It's probably going to be getting dark soon outside. It looks like it's going to storm soon" said Carolyn looking out the window always concerning herself with the comings and goings of nature.

"It does look that way, by golly. We'll probably eat supper at the feed store when we get there at some point in time. If it is OK with Amanda's parents, I would like to have us stay overnight there so that I'm not driving back in the dark with the winter roads. I promise to bring us back in the morning loaded down with Christmas gifts for under the tree" said Ralph.

"Well, you'd better get going. The sooner you go, the sooner you'll be back" said Tom hiding a tear from his eye crying inside that he would be missing his daughter again. And, she was leaving so soon after coming home to him.

Still, she was an adult woman now. He knew in his heart that she would do what she wants now whether her father liked it or not. He had her love as a child. He had to keep that in mind now. Tommy was gone from him. He couldn't afford to lose her as well. So, in that case, he welcomed Ralph and Amanda doing whatever got them through this Holiday in one piece.

It was only a matter of time before she was a married woman as it is. He would have to share her with her new family then. Tom sighed. It made Carolyn smile. She knew that he suffered inside as a parent because she suffered, too.

Ralph made it into town with his precious cargo: Amanda. He couldn't wait to show off the feed store. Once the door opened to the store, he turned on the Christmas lights. Amanda "oohed" at the prettiness of it all.

Ralph took her to the gift baskets to select what they wanted to take back for under the

Christmas tree so that they wouldn't forget when they promised Amanda's parents. He wasn't going to be selling these items at full price after Christmas. So, this was a good time to be generous to impress Amanda's parents now that they had bedded down together.

Carolyn would get a gift basket of garden tools and garden gloves with a red bow on it. Tom would get a gift basket of hand tools with work gloves with a green bow on it. Ralph also had some extra gift baskets with teas and dehydrated soups and such. In all, Amanda and Ralph selected six gift baskets to take back to her parents for Christmas presents which Amanda told him that they would love having.

There were matching soup bowls and glasses there. There was a ceramic teapot in another basket there. There was a hand drill for Tom in another basket there. Ralph wanted to start on the right foot with Amanda's parents as much as he could.

"I want to take you upstairs to show you where we are sleeping tonight" said Ralph grabbing her by the hand leading the way up the stairs.

Amanda passed by a bedroom, a large living room, a kitchen, a second bedroom and another bedroom before entering the front master bedroom with its own private bathroom, that faced the main street. There standing next to the bed, Ralph unbuttoned her blouse and unzipped her skirt revealing her standing in front of him wearing a satin white slip.

Amanda pulled the slip over her head. She came prepared to be with him. She had no other under garments on. She pulled back the sheets of the bed and lay down in the bed waiting for Ralph to disrobe which he did eagerly. They were already an old married couple. They were used to each other by now.

Ralph lay next to Amanda allowing her to touch him where she wanted. He was interested in pleasing her to no end. She reached down to what was between his legs to touch what was under the sheets until it was aroused enough for Ralph to climb inside her while they kissed into the night.

They had forgotten to eat supper as they promised Amanda's parents. And, they were painfully aware of the delicate situation their love created for the family. Ralph didn't care to think of it right now while in the arms of his lovely Amanda. She was all that mattered to him now. He didn't want to ever lose her.

In the morning, Amanda and Ralph talked but, only after making love to each other all night. "Making love is a wonderful way of saying having sex because it says so much about the importance of sex in a relationship" said Ralph.

Amanda nodded.

"My mother knows about us, by the way. Just for you to know, we aren't to tell my father for right now" said Amanda.

Ralph nodded.

"Love is love. We will have to figure out a way to make this work" said Ralph.

"That's what my mother said" said Amanda.

Ralph gave Amanda a hug and a kiss on the forehead.

He was so in love he could hardly stand himself. He hoped Amanda was a woman in love with him. He secretly thanked God for this lovely lady: his Amanda.

They hadn't realized how much of the day had passed. They decided to shower quickly and get dressed. They had the car to load up with the Christmas goodies for Amanda's parents that they had promised to bring back with them. They were too in love to eat, anyway.

They would grab something from the refrigerator to take with them to tide them over until they got back to the farm. They would look forward to home cooking again from Amanda's mother. And, Ralph wanted to get off on the right foot with these Christmas gifts for Amanda's parents. He wanted to load them down with Christmas gifts so that they would definitely love him—which he knew they did. But, still he wanted to please Amanda's parents a lot. He wanted to be a permanent family member beyond a shadow of a doubt. He loved Tom and Carolyn with his whole heart. And, he loved their daughter with his whole heart.

So, while Ralph was packing up the car, Amanda like a seasoned wife was making scrambled egg sandwiches to go with a thermos of coffee. And, she even washed the dishes before they locked up the place since they would be gone for the weekend at the farm.

Tom practically ran out the door to hug Amanda when she showed up. Carolyn followed. Neither had their winter coat on. So, Amanda was quick to enter the house knowing her parents would follow her while Ralph unloaded the car. He was proud to be able to provide these gifts from his own store for the Millers. He put them under the tree. Amanda's present was already there from him from the day before.

Christmas was on in the Miller household one more overnight until Christmas. This was Christmas Eve. Ralph had kept his promise of returning Tom and Carolyn's daughter to them in time for Christmas.

Carolyn went all out for Christmas Eve dinner. She had been cooking since Ralph and Amanda had left for the feed store so that it would be special for everyone.

Carolyn decided on baked pork chops; sautéed red and green bell peppers with onion slices; and sweet potato cups. Carolyn pulled out her recipes that she planned to give to Amanda when she got married for her family's meals.

First recipe:

## DOUBLE BREADED PORK CHOPS

Ingredients:

4 pork chops
1 cup bread crumbs poured on a dinner plate (use extra bread crumbs if needed)
2 beaten eggs with 2 tablespoon of water in a bowl
2-3 tablespoons of cooking oil

Directions

Preheat oven at 375° for 10 minutes. Then, put the cooking oil in the bottom of a frying pan on low heat. Then, dip the pork chops in the egg mixture on both sides until completely covered. Then, dip the pork chops in the bread crumbs until completely covered. Then, dip the pork chops again in egg mixture. After that, dip the pork chops in the bread crumbs. Place gently side by side in the frying pan browning each side. While frying the pork chops, line a cookie sheet with aluminum foil. Lay the fried pork chops on the foil. Place a sheet of foil on top of the pork chops crimping the sides of the foil to seal in the meat. Bake for approximately 1½ hours in the oven.

In the meantime, Carolyn wrapped 4 sweet potatoes individually in aluminum foil and placed them in the oven next to the pork chops. So now, Carolyn was ready for her second recipe:


## SWEET POTATO CUPS

### Ingredients

4 sweet potatoes washed, dried, and wrapped individually in aluminum foil
4 maraschino cherries
miniature marshmallows
milk

### Directions

Bake the sweet potatoes in the oven at 375° until can be pierced easily with a fork. Usually 1-1½ hours. Then, take the skin off the potatoes. Put the potatoes in a mixing bowl. With a mixer, beat the potatoes with milk leaving the mixture thick comparable to the consistency of mashed potatoes. Put the mixture in individual serving dishes. As a decoration and for taste while the potatoes are steamy hot, around the rim of each cup push a marshmallow side by side around the edge of each cup. Then, garnish with a maraschino cherry in the middle of the cup.

So, while everything was baking in the oven, Carolyn prepared her third recipe:

## RED AND GREEN PEPPER SAUTEE

## Ingredients

1 red pepper—cored, cleaned, and sliced in strips
1 green bell pepper—cored, cleaned, and sliced in strips
1 yellow onion, medium size, peeled and sliced thinly
2-3 tablespoons of cooking oil

## Directions

Pour cooking oil on the bottom of a frying pan on low heat. Then, pour in the red and green peppers with the yellow onion slices. Move around the mixture until the peppers are completely cooked and the onions are translucent. Put a lid on the top of the frying pan to keep the mixture warm and place the frying pan where there is no heat under it until ready to serve.

Everybody at the dinner table complimented Carolyn on how Christmassy the dinner was. The red and green peppers sat on the dinner plate next to the sizzling hot pork chops that you could hear it sizzling on the dinner plates. The marshmallows were melting in pools of moist hot sweet potatoes. Carolyn even complimented the colors of the peppers with red and green dinner candles that sat lit in the middle of the dinner table.

After dinner, Carolyn hurried everyone to bed since Christmas day of opening presents came early in the morning at the Miller household. Carolyn knew where Ralph would be spending the night. This Christmas, she didn't care as long as this was what Amanda wanted which it obviously was. And, as long as her husband didn't find out—at least not yet. Carolyn couldn't bear Christmas getting ruined this year for anyone.

Christmas came off without a hitch. "Santa Claus has been good to us" said Tom as he opened up Ralph's presents. Carolyn nodded. They even gave Ralph a thank you kiss on the cheek which pleased him to no end. And, as with everything, including Christmas, it had to end until another year. It was time reluctantly to take Amanda back home with her roommate, Sarah. Carolyn cried which she never does. Amanda hugged her telling her that she would return soon and loved her which seemed to help soothe her mother some. Amanda knew that it was hard to leave loved ones because that is what she went through all the time anymore.

Ralph asked if he could come along to say goodbye to Amanda at the apartment. Tom nodded in agreement. Tom had bought his daughter a new black winter coat that sat in the back seat with Ralph. Carolyn made her daughter a knitted light and dark blue blanket to keep Amanda warm that sat in the back seat of the car with Ralph. And then, there was the stunning real pearl necklace that Ralph had bought Amanda for Christmas that just floored Tom and Carolyn when they saw this beautiful expression of love for Amanda.

Tom drove home to Amanda's apartment silently. Amanda just smiled all the way. She told her father that she was with her "favorite two fellows." She kissed her father's cheek as he drove. She hoped that it made him feel better about things.

"I'll be back, dad. You know that I love you" said Amanda as she brushed away a tear from his cheek startled to see her own father cry. She was sorry that she had to ruin everything for her father by growing up and all. Truly. She knew that it broke his heart to have that happen.

Amanda was happy to see her old apartment again. But she was not happy to leave the farm and her parents. And, she certainly wasn't happy to leave Ralph after what had happened between them.

She would definitely tell Sarah, her roommate, and Jerry what had happened. She hoped that Jerry would take it well. She had forgotten all about Jerry in all the excitement. She loved Jerry. Truly.

She hoped that Jerry would be happy for her because it just happened that way. And, she knew that she wanted to spend the rest of her life with Ralph. She knew that after the lovemaking between them. She would have to face Jerry. He deserved that from her. He was a sweet and loving boyfriend. She hoped that they would somehow remain friends. That meant a lot to her.

Tom kissed Amanda goodbye first handing her suitcase to her. Ralph carried up her Christmas presents to the apartment for her. He came near to kiss her goodbye. He forgot himself in front of Tom. He actually kissed Amanda goodbye on the lips.

"See you both soon" said Amanda waving goodbye as she entered the dark apartment by herself.

She cried in the dark as she sat on the couch. So much emotion had gone through her body in one short Christmas weekend, it was incredible. She didn't know if she was crying tears of happiness or sadness. Probably both.

Tom drove home to the farm with Ralph in the front seat of the car. Ralph was afraid to speak first. He was a little afraid of Tom. He wanted to stay on his good side. He would let him have his say as a man if he had anything to say at all.

They must have drove for a good 20 minutes when Tom finally spoke. "You're sleeping with my daughter, aren't you?" said Tom.

Ralph wished that he could just jump out of the car about now. He didn't want to answer. A silence hung in the air that just felt like an eternity. Finally, he managed an almost inaudible "yes."

"You know how I feel about this" said Tom back.

"I do" said Ralph. The silence was a killer all the way home. Ralph didn't like making Tom unhappy. But, he loved Amanda. And, she loved him.

Ralph's car waited for him at the farm. Carolyn had waiting for him a homemade apple pie for him to take home with him and some homemade apple jelly from the farm's orchard that he loved so. And, he had some work clothes that Tom and Carolyn had bought him: some assorted flannel shirts to keep him warm while working that they knew he loved wearing. And, Amanda had bought him a new wristwatch with a silver band that she brought from the big city. She knew that he wanted that for Christmas.

Ralph was a happy man because he had Amanda's love. But, he wasn't happy to return her back to the apartment far away from him.

And, Tom wasn't happy either with Amanda's choice in life even though he clearly loved Ralph and accepted him as family. He just didn't accept him as his son-in-law and Amanda's husband.

Returning home, he decided to express his discontent to his only son. Perhaps he could get Tommy to talk some sense to Amanda. Somebody had to do that. "Dear Tommy" he wrote.

## Chapter 8

Amanda wished she knew where home was anymore. She just kept running back and forth from place to place. Her parents wanted her home at the farm with them. Sarah and Jerry wanted her at the apartment. And, then Ralph needed her with him at the feed store. She was starting to feel exhausted instead of rested from the Christmas Holiday.

She needed to return back to work tomorrow to begin the work week. And, then it was New Year's weekend where she would have to travel back home again. And, she had yet to make arrangements for her father to pick her up for the Holidays. She knew that it was a family obligation, too.

"Hello, dad" said Amanda on the phone.

"What, Amanda?" said Tom.

"I'm coming home for New Year's. Ralph knows. But, mom needs to know. Tell her for me, please. And, I need a ride home. Please, dad," said Amanda.

"It will be my honor to pick up my only daughter to be home for New Year's. Your mother will be delighted to have you home again so soon. She really loves you, you know" says Tom.

"I know dad" said Amanda.

"Meet you at the apartment on Friday at say around 5ish" said Tom.

"Perfect. It will give me just enough time to walk to the apartment after work and grab my suitcase before we take off" said Amanda.

"OK. I'll see you then. Love you" said Tom.

"Love you too" said Amanda just before hanging up the phone. Now, all she had to do is wait on Sarah and Jerry's plans for the Holidays. They could always tag along to the farm. She never liked leaving loved ones alone especially at the Holidays.

"Growing up sucks" said Amanda under her breath.

"It breaks up a family. Just when everyone gets used to everyone and everything, you end up living without the people you love most" said Amanda.

But, she was starting to get a new life here with friends and work. It was beginning to be home, too.

"Well, it never hurts to have two homes" said Amanda to herself. She couldn't wait until she got to see Jerry and Sarah. She missed them so.

Amanda picked up her phone that was ringing "Hey Amanda. You're home. Great" said Sarah.

"Yes, I just got here awhile ago" said Amanda.

"Listen. I'm calling to let you know I'll be coming home late tonight. I have a date. And, I don't want to skip the date because he might never ask me out again. OK. We're cool" said Sarah.

"Yes, of course. We're cool" said Amanda.

"But, I am having a special dinner for you tomorrow at the apartment. See you later tonight to tell you about my new guy. Cross your fingers for me. And, oh, you have mail sitting on the kitchen table. Love ya'" said Sarah.

"Love you, too" said Amanda hanging up the phone.

Amanda turned to the kitchen table. She saw what seemed to be a stack of circulars and ads. The usual. But, there as she shuffled through the pile was a letter that said the return address was from Jerry Benson.

"What is this? It probably is a Christmas card" said Amanda as she tore through the envelope. She loved Christmas cards ever since she was a kid. The Christmas tree was still up in the apartment. She planned to put the card around the branches of the tree as she loved to do.

Amanda was surprised to not find a card at all. It was a letter from Jerry.

It said:

Dear Amanda

I would have liked to tell you in person but, I couldn't because I didn't know yet until I came home to the family farm. My parents had me when they were older. My father's health is failing some. He is hardy enough to run the farm but, not by himself. He deserves his son to be there. He gave to me when I was a kid. I should be the one to give to him. I'm sure that I will remember that I did forever when I am older that I took this time.

I know that I am putting aside my dreams. But, if this family losses the farm, I will never hear the end of it from the rest of the family. And, I can't afford for them to hate me. It would break my heart if they did.

Even though it breaks my heart to not be there with you since we were doing so well together as a couple. At least, I thought that we were. And, I hope that you agree that we were "good" together. That's for sure.

But, my mom said that the time will pass quickly enough. She says it seems like only yesterday when she first married dad. And, she can hardly believe it herself that she has grown sons. But, she does.

But, once the family steadies itself, mom says that she understands I might leave the farm again to "spread my wings" once again as she puts it instead of staying "in the nest" where it has been home for generations of Bensons.

So, it is important to the family. My two brothers are up in Chicago right now. Both are in college pursuing their degrees. One is getting a degree in agriculture which is common for a farmer boy like myself. So, I know that he will be back sometime to take "the reins" of the family farm we all love—even me.

Even though I really wanted to be there pursuing my dreams and be with you, it would only be "selfish and heartless" to leave my parents now. I am the youngest son. Now, the whole family is "counting on me" to be there for them. So, I hope that you understand, Amanda. I love you. And, I love them.

We get stuck sometimes trying to stretch our lives in many directions. We can't be everywhere. And, we can't be with everyone we love at the same time—except in our hearts which is the most important place of all. At least, I think it is.

I will never forget you. You are so dear to me. I hadn't anyone before I met you in that city that I could actually say I loved because I was always working and only knew my roommate pretty much.

I hope that it made your life better knowing me. It isn't goodbye. We are still friends and family together as we promised we would be. And, I love you so much, Amanda.

Please, do write to me often while I am here. I will be lonely without you.

I am going to be really lonely. I will miss the city; my job; and you. For now, I will have to be content to know that I am doing a "good deed" for my parents. And, I have to be happy that we have this ol' farm that originally belonged to my great great-grandfather I am told.

So, goodbye for now.

Love, Jerry


Amanda just stood there holding the letter. "Now, I don't even have Jerry" said Amanda under her breath. Tears rolled down her cheeks. She put the letter to her chest.

"Well, if Ralph wasn't in the picture, Jerry would have been the one. He really was what her parents would have called the ideal husband material. He knew the farming life. He had brothers who were farmers. His family owns a farm, too" said Amanda thinking out loud.

He actually was quite a catch thought Amanda. What a personality. He was such fun to hang around. And he was so handsome too, with bright blue eyes. He was tall and strong looking with sandy blonde hair that had a red cast to it in the sunlight. And, he had a big toothy smile that made you smile when you saw it thought Amanda.

"I've been the lucky gal to have known you Mr. Jerry Benson" said Amanda out loud.

"And, I don't want you to ever leave my life either. You mean so much to me" said Amanda.

"I love you. I love you. I love you, Mr. Jerry Benson. That I do" said Amanda. And, with that she kissed softly the envelope right over his name.

"I wish you were here with me. Life won't be the same without you here" said Amanda.


Just then, the phone rang. It was Ralph. The voice on the other end said that he wanted to know if he could spend New Year's Eve at midnight with her at the apartment if her parents didn't mind. He had a special "dinner in mind" said Ralph.

"Well, I will have to tell my parents. I don't think that they will mind. They are just happy to see me back home again" said Amanda.

"Well, let me know. If I don't hear different, I'll pick you up Saturday during the early evening at the farm. And, if you think your parents won't mind, you can stay overnight so that I don't have to drive back in the dark" said Ralph.

"Well, my mom knows about us. But, dad doesn't yet. And, we aren't to tell him right now. Mom will have a fit. And, you know why" said Amanda. Ralph didn't want to say anything different about it to Amanda. Yikes! Tom and he had, in effect, words on the subject. He wasn't quite as stupid a man as Amanda had thought—or perhaps even her mother. He had put two-and-two together about their romance on his own.

"Have you heard from Tommy yet?" said Ralph.

"No. And, I don't know what his plans are about living on the farm. I'm surprised that he isn't back from the military, yet. He wasn't supposed to be there as long as he has. I'm happy for him if he liked the work and all. But, we need him to help run the farm. Dad can't do this forever by himself. He is a brave man all these years to hold the farm together with only us girls and a few farmhands to help" said Amanda.

"I know that you never want to lie to your dad. But, if you could somehow make him not worry about us and our sleeping arrangements for now, I would appreciate it. He comes into the store himself from time to time for the farm. And, I don't want to be confronted with questions. I won't know what I will be supposed to be saying without you there by my side if you know what I mean" said Ralph.

"I understand" said Amanda.

"I love you" said Ralph.

"I love you, too" said Amanda.

"Well, I'll see you Saturday then unless I hear differently" said Ralph.

"Alright" said Amanda. And, with that Ralph hung up.

Amanda stood there all filled with so many emotions that she wasn't used to having inside of her. Jerry. Ralph. Her parents. Tommy. And, of course, Sarah, her roommate who only yesterday, they sat in class together in high school. Who would have guessed all this? thought Amanda. Ralph and Amanda were moving along awfully quick in this relationship she thought. So loved it. He made her feel so adult—so desired—so much a woman. And, she did love him, too thought Amanda.

She would be glad when her roommate would be home so that she would have a real person to talk to about all that happened to her recently. She hardly could believe it herself. And, Sarah would miss Jerry, too. They were good friends together, too.

Amanda sat herself near the Christmas tree and cried. She missed home with her parents. She missed Jerry. She missed Ralph. How was her life going to end up when so much going on in her life? thought Amanda with tears running down her cheeks about now.

"Tommy, please write to your sister, Amanda, soon" said Amanda.

And, just then the doorknob to the apartment turned. It was Sarah, her roommate.

"Hi, roommate" said Sarah as she hugged Amanda.

"Hi" said Amanda.

"Have a great time at the farm?" said Sarah.

"I did indeed" said Amanda as she returned the hugs. And, they spent the night talking about Jerry; her parents; and Ralph. And, she talked about her upcoming plans for New Year's so that she would know.

And, Sarah wanted Amanda to know about her new beau, John Goldman who was of all things, a chef who owned his own restaurant in downtown Indianapolis where Sarah was window shopping one day after work, when this man with bright brown piercing eyes waved at her as she looked in the window at the menu. She waved back. He invited her to dinner he made himself after the restaurant was closed.

"A candlelight dinner with beef au jus, carrots, and potatoes with hot apple potato salad, and house wine. The rest is history. He wants me to come to the restaurant for New Year's eve for dinner and dancing to celebrate the New Year with him" said Sarah.

"Perfect. I already promised my parents and Ralph I was coming home for New Year's. I will be leaving Friday after work. And, I will be back Sunday early evening" said Amanda.

"Perfect. I worried about our plans for New Year's eve. And, now we are all set" said Sarah.

"I know" said Amanda.

"It's perfect" said Amanda and Sarah together.

"How do we do that?" said Sarah.

"I don't know. But, it's perfect that we do all the same" said Amanda.

"How true" said Sarah.

And, they both laughed and hugged. And, they made plans to have a special dinner in the apartment as a get-together just the two of them when she returned home.

"Perfect" said Amanda and Sarah together again. And, they both laughed together so much until they got hiccups from the whole thing.

Just then, the phone rang. It was dad telling Amanda that he was home at the farm safely. Amanda was glad. He didn't like those winter roads because he couldn't see the ice there.

"Did you tell mom that I'll be home New Year's weekend?" said Amanda.

"Yes, I did. And, she is delighted. She is having some of the farmhands and their families stop by early Saturday if you don't mind to say howdy around 10 AM or so. It will be a brunch to celebrate the New Year" said Tom.

"I'll be there" said Amanda.

"I'm counting on it. We wanted to thank them for helping all these years on the farm. You know, show appreciation and all. Your mother thought that it was a good idea. And, they really are like family" said Tom.

"That's true" said Amanda.

"Oh dad. I almost forgot to tell you that Ralph called. He wants to know if he can pick me up at the farm early evening on Saturday so that we can spend New Year's Eve with me at the feed store. He wants me to stay overnight so that he doesn't have to drive me back in the dark on the winter roads. He'll bring me back mid-morning on Sunday so that I can spend some time with you and mom. I won't go if you don't want me to" said Amanda. She stood there crossing her fingers waiting for a response from her dad.

"Well, I wouldn't want Ralph to have to spend New Year's by himself if he wants you to come there. We are all family together" said Tom.

"I trust you to act like a proper lady there" said Tom.

"I'm an adult lady now, dad" said Amanda feeling her cheeks blush.

"Well, you are an adult lady. So, I can't tell you what to do anymore. But, I appreciate your respecting me enough to ask me all the same. Do you think that you could be home by 10 AM at least on Sunday? It would be nice to spend the day with my only daughter before I have to drive you back to your apartment" said Tom.

"I will" said Amanda.

"I love you, Amanda" said Tom.

"I love you too, dad" said Amanda. Amanda heard her father hang up the phone.

"Perfect" said Amanda as a feeling of guilt swept over her emotions. She never liked to lie to her father in the least. He was a good honest churchgoing man who raised his family right thought Amanda.

This will have to do for now. She loved her parents. She loved Ralph. She wanted everyone to be happy. She wished she was at the farm about now. If she was, she would walk to her grandfather's grave knee deep in snow.

She would pinch off one of the red geraniums her mother grew in the kitchen window sill in the winter. They always blossomed red flowers at Christmas time. They were a great Christmas flower with the large green leaves up against these red flowers thought Amanda. In the summer, they could go back outdoors in the garden to blossom once again.

But, right now Amanda wanted to hurry on home to put one of these Christmas blossoms that was one of Grandpa Jim's favorite flowers on his gravesite to pay respects to him. And, she wanted to sit there in the snow to tell him about all that has been happening to her life since she moved from the farm. Certainly, he would know the answers for her life. He was a very wise grandfather to her when he and her used to walk among the trees in the apple orchard on the farm to gather apples for his only daughter Carolyn to make apple pie that he loved. The recipe had come from his own wife Gertrude nicknamed Gertie.

"Oh, how he loved his red haired beauty of a wife" said Grandpa Jim who was Amanda's grandmother. Amanda didn't know her as well since she died when she only an infant. But, she did recall what she looked like somewhat. And, she loved her, too. She was buried next to her grandfather here. But, it was her grandfather who she knew best since he helped raise her.

And, it was her grandfather who had taught her that she could talk to him in heaven. "You can talk to Jesus" said Grandpa Jim handing Amanda a ripe red apple with a bright green leaf attached to the stem he just grabbed from the apple tree one autumn day when they were walking together as always.

"Yes" said Amanda.

"Well, I will be in the same place, Amanda, someday years from now. And, I want you to remember that you can always talk to me there, too. Promise me that you will remember that" said Grandpa Jim determined his granddaughter wouldn't cry when he had passed away.

"I promise" said Amanda as she tugged at her grandfather's navy blue jacket for him to lean down for her to kiss his cheek. He kissed her cheek back.

Her mind went back to her apartment. "I think that I will light a candle in the bedroom by my statue of the Virgin Mary and say a rosary. That always makes me feel better. I have my blue beaded rosary with me that mom gave me for a gift" said Amanda softly so as not to wake up Sarah who went to bed early. Blue was the special color in the Catholic Church to honor Mary, the Mother of

God, she was told by her mother. She could use the sweet love of my Mother of Perpetual Help as the nuns who helped raise her in school had taught her. I need spiritual help about now thought Amanda. And, with that, she sat in the glow of a blue candle lit in front of the Virgin Mary holding her blue rosary. She began her rosary: "In the name of the Father, the Son, and the Holy Spirit..." She believed in the power of the Sacred Heart of Mary and Jesus and the saints and angels in heaven as she was taught in the Church and by her mother, Carolyn. She also believed in what her father had taught her about God. Amanda was filled with the Spirit of the Lord with hope of Mary's sweet intercession for her to her son, Jesus Christ.

She blew out the candles confident that her spiritual mother would watch over her through these times. She was glad to be home in her bed in her apartment for now. She felt safe with Sarah in the next bedroom.

She wondered what next year would be like about this time. But, sleep overtook her. And, this was something only God knew. It wasn't proper for her to think on things much that was the promise of God to unfold as was His will. Tomorrow was a day of relaxing and waiting on Sarah's special dinner.

"Goodnight dad. Goodnight mom" Amanda called out softly before falling asleep. It made her somehow feel that she wasn't alone and not be so far away from what was familiar with. She knew that she was a blessed lady to be surrounded by so much love.

"Goodnight, Jesus. Goodnight St. Mary" said Amanda softly as Amanda threw a kiss to Mary's statue on the dresser before her. Jesus and Mary were family to her, too.

# Chapter 9

Amanda opened the door to her parents' home to the smell of bacon in the air. Carolyn had decided to have a buffet style brunch because of the large number of houseguests. There was Larry, who was a farmhand, and his wife, Mary. There was Zach, who also was a farmhand, who was Amish and his wife, Rita, who wasn't of Amish heritage. And, John who was the only farm hand who wasn't married. His wife had died some years back. He liked living on the farm. The Millers liked having him on the farm pretty much 24/7 being that it was a farm and all. Without him, Tom was the only male on the farm at all to work the farm and watch over it. So, without a wife to watch over, he could afford to hang around more than the other farmhands. He was a hard working quiet man. He was especially loved by the Millers.

The eight of them sat at the long table Tom had opened up, covered with Carolyn's white linen table cloth. Carolyn sat at one end of the table. Tom sat on the other end of the table.

Tom began grace:

Dear Lord: Thank you for blessing us with these wonderful folk coming to our breakfast brunch to celebrate the beginning of the New Year and the good work done for the Miller farm this year. We had an especially good harvest this year. Please help us have a good year again this year. And, thank you Lord for Amanda, our dear daughter, being with us to celebrate the New Year. Amen.

Everyone said: "Amen". And, everyone praised Carolyn's attractive breakfast brunch. Along the length of the table there was hot homemade cranberry muffins and butter; cooked bacon; hot pork sausage; and a platter of scrambled eggs. And, there were two glass pitchers of orange juice that sat at both ends of the table. Fresh coffee brewed in the background.

Carolyn planned for everyone to join her and her husband after to the living room to sit around the Christmas tree to visit. The Millers never had time to just chat since they were always working on the farm. And, Carolyn had belated Christmas gifts for everyone to take home with them.

So, everyone automatically gravitated to the living room.

Carolyn handed Larry, Zach, and John 3 gift baskets Carolyn had made herself for each of them. "This is kind of a late Christmas present for you" said Carolyn. In each was a jar of homemade strawberry jam; homemade apple jelly; and a homemade apple pie wrapped in plastic with a red bow on it.

"These all come from the farm. I made them myself for you" said Carolyn beaming. Everyone agreed that these were the best presents ever since they were coming from Carolyn and their boss, Tom. They were grateful to be appreciated by their boss and his wife in their home. They understand that they were at their job in many ways. And, therefore, they had to be on their best behavior.

But, all the same, it was nice to relax for once on the farm and actually enjoy the place for once instead of just work there.

Since it started to snow outside, everyone decided it would be a great time to go skating on the farm together to enjoy the day. In the back of the farm was a small pond. So in the background of the farm with the snow sparkling pink, green, and yellow in the sun, donning ice skates everyone skated for what seemed like hours.

Tommy had liked coming here with the family when the pond was frozen thick enough for ice skating. In the summer, the pond was stocked with fish for fishing. That was Tom and Tommy's pastime together.

Back at the house, John was the first to get up to say goodbye. "I'm going upstairs to nap. I've had such a nice time. Thank you for inviting me" said John. He reached over to Carolyn to hug her. He shook Tom's hand. John was always welcome to use the attic bedroom which doubled as a mini-apartment. He was family. Amanda regarded him as a blessing. She didn't like the idea of her parents being all alone while she was gone in the big city and with Tommy gone and all.

Shortly after that Larry and Zach grabbed their wives coats to help them put it on. Having their own coats zipped up and their Christmas gifts under their arms, they thanked their boss and his wife for the invite.

Tom wished them a safe trip home. They lived a few miles from the farm in a house near each other. Larry and Zach traveled in to the farm together. Today, they and their wives would travel back together with memories of this day together to talk about on the way back there. Monday would come soon enough for both men to have to return to work.

Everyone kissed and hugged each other goodbye in the warmth of the house. Carolyn would miss everyone's company. In her heart, she knew that she was part a city girl who would have loved living in the city around lots of people just as much as here. But, she loved her husband, Tom. So, wherever he went she went and determined to love every moment.

Right after brunch, Ralph showed up eager to pick up Amanda as he had promised her. She had her suitcase packed for her overnight stay. Her mother had made a homemade apple pie for Amanda to take to dinner. She knew Ralph loved Carolyn's apple pie. "It made Carolyn feel more like family with Ralph" said Carolyn as she handed it to Amanda wrapped in a clean red and white linen towel to keep it warm on the trip to the feed store.

The roads were slick with snow drifts being blown hard. The car shook as Ralph made his way down the road. Ralph came prepared with a thermos of hot coffee to keep them warm on the way. He brought a blanket for Amanda's lap to keep her warm. And, he had a blanket in the back seat of the car for himself in case he needed it.

The roads were plowed somewhat recently thought Ralph. But, the roads were starting to be covered by drifts of snow off the farm fields.

"It is really pretty in the snow but, it makes my hands sweaty to try to keep us on the road. We'll drive extra slow. Thank God there aren't any other cars on the road" said Ralph.

Amanda nodded in agreement not wanting to shake up Ralph worse than he was. He hardly even left that small city where the feed store was in. And, he could do everything on foot there. So, the snow was never a worry for him. If anything happened to him in that weather for his having to come get her, she would never forgive herself thought Amanda.

Ralph parked his car in the garage behind the feed store. Going inside, Ralph reached up to Amanda's hands to rub them to warm them from the cold outside. He then began to kiss them. "Let's go upstairs under the blankets to warm you up and give you a proper welcoming home" said Ralph.

"You mean make love" said Amanda.

"Yep" said Ralph as he took her hand to lead her up the apartment stairs to their bedroom.

"Oh good" said Amanda wanting so much to lay next to Ralph once again.

Ralph carried Amanda's suitcase upstairs to the apartment. Amanda's cheeks were bright pink from the cold air outside. Snowflakes sat in her dark hair which sparkled when the hall light shown on it like miniature jewels around her face. Ralph thought that she looked especially beautiful this evening.

She was wearing a green dress and green emerald earrings shaped like a flower that matched her eyes shining green. She is a beauty thought Ralph.

Amanda followed Ralph into the bedroom. He laid the suitcase next to the dresser.

"Well, welcome home" said Ralph.

"Thank you. It's good to be home" said Amanda as she looked around the room taking it in. By then, Amanda had closed the bedroom door. It kept the draft from the hall from coming into the bedroom. But, it felt so comfortable in the apartment compared to outdoors. Amanda took off her coat. And, she handed it to Ralph. He laid it on the chair by the dresser to dry some from the melted snow before hanging it.

"You look ravishing" said Ralph as he pulled her body close to him.

"I've missed you. I've thought about you all the time" said Ralph. With that, he leaned toward her lips to kiss her. Her lips parted. She could feel his warm breath on her. His breathing quickened as he kissed her lips—then her neck and her chest.

Her nipples were hard. She could feel them under her dress. She didn't know if she was responding to him or the cold weather. But, she could feel him rubbing up against her as he kissed her.

She was planning on wearing this dress to her parents. She decided to start pulling it up above her pants. Ralph pulled it over her head.

She stood there naked in front of him. Amanda grabbed at his snap and zipper. He stepped out from his jeans.

He kissed her again feeling her flesh against his. She could feel his heart beat in his chest. She reached to kiss him there. He, in turn, reached to kiss her there. It was their special symbol together to remember the heart that beat in their chest for each other!

He took her by the hand to bed. He stripped down under the covers to nakedness. By now, they were used to each others look and feel.

He laid by her kissing first her lips working his way down to her nipples which were still hard and responsive to his touch. Amanda spread her legs as Ralph kissed her to arouse her before he came inside her. Ralph could hear her groan as he kissed her. And then, she arched her back as she climaxed. Ralph pushed himself inside her with rapid thrusts to orgasm. And, he then lay on top of her as they breathed deeply together.

He then pulled her on top of him. He pulled the blanket over her. "Sleep for awhile, honey. I want to feel you on top of me for awhile while I rest myself while listening to the snow outside. It sounds like it really is coming down outside" said Ralph.

"Yes, it does" said Amanda closing her eyes to drift off.

Ralph laid into the dusk feeling Amanda's heart beat on top of him. He laid like that until he could hear her very softy snoring.

And, Ralph was starting to drift off. He couldn't afford to sleep the entire evening away. He had a special dinner planned for himself and Amanda.

So, he carefully rolled her next to him without awakening her. And, he got up to pull the drape over the window to block out the sun. And, he set the clock for an hour from now.

He would let Amanda sleep in if he could. He would sneak to the kitchen to prepare the New Year's dinner. He was so happy to have her home with him.

He looked at her as she slept. Ralph leaned down to kiss her lips as she slept. He laid next to her pulling her into his arms careful not to wake her. Carefully, he pulled the blanket over him and her for warmth. And, Ralph drifted off to sleep thinking he must be the happiest man on earth. He wished he could sleep like this every day for the rest of his life Ralph thought before falling asleep.

The clock rang. Ralph decided to shower in the bathroom next to the bedroom while Amanda slept. He dressed pulling up his jeans and putting on a brand new blue plaid flannel shirt. He was ready to tackle the rest of the New Year's dinner. He had some of the food ready in the refrigerator. He already had the kitchen table set.

He had purchased a gold candle that he set in the middle of the table. He rolled a white linen napkin with a gold bow on it over each white dinner plate edged in gold. It went well with the long stemmed glasses edged in gold, where he planned to pour chilled red burgundy wine.

He hoped that Amanda would like what he had cooked for them. He wanted it to be special. The cook across the street at the restaurant from the feed store had helped him decide what would be nice.

In a mixing bowl in the refrigerator was already chopped in thin cooked strips red, green, and yellow peppers.

# RALPH'S 3-COLOR PEPPER SAUTEE

## Ingredients

One red bell pepper, chopped in small pieces
One yellow bell pepper, chopped in small pieces
One green bell pepper, chopped in small pieces
Butter, melted

## Directions

Mix all the peppers in a mixing bowl making sure that all the three colors of the peppers are evenly distributed throughout the ingredients. Then, over very low heat, melt butter one tablespoon at a time since (this is for taste) and used as needed. OK to brown some of the peppers slightly while they are cooking. Using real butter to add a nice sweetness to the peppers. Have to mix often with a spoon to help cook all of the ingredients at one time. Add butter as needed to keep the mixture moist but, using sparingly. Keep a lid on the frying pan as cooking to help keep in the heat to the ingredients. Stop cooking when all the ingredients are evenly cooked. Usually the peppers change slightly in color and texture from fresh when this happens! Move immediately into a mixing bowl such as a casserole dish with a lid once the peppers are cooked until ready to serve. Can pre-warm the serving bowl by placing it and its lid in a sink (that has been previously been cleaned) in very warm water to make it warmed (instead of putting warmed and cooked peppers in a cold to the touch serving dish).And, then dry it quickly to keep in the warmth with a clean towel! Can coat the surface of the serving bowl with a non-stick cooking spray before putting in the cooked peppers to keep ingredients from sticking. Note: If you have to reheat the ingredients to be served at a later time, reheat on a very low heat mixing often with a spoon and using a lid to the pan as needed to keep in the heat. Serve immediately while warm.

Ralph placed shredded lettuce, carrots, and red cabbage on small dinner plates. He had put the spoon, knife, and fork on top of the dinner plate next to the linen napkins.

He saved for last two rib-eye steaks in the refrigerator that he put in the broiler at the bottom of the stove to cook for the main course. He had a glass on the table filled with V&O salad dressing for the salad dressing for the salad.

## RALPH'S BROILED STEAKS

## Ingredients

Two rib-eye steaks (or any other steaks that can be broiled)

## Directions

Place the meat inside the broil drawer in the stove. Turn on the broiler. Keep the heat to the desired temperature to get the meat to brown and cook inside. Keep the broiler drawer completely closed while cooking. Check often to see meat browning as desired. After, using an oven mitt and fork to pierce the steaks, turn the steaks over to the uncooked side and repeat same directions above. Once cooked, slice each steak with a sharp knife, slitting down part of the center of the meat to see if it is cooked enough. If so, close the broiler drawer again to keep the meat warm until serving. If not, place the meat into the broiler again and continue cooking. Once cooked, turn off the broiler and keep the broiler door closed to keep meat warm until serving.

"Perfect" said Ralph eyeing everything before heading off to the bedroom.

"Honey, wake up. Dinner is almost ready" said Ralph. Amanda opened her eyes. She put her arms around Ralph kissing his lips. He kissed her back.

"I'll get dressed" said Amanda.

"Dinner will be probably ready in about 20 minutes" said Ralph.

"Good. I'm hungry" said Amanda.

"What should I wear?" said Amanda calling back at Ralph.

"Anything that is comfortable" said Ralph calling back from the kitchen.

"Good. I'll wear my black negligee that I couldn't resist buying that was sitting in the store window near the apartment" said Amanda.

"OK" said Ralph calling back to Amanda. Ralph's hands shook as he lit the candle in the middle of the table. He turned off the bright kitchen light for cooking. The broiler was off now. The meat was cooked and ready for serving. The burner was off on top of the stove. The lid was on top of the skillet to keep the peppers warm.

The glow of the hall light shined softly into the kitchen giving a soft glow to the room. Just then, Amanda walked into the kitchen. She was barefoot and wearing a black lacy negligee. Ralph gasped at the sight of her. She was so ravishing. He wanted her now.

"Please sit down. You look beautiful. I hope that you like what I made for you" said Ralph.

"I'm sure that I will" said Amanda as he leaned down to kiss her. He looked tense. He sat down on the chair across from her watching her.

"Aren't you going to serve the food?" asked Amanda.

"I will in a minute. I just want you to get situated first. Nice and comfy" said Ralph.

"I'm OK" said Amanda.

"Everything looks so beautiful. You must have done a lot of work" said Amanda as she looked at the table setting.

Ralph nodded as he watched Amanda untie the gold bow on her linen napkin to place on her lap to begin eating. Just then, Amanda felt something hard in her napkin.

"What is this?" said Amanda as she unfolded the napkin to see a gold ring with a diamond.

Just then, Ralph knelt in front of Amanda on one knee. "Amanda, will you marry me?" said Ralph.

Amanda looked at Ralph. She knew that she couldn't turn Ralph away.

"Yes" said Amanda.

Ralph overwhelmed with happiness swept Amanda in his arms. He took her to bed filled with love and desire that had to be quenched this moment. She wrapped her arms around his neck. He pulled up her negligee above her waist. And, he pulled down his shorts and jeans. And, in the soft glow of the hall light came inside of her thrusting over and over to orgasm as she groaned softly with each thrust.

Then, without a word, he pulled his shorts and pants back up and carried her back to the kitchen where she put her engagement ring on for the first time on her finger.

"It says 'Ralph and Amanda in love forever inside'" said Ralph. Amanda reached up to kiss him.

"How did you know my size?" said Amanda.

"Your mother told me. But, your father doesn't know yet" said Ralph.

"We'll have to work it out somehow" said Amanda.

"Sweetie, we will" said Ralph pulling back the chair for her to sit at the dinner table. This evening couldn't have been more perfect. He knew that he would have her again tonight. It made him smile as he served the dinner for him and Amanda. They were in love. They would be man and wife.

They sat quietly by candlelight eating their first dinner in their apartment together. Amanda was content. She had her husband as far as she was concerned. She had her home with him in his apartment above his own store that was his. Her parents that she loved lived nearby.

She decided that Jerry would have to be there if she could tear him away from the farm long enough. She would ask. And, Sarah would be the bridesmaid she thought.

But, that was down the road. She wanted to enjoy the moment. But, all these thoughts were rolling around in her head. And, poor dad with his dream of a farmer husband for her with good ol' hardy brothers to help.

And, the farm was a love of hers, too. But, nothing was going to be solved tonight thought Amanda. And, she didn't want to miss out on the memory of this evening.

"This is really good" said Amanda.

"I'm so happy that you like it, honey" said Ralph beaming.

Ralph blew out the candle. "Let's do the dishes in the morning so that we can get an early jump in getting up early in the morning" said Ralph.

"Good idea" said Amanda. Ralph could barely contain himself with desire for Amanda. He couldn't spend his time washing dishes about now. He had to have her.

He walked over to the drape opening it so that the soft street lights would glow in the room.

He turned off the lamp on the nightstand. Amanda was already in bed.

He lay next to her kissing her repeatedly as she could feel him rubbing against her. He stripped off his clothes. She put her mouth over his hardness to ready it for her. He climbed on top of her trusting harder and faster than ever before rubbing himself against her to arouse her as he came.

"I hope you know how much I love you. You mean so much to me. You made me a happy man" said Ralph.

"I'm glad" said Amanda caressing his back softly as she spoke.

"Let's go to sleep, honey. I want to take you down to the feed store tomorrow so that you can see it, again" said Ralph.

"OK" said Amanda as they kissed each other goodnight.

Ralph and Amanda woke up early as Amanda climbed on top of Ralph to bring him to orgasm. She woke him from his sleep. Ralph smiled as she pushed up and down on top of him.

"Well, you sure know how to wake up a man" said Ralph kissing Amanda good morning.

"I'm glad you like it" said Amanda.

"Me too" said Ralph as he came.

"Let's get dressed. We've got things to do before we head back to your parents" said Ralph. They both ran to the bathroom to shower.

Dressed Amanda said: "What's for breakfast?"

"You'll see" said Ralph grabbing Amanda's hand as they headed downstairs to the feed store.

Inside Amanda saw how pretty the store was. It brought back memories. Good ones.

Just then, someone was knocking on the door to the store. I didn't know the store was open on Sunday" said Amanda.

"It isn't. I wonder who it could be?" said Ralph as he opened the door.

"Surprise" people shouted as they poured into the store carrying covered dishes and covered pots of food.

"We're having a New Year's breakfast together. You're the honored guest" said Ralph.

"I am" said Amanda smiling.

Some of the men opened up a long table from the back and folding chairs. The women walked around the table laying down paper plates and cups and plastic silverware equal to the number of guests. And, Ralph began grace at the head of the table with Amanda on the other end of the table.

Dear heavenly Father: We want to thank God for our good friends sharing our first New Year's dinner of the year together. And, thank you God for bringing Amanda here today to having this dinner with our friends we love. Amen.

"Speech. Speech" people called out to Amanda.

Obliging, Amanda stood up at the other end of the table. Picking up a paper cup filled with orange juice, Amanda said: "I wish to toast in the New Year with my dear friends. I want to thank you for bringing this lovely breakfast food to ring in New Year with us. All the homemade breads, bacon, sausage, eggs and everything else has been a wonderful surprise for me and a wonderful memory for me. I love you all" said Amanda as everyone smiled at hearing this.

"And, I want to be the first to tell you that Ralph and I are engaged to be married" said Amanda. Amanda threw a kiss to Ralph. He caught it. And, he then threw a kiss back to Amanda.

Everyone got up to kiss and hug Amanda and Ralph. "Congratulations" people said to Amanda and Ralph. Everyone was happy for them. The Christmas tree was lit adding to the cheer. One of the men grabbed a camera to shoot a photo of Amanda and Ralph. Amanda hated to see everyone go since everyone was in such a festive mood. She hoped everyone would return next year for another New Year's get-together at the store with her and Ralph.

"Let's really celebrate the New Year" said Amanda.

He laid down on the bed naked. She stood in front of him allowing him to see her naked in full view. Then, she began kissing him warmly and deeply on the lips and between his legs before he came to orgasm. Then, he laid her down next to him. And, he did the same to her.

"I love you, Amanda" said Ralph.

"I love you, Ralph" said Amanda.

The day was getting late. They had promised to be back at the farm early. They ran to the shower to bathe and dress quickly.

Amanda threw her things in the suitcase barely folding them. "I'll do that later" said Amanda.

"Good idea" said Ralph grabbing her by the hand running down the stairs of the apartment. She was wearing jeans and white tennis shoes making it easier to walk on the ice and snow. Ralph threw her suitcase in the back seat.

"You had better hide your engagement ring before you get to the farm" said Ralph eyeing her ring on her finger.

"Oh, you're right" said Amanda turning around to put it in the zippered section of the suitcase for safekeeping.

"I'm glad that you remembered" said Amanda.

"So am I because I don't want to upset your father right now" said Ralph as he pulled out of the garage leaving the door open to drive down the road. He had no time to close it. He had to get to the farm as he promised Carolyn and Tom. Being late wouldn't be a good way to start the marriage.

Amanda and Ralph drove to the farm the rest of the way quietly and listening to the Christmas music on the radio. It just started to snow. Amanda looked out the window of the car.

"It looks like a Christmas card" said Amanda eyeing the trees with snow and icicles glazing their trunks and limbs.

"It sure does" said Ralph.

Just then, they pulled into the driveway of Amanda's parents' house. Amanda was relieved. She looked at her watch. It said 9:45 AM. She never would have made it down these roads like that being so slick. Ralph was really such a good winter driver. He drove mighty slow down these roads.

But at least he got us here OK all the same.

"We had better hurry in" said Amanda pushing open the car door to the sound of the door cracking ice off the door. Amanda slammed the car door as more snowfall fell off the side of the door.

Amanda waited for Ralph to come around the side to help her walk safely up the steps. As he did that taking Amanda's hand with one hand, he carried with him a gift bag from the store with a red metal tool box to give to Tom that he had admired at the store. He also had nice matching pots and pans with strawberries and strawberry blossoms all the way around on them that Carolyn would like since she grew a strawberry patch in her garden.

These were really pre-marriage presents for his future in-laws. He wanted them to know that they could count on him as a son-in-law as best he could. He wanted the marriage to start out right.

"The day has gone by so fast. My dad is going to be driving me back soon to get to the apartment. He won't drive in the dark in the winter roads. Too dangerous. We are going to have to say goodbyes now" said Amanda turning to Ralph.

It made Amanda feel bad because it looked like Ralph was beginning to cry. On top of it, her parents looked like they were beginning to tear up.

Tom threw Amanda's suitcase in the vehicle. He stood there with Amanda, Ralph, and Carolyn. "Well" said Tom to Amanda because she wasn't getting inside. He was growing impatient.

Carolyn grabbed Tom by the arm. "Let's give these kids some privacy."

Tom frowned making Amanda smile since she was always daddy's little girl. Her parents went inside.

Carolyn went to the kitchen to make a pot of coffee. Tom stood inside looking out the living room window. He saw Amanda and Ralph embrace and kiss. Tom frowned.

Ralph began to drive away. "Tell your parents goodbye for me and thanks for everything. I know that your dad has to be heading soon to Indianapolis to drop you off at the apartment and get back to the farm today. And, I have to get back to the store" said Ralph waving goodbye.

"I will" said Amanda waving at Ralph as he rolled down the road.

Then, she ran inside calling out to her dad. "Let's go, dad" said Amanda.

"Now, she wants to go" said Tom. Carolyn came running to the door to hug Amanda. She handed Amanda a jar of homemade strawberry jam that she made from the strawberry patch on the farm.

"Ralph was given a jar of strawberry jam to take home with him, also" said Carolyn.

"Great, mom. He said 'thanks for everything' to you and dad, by the way" said Amanda.

"He's such a nice man" said Carolyn.

"Yes, he is" said Amanda grateful to have him.

Soon Tom and Amanda headed down the road. Tom was quiet the whole way to the apartment. Amanda felt bad because it looked like he was tearing up. He probably knew about Ralph and her. He was bound to find out sometime anyway. But, she didn't want him to find out, now. She needed more time.

She never liked to displease her father. He was everything to her. And, she loved the farm just as much as he did. It was her home, too.

But, she loved Ralph and wanted to marry him. And, she hoped her mother would know how to save the farm and Amanda keep Ralph for her husband. For now, she didn't know the answers. So, she drove in silence next to her dad she loved so heading to the apartment to tell Sarah the good news about her and Ralph.

Her father being always the good guy in her life drove her in front of her apartment as usual.

"I love you, daughter" said Tom as he handed her the suitcase as before.

"I love you too, dad. Kiss mom for me" said Amanda.

"I will" said Tom looking really sad and broken.

"We'll stay in touch, dad" said Amanda feeling bad for her dad.

He threw her a kiss as he drove off.

Amanda ran up the stairs with her good news to be greeted with Sarah letting her know of her own good news. She showed Amanda her engagement ring she had gotten from her boyfriend, the chef, she adored and thought of as "Mr. Perfect." The girls were elated and hugged.

Tom drove back home to the farm by himself. He fought the tears from running down his cheeks. He loved Ralph. But, he had in mind a different kind of husband for Amanda that would continue the traditions of the farm and help save the family farm that had been in the family for years for the Millers to the end of time.

When he got home, he asked Carolyn for some quiet time. He sat at his desk that he did his thinking about his farm and family. And, he resolved to swallow his pride and ask his only son for help since it was always the other way around.

Tom wrote:

Dear Tommy
Please come home, son. Soon. We need you here for the farm's sake and the family's sake. Love, Dad

# Chapter 10

The office was a buzz of gossip about Sarah's upcoming wedding. "Just think. Soon, I'll be Mrs. John Goldman, wife of a chef and successful restaurant owner. Wow!" said Sarah to Amanda.

"Wow, indeed. And, I will meet for the fitting since I will be the bridesmaid. And, Jerry will be in town for the wedding. He says that he wants to be the ring bearer at your wedding" said Amanda.

"Tell him thank you for me. And, yes, I want him for my ring bearer. I will love it. We will be measuring the gowns at 2:30 PM this Saturday at the apartment. The gowns are 'drop dead gorgeous' with very pastel blue colored beads and sequins sewn under the top veil of the skirt. They are custom made. John's sister is a seamstress and owns a shop. She will bring the gowns over to the apartment. I hope you like the color blue" said Sarah.

"I love the color blue" said Amanda.

"Great. I wanted something for a gown that was so beautiful that you could have it for a keepsake or re-wear it for a special occasion. I didn't want it to be too bridesmaid—like so that you could wear it everywhere. The bodice has sewn in beads and sequins in the shape of flowers that will match the same designs in my gown except mine will be white. I think it will be beautiful" said Sarah.

"It sure seems that way" said Amanda.

"We will be having the reception at John's restaurant at 5:30 PM after the church service. John is cooking the food with his assistant chef. And, the staff has agreed to stay late to serve the food and clean-up after" said Sarah.

"Great. Jerry is staying overnight on your wedding weekend and probably a few days after at the apartment. He already told his parents ahead of time so that they wouldn't worry. And, it will be good to see him. And, my parents are coming up for the weekend as well. They will be arriving Saturday" said Amanda.

"Sounds like a plan" said Sarah.

"It sure is. But, I'm going to miss you, roommate" said Sarah.

"Me, too" said Amanda.

"But, life goes on. But, there will be the christenings and other family events. And, you are going to be my kids' Godmother" said Sarah.

"Of course" said Amanda.

"So, you may be losing your roommate, but you are gaining a whole family. And, that is important to remember before you tear up on me again" said Sarah.

Amanda smiled while a tear fell down her cheek. "Alright, I'll try to be a brave little soldier through it all" said Amanda saluting while she spoke. Sarah saluted back at Amanda. And, then she hugged her friend.

"Well, I have to get back to work, you know. Oh, by the way, we only have two bedrooms. Where will everyone be sleeping?" said Sarah.

"It's only one overnight before the wedding. Jerry will sleep on the couch as usual. My parents are going to sleep in my bed. And, I'm borrowing a camping cot from our co-worker, Mike, who is dropping it by since he isn't using it for right now while the weather is still cold outside. I'll sleep in my parents' room" said Amanda.

"Perfect. I will be out of the apartment by then. John and I are honeymooning in our apartment above the restaurant where we will be living. It works out really well since the reception is downstairs in John's restaurant. I'll be close by if you need me" said Sarah.

"Good. I will want to stay in touch. For one thing, the apartment is filled with your things. I won't know what to do with them. I will box them up for you—what you have in your bedroom so that you can stay on your honeymoon longer" said Amanda.

"Gee. I really appreciate it. You can keep the furniture if you need it since John already has furniture in his apartment for us. I already have some of my clothes in John's apartment to get going" said Sarah.

"Good. And, we had better get back to work" said Sarah walking down the hall to her desk. Amanda sat at her desk contemplating the wedding and thinking about all the things that had happened to her since graduating from high school. Who would have guessed all of this? She looked down at her own engagement ring. She thought about her marriage to Ralph. It made her smile to think how much she loved him. To think how much she had to look forward to being Mrs. Ralph Tomlinson.

She couldn't wait. She wanted Sarah to be her bridesmaid, too. And, she wanted Sarah to be the Godmother to her and Ralph's kids. And, she wanted Jerry to be a big part of the wedding. If there was such a thing as a second bridesmaid that is a man, she would have that. In fact, that is what she wanted.

Her father would give her away. With that, Amanda frowned. What was she going to do about her dad and his wish for her? And, if this family lost their farm that belonged to Grandpa Jim because of her selfishness, her family would have a fit.

She wished that Tommy would write back to her. He probably was overseas somewhere...goodness knows where. She wondered what was running through his mind about the family farm and his role in it. She wondered if he would make it back for her wedding. She would love to see him again. He had been away for such a long time. Her parents missed him. She didn't know if they would be able to bear having him leave again if he came since he was their only son. I had better write to him tonight to tell him that I would like him to come if he would be able to make it.

Amanda's job was one of mostly being a receptionist in case someone came in the door or called in. In between, she did some typing once in a while. But, since she had to man the phone and be there at attention when someone came to the door, mostly she just sat there trying to keep her mind busy. She was allowed to sneak in a novel or two to read. Her boss said that as long as no one saw her reading it when they come to the desk, then it was

OK. She hid her book behind a vase of artificial flowers sitting at the desk that matched the flowers on the painting on the wall across from the desk and the pattern in the drapes. After all, Amanda worked for a commercial interior design company.

Everything had to look fashionable and eloquent. There were many businesses in the downtown area. This company was responsible for decorating from upscale restaurants to hotels. Very posh surroundings for business folk. There was swatches and mock up designs and color schemes. The whole nine yards. It is nice to have something to be proud of thought Amanda. Not a bad job for a first job, either thought Amanda. It will look good on my resume. The Sullivan Interior Design Company. A legacy of beauty and eloquence was its motto.

Jerry was the first to arrive to the apartment. A dark navy blue tuxedo with a pale blue shirt was sitting on the back of the couch for him. The collar of the shirt had sewn beads and sequins in the design of flowers that matched the bridesmaids and the bride's gowns. John's sister wanted everything matching. Sarah's veil even had the same design with beaded sequined flowers that sparkled under the top layer of veil that flowed down to her ankles.

Her bouquet was of white roses with baby's breath for good luck for all the babies John and Sarah would have. And, in the refrigerator in the apartment sat Jerry's white rosebud boutonniere with baby's breath around it to pin to his tuxedo's lapel. Amanda was to have one single rose with baby's breath pinned to the gown right between her breasts. Sarah called it a mini-bouquet. And, all the other women in the wedding party wore the same attire from Sarah's mother, Jean to John's sister, Mary who also had a similar gown to Amanda who was the bridesmaid.

The service was being held at the Catholic Church even though John was Jewish. He respected Sarah's right to still be Catholic and raise the kids Catholic. He only wanted a happy and healthy family. Nice guy thought Amanda.

"Well, come here for a hug. Long time no see" said Amanda reaching out her arms to Jerry. Jerry embraced Amanda and kissed her cheek.

"So, when are your parents coming?" said Jerry to Amanda.

"Anytime. Well have supper together in the apartment" said Amanda.

"I'll make it. It will be just like old times" said Jerry.

"Sort of" said Amanda.

"I know that a lot has happened. "We'll have to catch up. Is that my tux?" said Jerry heading for the couch.

"It sure is" said Amanda.

"Well, it looks like my size, anyway. I want to do a good job of this" said Jerry.

"You will. Sarah's mom will help you. Just go where she takes you. She has already been to the church rehearsal for you both" said Sarah.

"Well, that's a relief" said Jerry.

Amanda and Jerry talked on the living room couch for hours. Jerry congratulated Amanda on her engagement. He told her that he had news, too. He was planning on asking his high school sweetheart to marry him. He had worried that it would hurt her if he did. But, now that Ralph has come into her life like this, he felt more comfortable to go ahead with his plans. He had dated her a couple of times after he returned to the farm. "She was pretty and available." And, she would make a good farmer's wife.

Amanda discussed her worry about her dad not knowing about her and Ralph and asked him not to tell her dad until she broke the news to him. He would take it hard she knew even though he loved Ralph as much as she did. They both sat on the couch in each other's arms after that for hours. They were that close. In front of them on the living room coffee table was a glass of diet cola for each of them with melting ice cubes that was melting more by the minute.

Amanda was the first to hear her father's familiar car door shut outside the apartment. She jumped up from the couch. She headed for the window.

"It's my parents" said Amanda to Jerry.

"Great. I look forward to meeting them" said Jerry. Amanda walked to her apartment door to greet her parents. She had put her engagement ring in her jean's pocket for safekeeping far away from her father for right now.

Amanda's parents hugged Amanda and then Jerry. "Dad. Mom. This is Jerry" said Amanda.

"We've heard so much about you" said Carolyn.

"I hope all good" said Jerry.

"Oh yes" said Carolyn. Amanda showed her parents to her bedroom where they were sleeping. Jerry snuck off to the kitchen to prepare supper. He loved to cook. And, this was an occasion to be sure.

He found the fixings to homemade spaghetti:

# JERRY'S SPAGHETTI

## Ingredients

One medium onion, minced
One pound of lean hamburger (can use more if needed)
One to two tablespoons of cooking oil (corn oil)
One jar of spaghetti sauce (any flavor, any size)
One box of spaghetti noodles, enough to make 2 to 4 cups of cooked noodles (can use more if needed)
Grated parmesan cheese

## Directions

Roll onion and hamburger into small to medium size meatballs. Have a frying pan on low heat with the cooking oil poured into the bottom of the frying pan. Place meatballs gently in the bottom of the pan. While cooking, move around gently with spoon to see meatballs are browned on all sides. Using a slitted spoon after that, gently place on a plate. This will help drain any excess grease from the meatballs. Can place them on a clean paper towel to make sure that the meatballs aren't sitting in any excess grease! While the meatballs are browning, have a pot of water possibly with a teaspoon of salt or so in it to help it boil better using medium heat to do so. Put the uncooked spaghetti noodles in this water making sure that it is completely in the water while cooking. Good if water is boiling while cooking noodles. This will help them to cook. Gently stir often with a spoon to make sure that the noodles don't stick together while cooking. Place a clean colander in a clean sink. When noodles are soft which is usually around 10 minutes or so, pour the noodles into a colander to drain the excess water. Drain noodles in the sink. Rinse the noodles by pouring cool tap water over the noodles to remove excess starch from the noodles. Gently shake the colander with the noodles in it to remove the excess water from the noodles. Rinse out the pot that the noodles were cooked in with fresh cool tap water to remove excess starch and dry with a clean towel. Now, place the noodles back into the pot. Then, add the meatballs to that. Mix gently (which will keep the meatballs intact) together using a spoon to do so. Now, add spaghetti sauce to this mixture adding a little at a time until get to the desired amount of liquid desired. Use a spoon to gently mix the mixture together each time adding spaghetti sauce. Now, using low heat, warm all the ingredients together stirring often and gently to keep the ingredients from burning at the bottom. Keep a lid on the pot as you heat this to help keep the ingredients warm. Once ready to serve, move the pot from under the heat (using an oven mitt if need be to do so) to keep the spaghetti from cooking more. Keep the lid on the pot to keep warm. Can check if spaghetti is warm enough by carefully touching one of the noodles in the pot to see if feels warm enough (to serve) to the touch! Once done, using a spoon or any handy utensil, put desired portion of the spaghetti on dinner plate for each person's serving. Sprinkle with grated parmesan cheese over the mixture for a garnish. Now, the spaghetti is ready to serve. Can reheat leftovers for further meals over low heat mixing often (and gently) with a spoon to warm all the ingredients together and to keep the spaghetti from burning. Can add extra spaghetti sauce to leftovers before reheating if want to add more moisture to the ingredients. Garnish with grated parmesan cheese before serving. Serve immediately while warm!

And next to that, he put V&O salad dressing for the salad that he had put in salad bowls of chopped lettuce, carrots, and cabbage. He had a bottle of red wine chilled in the refrigerator. He brought out four long stemmed glasses for the wine.

"Supper will be ready in a minute. I thought you might be hungry" said Jerry.

"Thanks. You are so kind" said Carolyn thinking he was about the sweetest little boy she ever saw. She was glad that he was Amanda's friend.

They rested on the couch while he cooked.

Jerry decided to make garlic bread to go with the spaghetti:

# JERRY'S GARLIC BREAD

## Ingredients

Four slices of bread, any kind (wheat does well or white bread for this)
Butter, real butter is best (softened)
Powdered garlic

## Directions

Using a butter knife and soft butter, spread a thin layer of butter over one side of the bread. Sprinkle lightly over the buttered side of the bread some powdered garlic. Make sure to use a little at a time so that it has the desired amount of garlic. Place the bread butter side up in the stove's broiler on low heat checking often to see doesn't over brown the surface. Once the butter is melted and the surface of the bread is lightly browned, turn off the broiler and lift bread out of broiler with a spatula. Use an oven mitt while doing this since the broiler will be very hot to the touch. Place bread on a platter. Serve at once while warm.

"Come to dinner" shouted Jerry. By then, the wine glasses were filled. And, as a final touch, he lit a three-wick red candle that he put in the center of the table.

"It really is a Christmas candle. But, it goes well, anyway" said Jerry. Tom smiled approvingly.

Tom said: "Let's join hands in prayer."

Heavenly father, we thank you for this food that our dear family member Jerry cooked for us and bringing us here today so that we can celebrate Sarah and John's wedding and be with our lovely daughter, Amanda.

Everyone smiled and laughed through the night. They all loved each other. It made Amanda happy. She loved Jerry and him in her family forever. He was so dear to her. She couldn't help looking at him thinking of the good times with him.

His face just shined in the soft light of the candle light. She was blessed to have met Jerry when she did. God love him for being Jerry thought Amanda as she ate his homemade spaghetti that she already loved since he cooked it.

"We had better head over to bed" said Tom wiping his face on the paper napkin at the kitchen table.

"Yes. Morning will come soon enough. And, tomorrow is the wedding" said Carolyn.

"I will make breakfast" said Jerry.

"You'll be sleeping on the couch tonight. I already have your blankets and a pillow there" said Amanda. Everyone hugged goodnight. Amanda headed for her camping cot. Her parents were to see her room decked out with reminders of God and respect to God. They were happy that they brought her up right that way.

Amanda could hear her parents snoring before she fell asleep. She never slept in the same room with her parents before. She felt like a little kid again somehow. But, it made her happy. She wanted to always be her parents little girl, anyway.

Amanda woke up to the smell of bacon cooking in the kitchen and coffee brewing. It gave Carolyn a break since she was the one who usually did all the work in the house. She never minded but, still she deserved the rest thought Amanda. And, it was one of the things she loved about Jerry. He was so sweet.

Amanda kissed Jerry's cheek while he scrambled the eggs.

"Go wake up your parents. Breakfast is almost ready. We have a full day ahead" said Jerry.

"OK" said Amanda as she nudged her parents awake.

"We'll be there in a minute. We'll want to jump in the shower and dress" said Carolyn.

In a minute, they were again saying grace with Tom thanking God for the beautiful breakfast that to him was the most beautiful meal he ever had since it was the one sitting in the front of him and especially so since Amanda's friend Jerry made it. Carolyn and Tom had agreed the night before that Jerry was. He was so "dear."

"Dear. You are an absolute angel. How thoughtful of you to make this lovely breakfast" said Carolyn squeezing Jerry's hand.

Jerry blushed. These kind of things just came natural to him. It was what he loved to do. He hoped his wife would let him in the kitchen. He didn't know if he could bear it if she didn't even if he was a guy. He just loved cooking. But, Jerry thanked Carolyn all the same while Tom and Amanda smiled.

Dressed with Amanda placing a white rose boutonniere on her dad's lapel and a corsage of a white rose with baby's breath pinned to her mom's dress. Once done, they poured into Tom's car heading for the church. Amanda had promised not to cry. But, she had a clean tissue in her bra for just in case.

Jerry took the cue of walking just behind Sarah's mom and dad down the aisle. Jerry carried the wedding rings down the aisle to the altar where John and Sarah were exchanging their vows. He smiled at Amanda as she walked down the aisle behind the bride. Sarah's five-year-old niece who was the flower girl threw white roses on the white sheet that lay on the carpet all the way to the altar. She, too, had a pale blue matching outfit identical to the bridesmaid.

John and Sarah exchanged vows in front of all their loved ones. Then they took their wedding rings from the satin pillow Jerry was holding and placed it on each other's fingers.

Amanda silently wished them well. John's restaurant was nearby and already decorated to celebrate the occasion. She was sure that it would be as pretty as this beautiful church was right this moment.

Everyone applauded after John and Sarah said "I do." They turned to the crowd and threw kisses to everyone. Then, they smiled as they marched down the aisle to the car waiting for them. John had rented a black limo for the occasion. He wanted to start the marriage with "class." Everyone followed behind them to the wedding reception at the restaurant.

The Catholic priest who presided the wedding traveled in Tom's car to the reception. "You have to have some of John's cooking. He's a chef you know" said Tom turning to the priest beaming from ear-to-ear to have an actual priest in his car. He knew that it would make Carolyn happy since she was born in the Faith.

The restaurant was only about 10 minutes away from the church which was good. The food was warming up when the crowd arrived with a good 50 guests to serve an early dinner. John had closed the restaurant early. He would risk losing a little business to be able to have his reception in his own restaurant. That was the best memory he could possibly imagine.

The apartment upstairs had brand new white satin sheets with matching white comforter. He planned to scatter white rose petals on the sheets before making love to his wife for the first time. He hoped that she would think it romantic.

He was planning on spending the week in the apartment with her for their honeymoon so that they could spend time together. He had asked her boss for permission for her to have the week off if he allowed in return a catered dinner for him and his wife at the restaurant on him for their wedding anniversary. It was a good trade off. He hoped that it made her happy and was a good way to start off the marriage.

The guests would be served an early dinner of roast beef; baked potato with butter and sour cream; and roasted baked carrots. And, planted in the middle of the dinner table, were hot homemade buns covered in linens in a basket to keep them warm. Champagne was passed around in long stem glasses to toast the bride and groom.

A three-tiered wedding cake in white frosting with white roses and green leaves adorned the center of the serving table with plates and forks for all. The plastic bride and groom was at the top of the cake. The frosting on top of the cake read

"Congratulations John and Sarah Goldman." Sarah loved the cake. It had roses everywhere in clusters of 3 along the sides and top of the cake.

After everyone ate, the bride and groom cut the cake. Photos were taken. And, everyone left a pile of wedding gifts for the bride and groom.

Sarah and John danced the first dance. Her white dress sparkled from sequins as she moved. John wore the same shirt as Jerry except that it was white. His tuxedo was very dark navy blue which was almost black in color. He wore a single white rose with baby's breath in his left lapel. Sarah got the typical garter which was blue in color put on her leg to the band playing. She had borrowed it from Mary, her sister-in-law's own wedding. Everyone danced into the night.

John surprised everyone by having his staff bring out rollaway beds to accommodate all the guests since he said: "I don't want any of my loved ones on the road after drinking. We will all have breakfast in the restaurant together of crepes. There will be plenty of fresh strawberries; hot steamy coffee; and fresh squeezed orange juice. My restaurant staff will be here at 6 AM sharp to cook for you. They had better be. They are being paid time and a half" said John. The guests appreciated the hospitality. They all applauded.

John and Sarah stood in front of their guests waving goodbye and saying "goodnight." Then, John grabbed Sarah's hand. He took her upstairs to their apartment to start their marriage. The guests waved back before they retired, also. He also carried her over the threshold.

John had laying on top of the bed a sheer white negligee with beads and sequined flowers that matched the wedding dress. And, he would wear white satin pajamas with a collar that matched the shirt he wore at the wedding ceremony.

He thought that his wife was breathtakingly beautiful. Sarah was a virgin. John wanted it that way. Other than kissing and caressing, they never had gone all the way. Tonight was the night.

Sarah went into the bathroom to put on her negligee and primp herself. She was too elated to be nervous. She loved John with her whole heart. She believed he felt the same.

John peeled off his clothes. He felt himself becoming aroused. He was anxious. He put the satin pajamas on and stood before the mirror to comb his hair. He wanted everything perfect for the occasion. He went to the refrigerator to grab a container of white rose petals prepared for the occasion. He pulled back the comforter and top sheet. He scattered the rose petals on the sheets. He hoped that Sarah would love them and remember their wedding night forever. He lit a white three-wicked candle and dimmed the lights.

Sarah came out of the bathroom. He could see her pink nipples under her white gown. He wanted to touch them now with his lips but, all in good time.

He pressed her close in his arms. He kissed her lips. He picked her up. And, he carried her to the bed.

"I hope that you like our bed" said John softly.

"I do" said Sarah.

"I do too" said John as he laid her on top of the white rose petals. She felt the coolness of the white satin pajamas on top of her. They felt so soft but, she longed to feel the softness of his flesh next to her without cloth between them no matter how soft the feel of it.

John pressed his lips into her neck. His breath felt hot on her skin. Rose petal buttons opened to reveal her bare breasts. His hands caressed the sides of each breast as his lips surrounded each nipple licking each tip until he could hear her moan.

She unbuttoned his top. He took it off. And, she hungrily grabbed at his bottoms to reveal his genitals in full view for the first time. He was more well-endowed than she had imagined. She could see it erect. Her lips came on top of its head for the first time. She longed to taste it. She longed to have him. He yielded to her hands around his balls. He belonged to her from now on. He wanted her to want him.

He was about to burst from arousal as the warmth of her tongue came down on him. He pulled up her gown to see what he was after which was his heart's delight. Fingering the opening, he put himself inside her trusting as deeply inside her as he could. He wanted all of her. She was his. He came inside her feeling the walls of her vagina as he rubbed against it to pleasure himself.

He would want her every night like this his whole life. He came. He pulled off her negligee so that he could feel her whole body next to his. He pulled her body on top of him. He put the satin sheet on top of her and the comforter.

"Goodnight, Mrs. Goldman" said John.

"Goodnight, Mr. Goldman" said Sarah.

Sarah thought she had off of work on Monday so that she could afford to sleep in. She knew guests were downstairs for the wedding breakfast and send off. She thought that this was going to be the loveliest marriage ever since her husband was so romantic.

She loved him so. Soon, they were both sleeping in their wedding bed together as husband and wife. What could be more perfect!

# Chapter 11

Amanda had a couple of days off from work to visit with Jerry and her parents before everyone went home to resume their usual life. The apartment would seem empty without Sarah. And, she had to box up the rest of Sarah's belongings for her from her bedroom. Amanda didn't know what she was going to do with the apartment now that Sarah got married and all. She didn't know if she could afford the apartment by herself. And, she hated the idea of having a roommate she didn't know.

She would say a rosary on this for sure in her bedroom. Surely, God would reveal the answer to her in prayer.

She had a nice time at Sarah's wedding. John was quite a guy and a heck of a cook as well. She could see why Sarah chose him to be her husband.

Amanda decided to take off the rest of the week by herself. She would box up everything she could find that belonged to Sarah at all beginning with her bedroom. On Friday, Sarah and John were coming for the rest of her things.

The apartment would seem too quiet with Sarah gone. Amanda didn't know if she could bear it alone. First leaving the farm life. Now, leaving her home life with her roommate. It really hurt inside.

She wished Jerry could have stayed in the city but, she knew he had to go back to help his parents on the farm. And, he had his own life to live with the woman he wanted to marry there. She thought that she could have had a good marriage with Jerry her own self. He was a good man.

But, she was grateful to have Ralph. She loved him. He loved her. She knew that she would be happy with him as her husband. He was good to her.

But, she worried about the farm suffering and her dad because of her choice in spouse. She hoped that God knew the answers to this all because she surely didn't.

Amanda's father was a good farmer. Her mother, Carolyn, was a good farmer's wife. They loved their farm. They had a right, too. It was in their blood. It was meant to be passed from generation to generation to live off the land for a living on their own property and take pride in it. This was what Amanda thought on the subject that God knew.

Amanda's parents had never spent so many days from the farm but, they wanted to make sure their only daughter was OK. They didn't like the idea of her living alone. They just got used to the idea that she was going to be living with Sarah for the duration. It never came across their mind that Sarah would get married. It was just coming to Amanda's consciousness that she was alone.

"How completely miserable she was" said Amanda as she ate her first meal of her life alone. Never would she guess to ever eat a meal by herself in her life ever.

I suppose God now wants her to clean this apartment by herself. And how about grocery shopping that she loathed doing at all. She was a farm girl. And, now she would have to do it...and by herself or starve. Amanda cried.

Amanda decided to take the edge off her loneliness by calling Ralph. "Hi, sweetie" said Ralph on the other side of the phone.

"Hi. Sarah got married last weekend. My parents came up for the wedding. But, now I am here all by myself. I hate it" said Amanda crying.

"Dear heart. Maybe, it's time to set our wedding date. No use of you sitting there in your loneliness by yourself when your sweet teddy bear of a man, as you call me, wants to bring you here to live with me" said Ralph.

"You can sublease the apartment. How about we set a date for our wedding on the last Sunday of this month? We can have the wedding reception in your favorite restaurant if you want across the feed store. And, we'll get married in the Catholic Church in the city. Dry your tears, now, my dear lady. How's that?" said Ralph.

"It's better. But, I don't know what to tell dad" said Amanda.

"Don't worry about Tom. I'll go talk to him. We'll work everything out if I have to hire someone part-time at the feed store so that I can come on the farm myself to work side-by-side with your father. OK?" said Ralph.

"OK. I love you" said Amanda.

"I love you, too. And, when I get off the phone, I will take care of everything. I will have our wedding bands already here for when you come home. And, I will mail you a check for you to pick out a wedding dress there to bring here. I will rent a tuxedo for myself. Don't worry about anything. OK?" said Ralph.

"OK" said Amanda. Amanda felt better after hanging up from speaking to Ralph. This apartment seemed dreary without Sarah. Her spirit seemed to fill the apartment with her voice and laughter. Her personality lit up the room. It wouldn't be the same without her.

She would tell Sarah when she stopped by about her own wedding plans. She looked forward to being a wife instead of a child living in the big city pretending how adult she was. She was just a scared kid here.

With Ralph, she would be able to have kids and help him run the store. She would no longer worry about him being alone. She was relieved he would talk to dad instead of her. She knew that her mother would help.

Carolyn loved Ralph. And, Carolyn believed in a happy marriage and being a wife. Amanda would never find a better man than Ralph. He was dedicated to her. They both loved the feed store.

And, she would be close to her parents. They could be grandparents for once instead of just parents constantly worrying about their only son far away in the military. As much as they were patriotic, they would have preferred he stayed on the farm for his career.

Amanda boxed up her meager belongings in her bedroom. It was all that she brought with her.

Sarah decided to donate her furniture and the pots & pans and dishes to the local charity. Her apartment with John was already lavishly furnished. She only needed her clothing.

Sarah hugged Amanda goodbye and promised to show up to be the bridesmaid for her wedding. John would provide an appropriate dress for Sarah to wear since Amanda's wedding was on such short notice. He volunteered to bring the wedding cake from the restaurant to the reception that he would bake himself that would say: "Congratulations Amanda and Ralph." Brian, her old boss, said that he would pay for it.

Sarah promised to find someone to sublease the apartment by the first of the month. Amanda would give notice that she was leaving her employment since she was getting married instead. They decided to have a going away party with wedding gifts for Amanda to take with her for her new life as Mrs. Tomlinson. She was grateful for that. John drove Amanda to the apartment with these gifts since she didn't have a car.

On the following Saturday, Ralph showed up at the apartment. He told Amanda that he had a talk with Tom. "Tom was happy enough" said Ralph.

He came to take her boxes home so that she was out of the apartment by the first of the month. He was happily surprised to see the wedding gifts from her co-workers.

The last box Amanda put in the car was her boxed up wedding dress that Ralph bought for her. She didn't want him to see it for right now.

"Don't peek. It's my wedding dress. And, it's really, really beautiful. Wait until you see it on me" said Amanda kissing Ralph.

"I can't wait either for our wedding day. It's what I've dreamed of for such a long time for us" said Ralph with his arms around Amanda.

"I'm glad" said Amanda.

"We will have to send out thank you cards for our wedding gifts from your co-workers" said Ralph. She closed the door to the apartment for the last time.

From now on, her home was with Ralph. She was a happy woman to go home. So now, she was back to her old life in the feed store. Ralph was elated. So now, her life had come full circle. But, Amanda was happy. Instead of feeling out of place, she was with her own kind. She loved the big city and her friends there. But, she knew that she was a small town girl. That much she knew about herself.

Everyone welcomed Amanda back. Business picked up at the feed store as folks drifted in to give the couple good wishes and buy a thing or two whether they needed it or not just to be friendly and polite. "It was swell of them" said Amanda to Ralph.

Ralph was a happy man. He insisted on making supper. He wanted to be a man who could take care of her whenever the need arose no matter what. They were a team. They were a family.

She was already his wife to him. He didn't need a marriage certificate to tell him so. He knew it in his heart. That is what mattered. They slept in the same bed together. They bathed together. They ate together. And, they poured their love into their little feed store which was their livelihood and kept them going.

They knew that they had a special relationship. They couldn't seem to take their eyes off of each other. Ralph's arms were always around her in the store. She was constantly kissing him.

Mostly, they made love together before even considering eating supper after the hard work day since it was more important to them to fill their heart with intimacy and closeness than fill their stomach. Their need was that great. Amanda never wanted it any other way.

"Tell me you will always love me as much as you do now" said Amanda one evening while supper was heating on the stove.

"I promise" said Ralph.

"Tell me that you will always love me as much as you do now" said Ralph.

"I will" said Amanda.

"Good. Because I couldn't bear it if you didn't. I really couldn't" said Ralph pulling her close to him while they lay in bed together feeling the warmth of each other's bodies up against each other.

Once again, after supper, Ralph and Amanda made love. Amanda felt closer than ever. She could see her wedding dress hanging on the hook of the bedroom door. She would be glad when her wedding day arrived. She looked forward to it so.

Amanda woke up to the sunlight filtering through the glass of the bedroom. Ralph was still sleeping. She didn't want to wake him. The store wasn't due to open for a couple of hours yet. She would shower and make breakfast to surprise him.

Amanda returned to Ralph's side sitting on the bed. "Wake up, sleepy head" said Amanda. Amanda nudged him. He didn't move an inch.

"Boy, you must be really tired" said Amanda. She shook his body. He was laying on his side. He fell on his back. She put her head on his chest since she loved to feel his heart beat so.

"Oh my God" screamed Amanda. Amanda ran down the stairs. She left the door open to the apartment. She fled to the restaurant across the street. She tapped on the glass of the window. The waitress she had met the day she applied for the job opened the door.

"What do you want, sweetie? We are closed still" said the waitress.

"I think Ralph is dead. I put my head on his chest to give him a hug. And, I didn't hear his heart beat. And, I couldn't wake him up" screamed Amanda swinging her arms around franticly.

"Stay here. I'll run up to see if Ralph is OK. OK?" said the waitress.

"OK" said Amanda.

The ambulance drove Ralph away. Amanda felt like somebody had put a knife in her heart. How could God have let this happen to her and Ralph? Poor Ralph. He was so good. He deserved better. I loved him so. Now, I have to live the rest of my life without him.

I have to leave. I have to leave. I can't stay here. These things kept running though her head.

"Hello dad. Come get me. Ralph just died. I have to come home, I can't stay here right now. Please dad" said Amanda.

"I will be right there" said Tom.

Carolyn was waiting for Amanda when they drove up the drive with a hug and a kiss on her forehead.

Tom decided to bury Ralph next to Grandpa Jim on the family plot. Amanda thought that he would like that since he loved the farm by now, also. Amanda could talk to Ralph and Grandpa Jim though it wouldn't be the same as having them on earth by a long shot. The coroner said that Ralph died of a heart attack.

It hurt all the same to Amanda. She didn't care if she lived with him until he was a one hundred years old. As long as she got to live with him as his wife is all that mattered to her.

Amanda closed the feed store. She didn't know what she was going to do. At the reading of the will, all Ralph's worldly possessions went to her, except for a childhood cousin Ralph loved. He willed his childhood baseball card collection to his cousin, Leo.

The attorney had to find Ralph's only surviving relative who lived somewhere around

Michigan City, IN thought the attorney. Amanda wanted to meet this man that Ralph loved so. He was raised with Ralph like a brother.

Amanda returned to the feed store since it was hers now and the only thing she had of Ralph. But, it was unbearable to be there. Everything reminded her of Ralph.

One day, she thought that she saw Ralph. She thought that she was going crazy. The man was trying to introduce himself. He stood in front of the cash register. "Hello" he said. Amanda thought that she was going to pass out.

"Ralph?" said Amanda.

"No, I'm Leo—Ralph's only cousin" said Leo.

Leo" said Amanda putting out her hand to shake it.

"I'm sorry to hear about Ralph. We were raised like brothers together. I loved him a lot" said Leo.

"Me too" said Amanda.

"I am going crazy here in this store with all the memories of Ralph" said Amanda.

"Then why don't you leave" said Leo.

"I can't. The store is all I've got. And, if I lose it, I will have lost another part of Ralph" said Amanda.

"I know what you mean. But, you're young. I'm old. I'm retired. So, I can work in the store for you awhile until you get yourself together. Think about it" said Leo.

"Why don't I show you upstairs. There is a spare bedroom upstairs if you would like to stay for awhile. I could familiarize you with the store" said Amanda.

"I would be delighted" said Leo.

Leo and Amanda became best friends and family. Leo could tell Amanda stories about Ralph about his childhood that made her feel closer to Ralph and closer to Leo, too. And, she could tell Leo about what kind of man Ralph was as an adult man and what to do at the feed store if she decided to take off. Leo seemed a natural at the store like Ralph. Amanda was pleased even though she missed Ralph.

Amanda became a frequent visitor at the farm for her mother's hug and cooking. She wanted to sit next to her father to get a hug like she did when she was a kid. And, she wanted to visit Grandpa Jim and Ralph, too with conversations about the feed store and cousin Leo.

She brought Leo with her to the farm so that he would become part of the family. Her family was all that Leo had. She wanted to make sure his life was surrounded with love like hers was. He was a nice person. He deserved to be part of a good family like hers.

Amanda prayed about her future to God and the Mother of God who were her great love of her childhood. She sat in Ralph's backyard which was now hers at the St. Mary garden asking Mary to bless her life and help her through the pain and suffering.

"Ralph, I love you dear husband" said Amanda pointing to heaven where Jesus Christ was before she went to sleep at night. It comforted her right now to know someday she would be in heaven with him. She didn't want her parents to know that she felt that way. She was a young woman still. But, how could she go on without her husband?

"How could you have left me? I need you so" cried Amanda to sleep.

# Chapter 12

Amanda was seen everywhere with Leo in town. She wanted him to know everything there was to know about the business. It belonged to Ralph. And, Leo was Ralph's only surviving relative. Therefore, he was special to Amanda. She was getting used to seeing how much he looked like Ralph. It was amazing. He was the first cousin on his father's side of the family.

But, now that he was gone, this life didn't seem nearly as attractive. Working with Ralph was a dream life for her. The store was his life. Therefore, she wanted to share it with him every moment of the day.

She knew that she couldn't go back to living on the farm. Her parents wouldn't have her. She was too old to be returning home. And, she wasn't a strong male who could help the farm and pass on the inheritance and traditions of the farm from generation to generation. And besides, they knew that she had a nice apartment above the store that belonged to Ralph and her.

But, it was unbearable to live there. Her wedding dress still hung on the hook of the bedroom door. And, she didn't begin to go through Ralph's clothing to see what to keep and what to give away to a charity. Perhaps Leo would want some of Ralph's clothing. He was about the same size. But, she couldn't bear it for now.

She had one blessing: Leo. Ralph had never mentioned him even though Leo and Ralph were obviously close.

The snow was beginning to melt off. The spring bulbs were shooting up from the ground green sprigs and the trees were budding. Leo thought it was a good idea for Amanda and himself to work in the garden behind the store. "It needed grooming up anyway" said Leo after the spring thaw.

Amanda didn't like cutting grass much. So, Leo decided to plant the entire area with flowers and vegetables that they could either put in vases or that they could eat.

Leo decided to make three "4x4" gardens so that it would be easy to weed from all sides. "And besides" said Leo to Amanda: "I can put a mesh over these gardens to keep the rabbits from eating all the greens before we get a chance to have our lettuce for our lunch and supper."

"You're making me hungry already" said Amanda.

Amanda liked Leo's intensity in doing the garden to perfection. He said that there was nothing better tasting than home garden vegetables. He said that Ralph and himself had "victory gardens" when they were a kid. "And besides 'said Leo' the garden will be pretty. And, you won't have to mow it."

"OK. OK. I am interested in having a garden like Ralph had when he was a kid. And, I can get the flower and vegetable seeds; the garden tools; and the bags of soil and fertilizer for wholesale at the store. And, we rent out our rototillers, so we can use it for free instead of paying for it by the hour" said Amanda.

"Great. Let's get going then because we want to get the seeds in as early as the seed packets say we can grow them outdoors without danger of the frost killing the seedlings. So, somewhere around May or early June, we can begin growing our plants outdoors. And, we can get a jump on growing our seedlings by growing them on the kitchen windowsill until we can safely take them outdoors" said Leo.

So, Amanda and Leo planted the seeds in the soil in containers. They were watered. They were left in the indirect sun with clear plastic placed tightly over them until they sprouted. And then, they were put on the window sills to get the sun on them until they could be put in the garden to grow the rest of the way. It gave Amanda something useful to do instead of mourning all the time about Ralph.

She went out of the way to pray to God about it. And, she showed Ralph the garden that he loved when he was alive. She hoped that he could see it from heaven. Surely, that was where he was because if Jesus was there, so was Ralph. Ralph was a good man.

Therefore, he was in heaven with Jesus. And, if Amanda could talk to God in heaven, she should be able to talk to Ralph as well...It took away some of the suffering of it all.

Amanda still wore her engagement ring that was inscribed inside: "Ralph and Amanda in love forever." This is true! She planned to never take it off.


Leo dragged Amanda into the backyard to weed around the St. Mary's garden that Ralph loved. There was a wrought iron trellis that arched over the statue of Mary. Once it warmed enough outdoors to let the paint dry, Amanda figured it out that it would take only a pint of white paint and blue paint that Amanda sold in the store anyway—along with turpentine and paint brushes. Leo would paint on the St. Mary statue for Amanda.

It would keep Mary looking as pretty as she was meant to be to honor her. Amanda set aside several tea rose bushes to plant at the foot of Mary that she sold in the store anyway. Perhaps two on each side of the trellis that were pink with bright yellow stamens would give proper adoration. And, then directly in front of the feet of St. Mary, Amanda planted a rosebush that had blossoms at least four-inch across that were pink in color with yellow throats. Amanda loved the two colors of pink and yellow on the same petal.

She hoped that Ralph would love what she and his cousin was doing to re-furbish his St. Mary garden. In front of it was a stone bench. Obviously, Ralph sat here to pray to St. Mary so many times thought Amanda. She smiled as she sat on the bench with Leo looking at St. Mary.

"I loved your cousin" said Amanda her head on Leo's shoulder for comfort.

"I'm sure that he loved you a lot. After all, he was going to marry you. And, he gave you everything that he had in his will: his home which is the apartment that we both live in; his car sitting in the garage; and his business. A man can't do more than that to show his wife his love for her" said Leo.

"Thank you for saying that. I want you to know that you are welcome to stay here as long as you like. You can stay here forever. I really need you here. You are Ralph's only family" said Amanda.

"Thank you for saying that. I feel like family with you. Ralph was all I had. I was so filled with grief when I heard that he had passed on. He was so young to go like that. And, I would like to make this home. I had a job where I was at. But, I had no family there. I was never at ease. Here, I feel at peace. And, I can feel Ralph here" said Leo.

"Well, his personality is certainly here. I can feel Ralph too all the time. Sometimes, it comforts me because we were so close. Other times, it just upsets me so that I just want to cry since I can't be with him. And, I will never get to marry him. And, I will never have his children. He wanted children really bad. It would have been a good life together. I'm so upset about it" said Amanda.

"I know honey" said Leo squeezing the hand of Amanda to comfort her.

"I don't think that the pain is ever going to go away" said Amanda.

"Probably not. But, you'll learn to live with it over time. You don't have to ever stop loving Ralph just because he went to heaven, you know. He would want you to be happy for him that he is in heaven now with Jesus. And, he would want you to take care of yourself for him. You can do that, can't you?" said Leo.

Amanda buried her head into Leo's shoulder to weep. Leo rubbed her back to comfort her. "Tomorrow, I want to go to the farm to see Ralph. Will you come with me?" said Amanda.

"Of course" said Leo.

"I want to plant some spring flowers at the foot of his marker for him to look at" said Amanda.

"What flowers should we bring from the store to the farm?" said Leo.

"How about those hyacinths that we are selling. We have blooming pots of white, pink, and purple ones. They are very fragrant. He liked those when he was a kid" said Leo.

"Then, that's what we will plant. One miniature garden of each color with the white hyacinths in the middle. It will look like the prettiest. I will have to call my parents to let them know we are coming" said Amanda.

"OK. I will look forward to seeing them again. And, I enjoy Carolyn's cooking. Tell her that for me" said Leo.

"OK" said Amanda as she took off to get the phone to call her mother. Tomorrow would be a break in the routine. On Sunday, the store was usually closed anyway. Amanda hoped that these flowers were respectful to the memory of Ralph.

He loved flowers when he was on this earth. Geraniums grew in hanging flowers pots that were for decorations for the front of the store. Ralph loved to rub his fingers over the leaves. He loved the scent of it. And, he loved the red ones the best of all the colors.

Ralph took care of the geraniums in the window sills in the back of the store in the winter time to keep them alive until he could re-plant them in the garden.

They would blossom at Christmas which was very appropriate thought Ralph. "What a great Christmas flower. All green and bright red" said Ralph at the time.

Amanda wished that she had more time with Ralph before he died. Who knew. One day, dreams of a long marriage. And, next you know, he was gone.

The folks of the town did a good job of showing respects to the man. He had plenty of flowers at the funeral to show how much he was loved. Leo hadn't known that he had passed away until after that. He had expressed his wish that he had been there. Amanda thought otherwise if he loved him so.

She barely could stand sitting in the funeral home looking at Ralph laid out that way. She wanted to wake him and take him home. He didn't belong there. He belonged home with her and the kids they were going to have. What a shame thought Amanda.

She was really angry at God for doing this to her. And, she felt guilty for thinking this way and for even being alive. By what right did she have to even eat or enjoy anything ever again if Ralph couldn't?

God should have taken her instead thought Amanda. He was more deserving. The people of the town counted on him to keep them going. There was no other store like this for miles. And, some of the farmers would have a really hard time of it if it wasn't for the store of Ralph's.

In comparison, she was nothing. She was just a kid. She wasn't even that useful to her parents needs since she was born the wrong gender. She could do some of the things on the farm but, not any of the heavy labor. She didn't have the body strength of a man.

So, she could understand her father's point of view. But, there was nothing too much that she could do of any significant help so far except to pray and write to her brother Tommy pleading for him to come home.

And, the truth be known, she probably wouldn't of made it as well as she did at the feed store had not Leo showed up. He was a "natural" at the store. "It must be in the blood" said Amanda out loud to herself.

Then, Amanda put her flower pots, garden tools, and garden gloves by the front door of the feed store so that she wouldn't forget them. It was too long a drive to come back for them. Leo asked if he could bring a couple of the flower pots with daffodils that were white, yellow, and orange in color for Carolyn's garden. Amanda put them by the front door as well with the other flowers.

Amanda went upstairs with Leo to the apartment. Leo was making all the meals these days so that Amanda could rest. She slept very little these days.

Leo told her to rest while he cooked supper. He decided to make hamburger with macaroni noodles in tomato sauce. It was pretty much the only recipe that he knew. But, it tasted good and was nutritional.

He wrote out the recipe:

# LEO'S MACARONI & BEEF

## Ingredients

1-1½ pounds of hamburger
1 medium onion, chopped
Macaroni noodles (around 2-4 cups)
Tomato juice
Parmesan cheese

## Directions

On low heat, fry hamburger and onion turning often in the frying pan until the hamburger is browned and the onions are translucent. In a separate pot pour in at least 4-6 cups of water and bring to boil. Pour in macaroni noodles in of at least 2-4 cups cooking in boiling water until the noodles are soft. Drain the cooked noodles into a colander pouring cool water over the noodles. Drain the noodles shaking the colander to have excess water drip out. Then, pour the noodles back into the pot; then, with a slit spoon put the hamburger and onions in the pot. Then, pour in tomato juice over this until the mixture is mixed together. Put on low heat until heated. Pour enough juice to at least cover the mixture. Then, pour into a serving bowl with as much as desired for serving. Sprinkle parmesan cheese over the recipe.

Leo cooked the recipe at the stove. He then handed Amanda a bowl filled with the food he just made with a glass of milk. He turned on the TV softly. Neither cared what was on TV considering the circumstances. After all, Leo grieved too even though he never mentioned it to Amanda on his own. It only would increase the suffering thought Leo.

"You made this. It's delicious" said Amanda eating quickly since she was so hungry. She hadn't eaten well for days.

"We have more on the stove if you want it" said Leo. They both had seconds. They both needed their strength now.

It was a bright sunny day when Amanda and Leo pulled into the driveway of the Miller Farm with their flowers for Ralph—and also their flowers for Carolyn's garden.

Leo helped Carolyn to plant her daffodils in her garden right off. She planted them on the edge of her garden in the back of the house as a border to accent the garden. "They are just beautiful. I thank you for them" said Carolyn hugging Amanda and then Leo.

"It was Leo's idea to bring them for you. He thought you would like them" said Amanda.

"Well, I certainly do" said Carolyn.

"Well, if you don't mind, I want to take these flowers for Ralph to his gravesite with Leo for us to plant a little garden for him. We want to pay our respects and pray there together" said Amanda.

"Good. That's good of you to want to do that for yourself and Leo. Go now with your flowers while your mother makes your lunch for you. It should be ready when you get back" said Carolyn smiling.

"OK, mom" said Amanda while Leo started unloading the hyacinth pots out of the back seat of the car. He didn't like leaving flowers sitting in the hot sun in the car at all. So, the sooner they were in the ground getting their nutrients from the soil and their drink of rain from the heavens the better thought Leo.

Leo planted the flowers for Amanda just as she asked with the white hyacinths in the middle, the purple hyacinths on the left of them; and the pink hyacinths to the right of the white hyacinths. "I hope you really like this flower garden we planted for you today, Ralph. I hope you see them from heaven. Leo, your cousin, is with me now. He lives in the apartment now. And, he works in the feed store, too. I hope that makes you very happy from heaven. And, he looks so much like you in the face. You could be twins. We all love him. We all miss you here on earth. We wish you were with us though" said Amanda beginning to cry. Leo held her in his arms. He asked to say a rosary before they headed to the farmhouse which he did.

Lunch was Amanda's favorite: meatloaf. Carolyn gave Amanda the recipe to take home with her for Amanda and Leo.

## CAROLYN'S MEATLOAF

### Ingredients

1 cup oatmeal
½ cup to 1 cup of tomato juice
1 egg
1-1½ pounds of hamburger
1 medium size onions chopped finely

### Directions

Pre-heat oven at 375°. Mix all ingredients together. Pour into a loaf pan. Make the surface flat on the meat mixture. Bake in oven for 1-1½ hours or until thoroughly cooked and browned on top. Surface will look browned when completely baked. Serve hot or cold for sandwiches.

"The meatloaf is in the oven now so that we can eat soon" said Carolyn.

"Great. I'm really hungry. I'm sure Leo is too. And, thanks for the recipe. I am sure Leo and I will enjoy making this at the apartment. This will make some really great cold meatloaf sandwiches like I ate when I was a kid" said Amanda.

"Good" said Carolyn as she went to the oven to take out the family's early dinner. Tom as usual bowed his head with prayers at the dinner table.

Dear God: Thank you for this great food my lovely wife Carolyn has made for us and our new family member, Leo. I'm so hungry I have to eat now, God. Amen.

Everyone smiled to hear the prayer. They all agreed that they were really hungry. And, there they sat together while it poured rain heavily outside. There was no more pleasant a sound on the Miller Farm than spending the day listening to the rain.

In fact, it rained so much that the road leading out of the farm flooded out. Amanda and Leo decided to sleep over and leave in the morning because of it. Much safer roads that way they thought. Amanda's parents agreed.

And, Carolyn didn't mind at all getting up early in the morning to make breakfast. Amanda was secretly glad this happened since she wanted to be home a little longer. And, she longed to eat her mother's food again to comfort her.

Leo didn't care because he was just grateful to have family with the Millers. And though he missed Ralph and was sorry he passed away and all, he sure was grateful that he had the forethought to have a business for Leo to work at and an apartment for Leo to call home. He never was anything without his cousin Ralph by his side. And, even in his death, it was the same deal. And,

Leo didn't mind because Ralph was the one who always took care of Leo. And, why should it be any different now.

He could still feel his cousin's love. He was grateful. He, too, cried in the night like Amanda though he never wanted to tell her. Sometimes, it was tears of grief for Ralph passing and Leo's hard life up to now. He had no parents or siblings of his own. Ralph's parents took him in. He had no wife or kids of his own. He barely had much of a job until now. But, he managed somehow.

Amanda was like the daughter he never had. He cried in the night tears of happiness to have her in his life and his new life at the feed store. He finally was "home." He never had a real home before—until now. Ralph's parents were kind but, it was Ralph who took him in when it came to expressing any kind of real love for him.

Maybe, Ralph was letting Leo pay Ralph back now by him being here thought Leo. He hoped so. What would he ever do without Amanda? She was everything to him. He thought that he would just die literally without her.

Leo closed his eyes to sleep. He hoped God would bring him some comfort and peace to his life that he needed so his own self. "Thank you so much God" said Leo before he drifted off to sleep.

When Leo and Amanda returned home, Amanda told Leo that he was going to go to Indianapolis to visit Sarah for the day. He wanted Leo to stay at the store. She saw the worry in Leo's eyes.

"Don't worry. I'll be back. I'll only be gone for the day. I will ask dad to take me" said Amanda. Her arms went around Leo to comfort him. He was almost as bad "a basket case" as Amanda. What a shame Ralph isn't here with us now thought Amanda.

Amanda reached for the phone to call her dad. He agreed to come by tomorrow to get her. She was only staying the day, so that she had no reason to pack a bag. She was going to make a surprise visit at work to see Sarah, her boss, and her old friends at work. Her dad would wait for her.

She would have lunch at the Circle with her dad as a treat to him for driving her and to spend some time with him. And, she would bring back a box of chocolate for Leo and her mother which she thought they both would love to be remembered by her.

Amanda waved to Leo as Tom and Amanda drove away to Indianapolis. She assured him that he could manage the store for one day himself and Amanda wasn't leaving him. She could see the terror in his eyes.

Amanda could sense his deepening love for her as his only kin—plus her parents. He was afraid to be alone anymore even though that was the life that he lived before.

But, things were different now that he found Amanda and made his home here. Amanda vowed to herself to never ever take this away from him. This was his home forever! Bad enough that Ralph had left her. She couldn't bear Leo leaving her on top of it.

So, she understood his suffering. She truly did. She loved Leo with her whole heart. She sensed that he felt the same. God love Leo thought Amanda. "And, thank you for him God" said Amanda.

Brian, Amanda's old boss, was surprised to see Amanda standing in front of his desk like when she worked there. He came from behind the desk to hug her. "Sorry to hear about Ralph" said Brian.

"Thank you" said Amanda.

"Well, what brings you to the city?" said Brian.

"I came for my old job if I can have it. I am at loose ends now since Ralph passed away" said Amanda.

"I understand, truly. But, your old job is taken. I can always find you work here. You are a good employee. But, is that what you want to do?" said Brian.

"What do you mean?" said Amanda.

"Well, I understand that your old apartment is subleased now. Your old job is taken. So, why not do something new and exciting in life. Live a little. You deserve it" said Brian.

"I wouldn't know where to go. I wouldn't know what to do" said Amanda.

"Well, what do you like to do that isn't putting your nose to the grindstone all the time?—Though God knows that you do a good job of it. You were a good employee here. I suspect that you, would be a good employee anywhere" said Brian.

"I mean that I hate to see you suffer like this, Amanda. You're such a nice person. You should have a chance to have some of your dreams come true for you for once. You've been through so much and at such a young age" said Brian.

"Thanks. I appreciate all of this. But, the only thing that I know how to do for a job is what I've been doing here for a living or helping my parents on the farm. The only other thing that I am good at all is singing but, I don't know how to make that into a job at all around here. And, that's OK because this is where I was born. I love the people here. They are good folk" said Amanda.

"Yes, the people here are always great. It is why I've been in business like this all these years so well. Just sit there for a moment without fidgeting like you always do, Amanda" said Brian.

Brian sat for a moment staring at Amanda in disbelief. She was beautiful. She was talented. "Singing, huh. And, if I could get you a job singing would be happy for once?" said Brian.

"Who wouldn't. It's been a dream of mine since I was a kid to work as a singer. But, I'm just a farm girl and all" said Amanda.

Once again, Brian just sat there staring at Amanda in disbelief. He knew that he had to help her.

"You know what Amanda? I have a cousin who lives in Las Vegas who says that he is a talent agent and has connections with the stars there. If you like, I can give you his contact information. You never know. It might just be the thing for you for now. Give you a change of scenery" said Brian.

"You can always come back here to work later. You are always welcome as long as I am here. And, I'm the owner of this company as you well know" said Brian also.

"So anyway, let me write down his name, address and phone number for you. His name is Manny Coleman. Just mention my name. We grew up together. He was always a flashy fellow even as a kid. So, it was no surprise to the family when he moved to Las Vegas. But, he said that he is doing well there" said Brian.

Brian handed her the information about his cousin Manny to Amanda. She felt lightheaded about the thought of moving to Las Vegas. She never thought of ever leaving Indiana. It was her whole life. But, what Brian said made sense. She would be frightened to go so far away from home. But, a real singing career and a chance to be a star was hard to pass up.

"Thank you" said Amanda shaking his hand.

"Maybe, it will take your mind off Ralph for awhile until your emotions are a little more put together. It must have been a terrible shock to you. And oh, Sarah is down the hall working if you want to say hello before you leave and some of the other co-workers" said Brian smiling.

"Thanks" said Amanda as she left the office. Amanda could see why she liked Brian so. He was a good person. She headed down the hall.

Sarah was at the copier when Amanda's arms went around her to hug her.

"I'm only here for a moment. Dad is downstairs waiting for me. I was just inquiring about my old job since I don't know what I am doing with myself yet. And, I heard that our old apartment is subleased" said Amanda.

"I'm sorry to hear about Ralph" said Sarah.

"Thank you" said Amanda.

"Well, stay in touch. I'll tell John that you send your love. OK?" said Sarah hugging Amanda.

"OK. Tell the co-workers I said hello and all. I have to get back to dad who is waiting for me in the car" said Amanda. Amanda hurried down the hall. It must have been a good hour by now that her dad was waiting on her.

Amanda opened the passenger side of her dad's car to sit down. Amanda's dad turned to her with a smile on his face. "I'm glad that you are still my little girl" said Tom.

"Yes, I am" said Amanda beaming as they headed to the Circle for lunch and to pick up Leo's and her mother's gifts.

Soon, they were on the rainy roads heading back to the feed store. Tom stopped in to say "hello" to Leo since he thought it important for him to feel connected to family right now with Ralph passing away and all. That made Amanda happy since she wanted her parents to be family with Leo. It was important to her.

Then, Tom headed back to his beautiful wife, Carolyn at the Miller Farm with the box of chocolate sitting on the passenger seat for his wife from her thoughtful daughter, Amanda. He knew that

Carolyn would be so happy to have been remembered today by Amanda. She would love the gift.

# Chapter 13

Leo stood at the bus stop with tears falling down his cheeks. Amanda hated leaving him like that. And, she hated seeing a grown man cry either. What a deal!

But, she hadn't heard from Tommy yet, her brother. She suspected that he was overseas. And, that was why. And, with Ralph dead yet. Her life was so upset.

"It will be alright, Leo. Dad and mom will look after you while I am gone. I won't be gone forever. And, you know the feed store pretty well by now. So, you can run it yourself. And, I am only a phone call away if you need me. And, I am only about a 4 to 5 hour flight away from you if I must come back home" said Amanda.

"But, this is an opportunity that I can't let pass me by. A real talent agent that could make me a star in music and make me a millionaire. And, while I couldn't get my family the husband and family they needed to help me run the farm for it to pass on to the next generation, perhaps I can at least bring in the money the family can use to save the farm" said Amanda.

"And, people love my singing voice. They really do" said Amanda.

"This is true" said Tom hugging his only daughter goodbye as she hugged her dad and Leo goodbye.

"Tell mom I love her" said Amanda.

"I will" said Tom.

"I will call you, Leo every day. I promise" said Amanda wiping the tears from his cheeks as she said this.

"Me too?" said Tom.

"You too, dad. Tell mom so that she knows" said Amanda.

She knew that Leo was a blessing to be able to watch over the store so that she could run off for the music career. She had to do it for herself and her family including Leo. He was a keeper in the family. That's for sure!

"I love you both" said Amanda as she kissed first her dad's cheek and then Leo's cheek. She sat at the window of the bus waving goodbye. She was afraid since it was so different from home but looked forward to the opportunity.

"Thank God for her boss, Brian" said Amanda softly to herself. She would have to thank him after she is a big star and all. She really would. She needed the fast track for obvious reasons.

She glanced at her engagement ring still on her finger. What a shame to have missed out on marrying Ralph. She hoped Jerry was alright. She hadn't gotten a chance to write to him. She should do it now on her way there. It was important for her to stay close to him. He was one of her best and dearest friends. She hoped that he would have a long and happy marriage. It wouldn't be right to wish it was her under the circumstances just because Ralph was gone and Jerry wasn't. It wasn't Jerry's fault. And, it certainly wasn't Ralph's fault. He would be here if he could.

The Roman Catholic priest who counseled her after Ralph's death said that Ralph never left or could. "He is in your heart. So, when you are upset, point to your heart. It will remind you of his love for you" said the priest.

Amanda pointed to her heart! A tear fell down her right cheek. She wiped it quickly off her cheek. She didn't want anyone to see her cry. They might come to her aid to help her. There is nothing that they could do. Ralph was gone. No one could bring him back. If someone could, she would be the first to do so. But, the gesture brought comfort to her heart all the same.

The bus was rolling down the road farther and farther away from Indiana.

She pulled down the miniature table in front of her. She began to write:

Dear Jerry,

I am heading right now for Las Vegas, NV to start a singing career there. Brian, my old boss, in Indianapolis that you met has a relative who is a talent agent there who will help me.

I'm sorry that I haven't written yet to you. Everything has happened so quickly since Ralph passed away. Didn't even get to the altar with him. My wedding dress is still hanging on the hook on the bedroom of my apartment. Don't have the heart to move it. Haven't gone through Ralph's clothing or anything.

Leo, Ralph's only kin, who is his cousin is tending to the store. He is staying at the apartment. There are two bedrooms there. Thank God. I just left my things as is. I can take care of things when I return.

But, I went down to Indianapolis to talk to Brian about getting my old job back. He already hired someone to replace me at my old job there as receptionist. But, he said that he would find me something there if I needed it. But, he thought the singing career would do me better. Brian has a cousin in Las Vegas who is a talent agent and is connected there. So, that is why I am on my way.

Say "hello" to Sarah when you talk to her. We had good times together—all three of us. But, my old apartment there is subleased now. And, as it is, I split the rent with Sarah when I lived there. Can't do that since she is married.

Dad drove me to see my old boss. He waited in the car for me. He is nice that way. We ate lunch at the Circle before heading home at the farm. I bought Leo and mom a box of chocolates while we were there. Should have sent you a box also since I was there. But, next time in town I will.

By the time I mail this to you, I will be in Las Vegas, NV. You are one of my best and dearest friends, so I wanted to let you know what is going on. Writing to you on the bus to Las Vegas since I am sitting here by myself looking out the window at the view. Excited but, afraid some.

Promised to call dad and Leo every day. Will get a little money from the store to live off of that Leo will mail to me regularly since Ralph willed me all his worldly possessions.

Leo got Ralph's childhood baseball card collection which was one of the reasons that he was in town. He took a shining to me and Ralph's store. When we met, I just fell in love with him. He reminds me so much of Ralph.

He really had no place to go. So, I welcomed him into the family and told him that he could live in the apartment upstairs forever. He really is a good guy.

He is retired. So, he can afford to work in the feed store full-time helping the family out. And, he doesn't have to pay any rent. We are family now. So, it's a good deal all the way around.

Love, Amanda


Amanda tucked her letter in her purse that was sitting on the right hand side of her by her legs. She breathed a sigh of relief. She pulled back the seat to sleep for awhile. She might as well. Nothing to do for hours while the bus driver was getting us to Las Vegas, NV.

The ride there was really rigorous. The bus changed once on route. We had a new driver other than the original. We stopped a few times for restroom breaks and to stretch our legs. Fast food places on the way became our friend so that we had a bag of food and a drink along the way. It was all that we needed to get us there.

But, Amanda felt all cramped up sitting here in her bus seat by the window. So, she was grateful to see the bus pull into the terminal in downtown Las Vegas, NV.

She stood outside the terminal with her suitcase. There were plenty of taxis to choose from just sitting there. She hailed a cab.

The cabbie nodded as he opened the back door to the cab. "Where to?" said the cab driver.

"Take me to a cheap and clean hotel. I need to clean up after the long ride into town from the bus" said Amanda.

"Can do. I take it that you are new in town" said the cab driver.

"Just got in a few minutes ago. I am supposed to meet someone tomorrow. I'm from Indiana by the way" said Amanda proudly.

"Wow. That's a long way from home. But, I know just the place for you to stay tonight. My brother, Tom, works there as a bellhop. Mention my name. It's Mike McCullough. They'll find you something for me. You have to have connections in this town to make it" said Mike.

"Thanks. I appreciate it. I am starting a music career. I am going to be a star. My boss in Indiana has a relative who lives here who is a big time talent agent. I am going to see him tomorrow" said Amanda proudly.

"Well, good luck. I hope that you make it" said Mike as he pulled in front of a small hotel that Mike said was about 10 minutes away from the Strip. Manny lived near the major campus in town that Mike said she could "hoof it" there since it was close by enough. A lot of people walk here to where they are going, so, she will fit right in.

"Remember to tell them that Mike McCullough sent you. They will fix you up good here" said Mike.

"Thanks Mike" said Amanda as she handed him the cab fare and grabbed her suitcase. She pulled out her envelope to Jerry from her purse so that she wouldn't forget to mail it now that she was in Las Vegas.

At the reservation desk with her suitcase still in her hands, she said: "I need a room for the night. Mike McCullough said to mention his name" said Amanda.

The clerk perked up his eyes. He smiled at Amanda looking like she was on the inside track of life here instead of someone who just arrived. "Oh Mike. Fine gentleman. Let me take you to your room. I hope that it is to your liking" said the bellhop.

"Are you Tom?" said Amanda.

"Yes, Mike is my brother. I'm just helping at the desk while the manager is at lunch" said Tom as he turned the key to a bedroom with two double beds with a TV on the dresser. Tom handed her the key.

"You can settle up in the morning if you are leaving then. Check out is at 11 AM. Enjoy your stay" said Tom.

"Thank you. Oh, can you mail this for me?" said Amanda handing her Jerry's envelope. She had put a postage stamp on it before drifting off to sleep on the bus. Thank God. So, it was ready to go.

"I would be more than glad to do this for you. It will go out in the mail with the other guests' mail" said Tom bowing slightly in front of her. Amanda liked all the pageantry to this city it seemed to have. Tom was wearing a light gray uniform with a dark gray pin stripe down the leg. He must have forgotten to wear his name tag today.

"Thank you for everything" said Amanda as she began to close the door.

"No. Thank you. It's not every day that I meet a friend of my brother. Say 'hello' to my brother Mike for me" called out Tom as he walked down the hall of the hotel back to the front desk.

As Amanda closed the door, she wondered if she would ever see Mike again though Tom seemed sure that she would. She had better call up dad and Leo to let them know that she arrived safely so that they could rest easy. She hadn't talked to them since she boarded the bus. She needed the rest. And, she didn't want them freaking her out. She could do that herself without them.

Amanda could hear the phone picking up on the other end. "Hello, dad, this is your daughter, Amanda. I've arrived safely in Las Vegas, NV. I took a cab from the bus terminal. I am safely in a hotel right now. Tomorrow, I will see Manny, my boss' cousin, who is a 'big time' talent agent" said Amanda.

"Good" said Tom.

"I love you, dad. Tell mom that I love her, too" said Amanda.

"I will" said Tom.

"Well, I just wanted to let you know that I am here. I'm going to get off the phone now. I have to call Leo yet tonight to let him know that I arrived safely. I'll call you tomorrow after I get with Manny" said Amanda.

"OK" said Tom. And, Amanda could hear her father hang up. So now, Amanda called up to hear Leo on the phone who she worried over. Amanda could hear Leo pick up the phone on the other end.

"Leo, this is Amanda. How's everything at the store and with you? I called to let you know that I arrived safely. And, I am at a hotel for the night. Didn't want you to worry" said Amanda.

"I miss you, Amanda" said Leo.

"I miss you too" said Amanda.

"I'm taking care of the store good" said Leo.

"Good to hear. You are going have to tend to our garden out back including Ralph's St. Mary's garden. The tomato plants had yellow flowers on them when I left. I put metal hoops over them to protect them from any harsh winds. They look hardy though. The other things are sprouting in the garden. They will need watering and weeding as they grow" said Amanda.

"OK" said Leo.

"OK" said Amanda relieved that the garden would be tended to while she was gone.

"The customers are showing a lot of support to you while you are gone for your music career and love for Ralph. They are coming by with covered dishes of food for me and all. And, sales are up so far. I have to remember to open up on time and put out the wheel barrel in front of the store to remind people we are open for business" said Leo.

"OK. Good. Send me progress reports and money over and above our costs no matter how little. I'll need it to survive off of. I don't have an address yet for that. Tomorrow, I will walk to the post office to get a P. O. Box so that I will have a mailing address for you to write to me regularly. Maybe, you can send me photos of the garden and the store when you have special events there. And, maybe you can overnight me something from the garden as things get harvested before the hard frost. I am sure that some of it will ship well enough after I get a place to stay. And, presuming that I'm not back home by then" said Amanda.

"OK" said Leo.

"I love you. And, I will call you again tomorrow. I am supposed to see Manny tomorrow. You remember my mentioning my boss Brian in Indianapolis. Well, this is his cousin who is a big time talent agent here who is going to make me a star and a millionaire. Brian thought that I could maybe audition for his cousin. And, he could get me recording contracts and a job on the Strip singing with some of the stars here. I want to come home soon to the farm to give my parents a million dollars. I do. It will help save the family farm for them. Tommy is off to the military. I haven't heard from him for months. And, maybe we could re-furbish the apartment upstairs a little with the money" said Amanda.

"That would be great. But, it looks good the way it is. I'm just happy to be here and of use to you. I love you so much and your parents. I feel like real family" said Leo.

"You are real family. I love you so much, too. Hey, I have to get off the phone. I will call you again tomorrow after I see Manny. Goodbye, sweetheart, dear cousin of Ralph" said Amanda.

"Goodbye" said Leo. Amanda hoped she calmed Leo's nerves. She was jumping out of her skin herself. But, she better take her mind off of things for now. She grabbed the menu sitting on top of the TV using the phone next on the dresser. She called the front desk. "Yes, I am in room 30A. I would like room service. I would like a hamburger with French fries. And, a coke with plenty of ice. How much will that be?" said Amanda.

"Twelve dollars and fifty cents. It will be there at your room in about 30 minutes" said Tom recognizing her voice.

"Thank you" said Amanda as she hung up the phone. She was glad to have met Mike. She felt safer here to know Tom, also.

"Room service. It's something else" said Amanda. Not like the farm at all. I had better jump in the tub to freshen up while waiting. Well, I had better not jump in the tub. Better I step in the tub. Much safer that way. Amanda laughed at the thought. Why did anyone ever come up with saying "jump in" a tub? It would be your last tub experience. At least most likely.

"I am hard pressed to keep from falling without a bath mat for goodness sake" said Amanda. She carefully laid the white plastic mat at the bottom of the tub as she poured warm water in the tub. There were complimentary soaps and shampoos with conditioner. And, there was a white clean flannel robe that hung from the back of the bathroom door.

"Wow" said Amanda as she grabbed the bathrobe to put it on over her white cotton nightgown.

Just then, there was a knock on the door. Amanda peeked through the peep hole. It was Tom with her order. She handed him fifteen dollars. "That should include the tip. I hope that it is enough" said Amanda.

"I appreciate it" said Tom. Amanda felt embarrassed. She would have liked to give more but, she was afraid of running out of money. She didn't know if she would have a job here for awhile or what apartments cost or what. She would know better tomorrow after she saw Manny thought Amanda.

"But, this room service was alright. I didn't cook this or grow this or anything. Imagine people living like this every day. Las Vegas! What a place!" said Amanda as she opened up the top of her dinner to reveal her supper and turned on the TV.

She definitely wanted to jump on the bed before she left. And, she definitely wanted to go downstairs to the lobby before she left to purchase five postcards: one for her parents; one for Leo; one for Sarah and John; one for Brian, her boss and one for Jerry. She wanted everyone to know that she had arrived! And, she would even get a postcard for herself for a keepsake.

She was in Las Vegas, NV. She didn't know if she should regard herself as a tourist or a resident for now. But, she was here! And, she wanted to make the most of it.

Soon, she turned off the TV and threw away the paper container from her supper. She hadn't much interest in the food compared to the experience of it. The food was delicious. But, she could have hamburger and fries at home. Her mother would make it for her. But, she never had room service before and never in Las Vegas. That's for sure!

She would put that on her postcards to home. They would be happy for her. And, she wanted them to have a postcard from Las Vegas with the postmark on it. She had a wish for them to be part of this "happy experience" to be part of her "Las Vegas experience" and her rise to the top.

Tomorrow would be another day. Amanda called down to the front desk for a wakeup call at 6:30 AM. She would have to drag herself out of bed. There was breakfast served in the lobby, then. "It will be quite a spread" said Tom on the other end of the phone.

"Good. I'll be famished by them" said Amanda. The truth is that she only had so many dollars on her to tide her over for awhile. But, no worries. She was going to be a big star thanks to Manny.

But, right now, she had to get to bed. Amanda began to say her prayers before going to bed. "Thank you, God. If you could see me now, Ralph. I love you dear sweetheart, Ralph. I love you, Grandpa Jim, too" said Amanda. She turned on her side to fall asleep.

She could see the neon signs outside blinking from hotels and the side casinos a little off the Strip. How different it was from home. But, she couldn't miss her one of a kind chance in life.

It would never come again. She had been singing her whole life. Now, she would be a "glamorous lady" with gowns and limos driving her. "Oh, Ms. Miller, will you grace us with a song?" they will say as she stepped in a casino with cameras flashing everywhere.

"Of course" said Amanda who now was only wearing her white cotton nightgown. But, in her dream, her dress shimmered glints of silver from the sequins on the long dress in the reflection of shimmering glass chandeliers as she made her way to a shiny black grand piano to sing.

She nodded her head to the pianist to begin playing. And, everyone hung on every note she sang as if there was no other voice more beautiful to them. And, cameras flashed at her as she finished the song and bowed. Everyone applauded.

And, the crowds called out: "Amanda, we love you!" As she turned to throw a kiss at her adoring crowd before leaving the casinos to enter back into her black shiny limo that the chauffeur helped her enter by grabbing her right hand as she entered to drive away to more cameras flashing. It was spectacular!

The Strip displayed her name as a regular. "Now performing for one night only: the beautiful and talented Amanda Miller" said Amanda. That's what her concert halls were like. Complete adoration. People whistled in the crowd as she made her way to the microphone. And, the money she would send home to her parents would be tremendous as the concert hall filled up with paying loyal fans. It was a beautiful dream that Amanda wanted to never wake up from.

The phone rang at 6:30 AM sharp to wake her up. She poured on her jeans and a top and tennis shoes. "Forget about the socks. I have no time" said Amanda as she pushed the door to her room and ran down to the elevator at the end of the hall.

Tom was right about "the spread." There was a pitcher of orange juice; dry cereal; a pitcher of milk; coffee with creamer and sugar; toast with strawberry jam and grape jelly, hot tea in a silver pot; soft-boiled eggs wrapped in a white linen in a wicker basket; coffee cake with raisins and white frosting; butter; pork sausage; bacon; and green grapes. Amanda loaded up her plate like a kid at Halloween with a bag of treats before her.

"Las Vegas is 'something else'" said Amanda softly. She never saw the likes of this before! Free food for Amanda. Her stomach felt warm inside. She was so happy to be in Las Vegas, NV.

Finally, she would make a difference for her family and herself. She couldn't wait to meet Manny. Maybe he had a big contract in music she would sign today. She would be a celebrity. Her parents would see her CD's in the stores everywhere. They would be proud of her. She couldn't bear it if they weren't. "Wow" said Amanda taking it all in.

A fellow tourist chimed in sitting at the breakfast table with her. She was wearing a black business suit with a pale vanilla shirt leaning in toward Amanda wearing eyeglasses. She was probably 40 years old. "The food is quite good here" said the lady.

"Yes, the food is great. But, I'm not here for the food at all. Today, I'm going to meet a big time talent agent. I'm a singer. This person is going to make me a big star. I'm doing this to help my family and myself. We own a farm in Indiana. My name is Amanda Miller by the way" said Amanda shaking the lady's hand.

"Well, Amanda Miller, I wish you good luck. You have guts if nothing else. Sometimes, that's all you need. Believe me. It's half the battle" said the lady to Amanda.

Amanda thanked her for her kind words. Amanda liked this woman. The people around here as so kind and friendly thought Amanda. The woman took off down the hall.

Amanda's thoughts turned to her postcards. Amanda thought she had better get her postcards from the front desk before going to her room. She needed five of them. And, she needed one postcard as a keepsake for herself.

Amanda saw that the postcards were 25 cents each. She chose one that had many views of Las Vegas as the prettiest of all. She gave Tom who was at the front desk at the time the one dollar and fifty cents.

She sat at the couch in the front lobby of the hotel with her postcards. She wrote the same to everyone since she was in such a rush. Checkout was at 11 AM. And, she had a full day ahead of her. Her salutation was different but other than that she wanted them in the mail the first day she was in Las Vegas, NV.

Her first postcard said:

Dear Mom and Dad:
     Wanted you to have a postcard mailed to you the first day I was here in world famous Las Vegas, NV. Really different from home. Had room service for the first time in my life yesterday. It was just hamburger, fries, and a coke. But, it made me so happy. And, I got a free hot breakfast with all the fixings. It came with the room. They treat me like 'a queen' here.

                                                        Love, Amanda


Amanda had all five of her postcards filled out. Just then, she heard a voice from behind her "Hey, good looking" said Mike.

Amanda looked around until she saw Mike. "Good morning. Just filling out postcards to send to home. Have to go to my room to get my postage stamps to put on them before I send them off" said Amanda.

"No, you don't. They send off mail all the time for guests as a courtesy. They can afford to do this. This is Vegas. Give them to me. I'll put them on the stack with the other outgoing mail today" said Mike.

"Gee thanks" said Amanda looking puzzled to see him.

"I hang around here all the time to pick up fares to and from the airport and the Strip" said Mike.

"If you want I can take you over to your talent agent today. It's really close by. And, I wouldn't want you to get lost your first day here. How soon can you get ready?" said Mike.

"I have to check out at 11 AM. How about 10:30 AM?" said Amanda.

"No worries, kid. It's on me. All I ask in return is when you become this big singing star is lifetime free CD's and free front row seats at your concerts" said Mike smiling.

"You've got a deal" said Amanda shaking Mike's hand.

She made her way down the hall to her room to pack up her things. She had saved herself the money on the postage of the postcards and the shoe leather to walk to the talent agent. She wanted to look fresh and groomed when she saw him—not sweaty and tired.

People were so nice here thought Amanda. She missed home though quite a lot—especially her parents and Leo. She hoped they missed her as much as she missed them though she didn't want them to suffer because of it.

# Chapter 14

It turned out that Manny lived in an apartment about ten minutes away from the Strip somewhat near the campus of the major university in town. Mike found it right away. There was trash blowing in the wind rolling down the street with beer cans strewn about. It was quite a departure from the trimmed fashionable front lawn of the hotel where everything seemed like a world of beauty.

"Is this it?" said Mike.

Amanda looked at her address written down on the piece of paper her boss Brian gave her. "It's alright. How will I ever pay you?" said Amanda.

"No worries. It's not what you think. I had a daughter who you remind me of. She was a singer, too. But, she smoked heavy against the wishes of her father: me. She died of lung cancer 3 years ago. So I was glad to help" said Mike.

"There are all types here. Remember that. This isn't Indiana. So now, go see your talent agent man" said Mike.

"Thanks, Mike" said Amanda as she began walking through the apartment complex looking for Manny Coleman. She couldn't wait to meet him.

Just then, she saw a sign that said: office. Amanda opened the door to a blast of cold air conditioned air. The man stood at the counter waiting to hear what this young woman had to say. He had a torn gray undershirt on. It must have been white at some time. His hair wasn't combed. That is what there is of it. Just a few strands of gray sticking up everywhere.

Worse he had a half smoked cigar in his mouth. "Well, I don't have all day. What do you want?" said the man.

Amanda startled started heading out the door. "Miss, I didn't mean to startle you. But, you don't seem to be the type to be in this kind of neighborhood. How can I help you?" said the man.

"I'm looking for Manny Coleman" said Amanda her voice shaking.

"That's me. I hope that I don't owe a bill. You aren't a bounty hunter are you? I run a clean place here. I follow the law. I only made mistakes when I was a kid. I did my time. Please" begged Manny.

"No. It's nothing like that. Your cousin, Brian Sullivan told me to see you" said Amanda.

"Brian, you know Brian" said Manny. It had been years since he had seen Brian. He missed his folks but, his life had fallen so low that he was ashamed to ever step foot near them. And, he couldn't afford the plane ticket anyway which was a mixed blessing.

"Come" said Manny opening up the wooden half door next to the counter leading to his apartment. He sat on the living room couch. Amanda sat on the matching living room chair.

They sat staring at each other. Finally, the silence broke. "I'm from Indiana, by the way" said Amanda.

"Well, it figures that you aren't from around here. I don't see your tits showing at all for one thing. No skintight jeans either. You dress too modest. You look like a tourist to me from far away" said Manny.

"Well, I am from far away. I worked with your cousin, Brian Sullivan in downtown Indianapolis, IN for awhile as a receptionist. My parents own a farm about an hour's drive north of there where I grew up. I lived in Indianapolis with Sarah, my roommate, until she got married a month or so ago. I was supposed to be a married lady by now my own self but, my Ralph died suddenly" said Amanda.

"He willed me his feed store that is about a half hour north of my parent's farm. His cousin is watching over it for me. It will bring me some income. Don't know how much. There is an apartment upstairs where Leo is living. And, I was living there with Ralph since we were marrying soon" said Amanda.

"I have a brother, Tommy, who is in the military who we haven't seen for years. He is a career man there. We have written to him. Haven't heard back yet" said Amanda.

"I was having coping problems being at the feed store. I had considered returning to work for Brian there. He had heard me sing at work functions. Recommended I come here to get on my feet since you were a 'big talent agent' here that could make me a big star and make me a millionaire so that I can help my parents out with the farm and all. Ralph is buried on the farm. I can't afford to lose the place or the feed store. I need the break" said Amanda.

Manny just sat there like a frozen statue. He didn't speak for a long time. Finally, he spoke

"Tough break, kid. I can see why Brian sent you here. I thought that I was going to be a 'big talent agent' when I first came here" said Manny.

"But, I was lucky to get this job as an apartment manager of this dump. I never wanted to tell my folks the truth in Indiana. I didn't want them to think bad of me. And, I knew that they would never come to Las Vegas, NV. It's too far away. So, I could afford to keep the truth from them. It was better than breaking their heart" said Manny.

"I would love to see them again but, not in this condition. I am sorry that you came all this way for nothing. Brian is a fine man. He always was a good relative to me even as a kid" said Manny.

"I just messed up young. I never could get it back together again after that. And I never wanted to ask my folks for help. I wanted to save face. I don't want that to happen to you. I have no way to help you with a music career in singing. If I did, do you think that I would be living here? How much money do you have on you, by the way kid?" said Manny.

"Probably a few hundred dollars. Brian gave me the idea that you would fast track me to a singing contract in a casino on the Strip and an album contract that was worth millions" said Amanda in tears.

"Please, don't cry. I've cried enough about life for both of us. I'll help you with what I can to get you going—at least enough to keep you safe. It is the least I can do after my own cousin sending you here. But, you have to keep one promise to me in return" said Manny.

"What?" said Amanda.

"Never tell anyone especially Brian, the truth about me. He thinks that I live a fancy life than the bum I really am" said Manny.

"I promise" said Amanda.

"Good. Because I now want to show you your new temporary home away from home. This place comes with two bedrooms. It came furnished. You can use the second bedroom" said Manny.

"But, if asked who you are, by anyone, you can say you are my girlfriend. And, we sleep together because the people around here gossip. We don't want to point out my past or what you are doing here in this part of the country" said Manny.

"There are lots of rough people around. And, I don't want to see you getting hurt. And, I don't want to answer to Brian. He will have a fit if he liked you this much to send you here. Agreed?" said Manny.

"Agreed" said Amanda.

"You can't stay here forever. But, if you lay low, you can stay here long enough to get a job and an apartment of your own" said Manny. Amanda cried. Manny put his arms around her to comfort her.

He went on. Here, opening the door to the second bedroom. "There is a bed; a dresser; and a chair. It's not much but, it's better than the streets. And, I bet you barely have enough to get home. You might as well stay here for awhile. And see if you can stir up some 'good luck' for yourself " said Manny.

"Better than turning around like a 'dog with its tail between its legs' admitting defeat to your family. The refrigerator has food in it. Eat what you need. But, I need you to get on your feet and out from under soon. I am doing this for Brian because he was good to me when I was a kid" said Manny.

"You will be safe here despite the rough surroundings outside. I don't want you to walk around this part of town by yourself. Understood?" said Manny.

"Understood. And, thanks" said Amanda.

"Why don't you freshen up in the bathroom down the hall. We will talk after that" said Manny.

Amanda couldn't believe what had happened to her. She never wanted her parents to know or Leo. They counted on her. Sarah and John would advance her some money if she needed it. But, she didn't want it to leak back to Brian. He had been so good to her. She had to make it somehow.

Manny had some fried chicken; potato chips; and a dill pickle sitting on two plates with two cans of diet coke. "I thought that you might need lunch" said Manny.

"Thanks. I hope that we can be family and friends together after this mess clears up" said Amanda.

"Thanks. I would like that" said Manny.

"I wish that there was something I could do for you to make things better" said Amanda.

"Thanks. But, you are going to have to take care of yourself first. You can't help someone else if you can't help yourself. It's a rule of life" said Manny.

"I have so much to learn. And, I'm really scared" said Amanda.

"It's only natural. But, you've got Uncle Manny here to help you. Your best bet is to take a telemarketing job here. It's not the world. But, there are plenty of them around in this part of the country" said Manny.

"You'll have to get a newspaper. And, after you get some money together, we'll have to find you an apartment. You can't have an apartment here. It's too rough. Here, I'm only a bedroom away. OK?" said Manny.

"OK" said Amanda.

"Now eat your food. And, dry your tears. It's not going to help. Believe me. I've been there" said Manny.

"I have to go somewhere today" said Amanda.

"Where?" said Manny.

"I have to open up a P. O. Box at the post office so Leo that I told you about can send me my mail from Indiana" said Amanda.

"I'm not supposed to lock up during the day. But, I'm going to anyway. We'll walk to and from the post office together. And, we can pick up a newspaper on the way back. There will certainly be something there to get you going" said Manny.

"OK" said Amanda still crying inside. This isn't what she came to Las Vegas, NV for. How was she going to correct her life now that this happened? She couldn't understand why God did this to her. She needed Ralph even more today. He had such strength.

So Manny and Amanda walked together to the post office. She was an attractive woman. People stared as Manny said. "My new girlfriend" said Manny to a man passing by.

"Nice" said the man.

"That's Terry. He owns the convenience store at the corner" said Manny.

"But, you can see why I said what I did. Nothing like Indiana, is it?" said Manny.

"No, not quite" said Amanda walking briskly holding his hand for safety.

"You'll be alright" said Manny.

"I hope so" said Amanda. She didn't know what she would say to her parents or Leo when she called them today. She didn't want to lie. But, she didn't want to worry them with the truth either.

Amanda and Manny looked through the newspaper at the kitchen table of his apartment. He was blessed to not have been noticed that he was gone from his job for awhile today. Nobody had come by that he could tell. Amanda was blessed to have Manny and his spare bedroom.

She regarded him as a relative. She didn't want to ever lose him or leave him as a family member to protect her from what was out there which really scared her. She wanted to go home to her childhood bedroom at the farm. It was safe there.

But, if she didn't help the family, there might not be a farm someday. Her parents couldn't go on forever. And, she didn't dare to tell Tommy about this and worry him until things were infinitely better. She could only imagine how he would feel being in the military and so far away from home with news like this.

She never wanted to tell anyone about this. It was too horrid a story. Better it was long ago and forgotten about. Just some bad memory from the past that will never happen again.


"Here's a job that looks interesting" said Manny circling it in the newspaper. Amanda read the ad:


Call center work. No experience required. Pays $10+ commission. Start immediately. Come in person.


"I'll bet you get that one. The address is listed. You are going tomorrow. I'm going to send you on the bus. I'll take you. I have no car here. I couldn't afford it. You can call me on your cell phone when you get off that bus to come home. I will come get you. You stay put there until I get there" said Manny.

"OK" said Amanda relieved that Manny knew his way around the rougher parts of town and kept her safe.

"It isn't that these people are necessarily bad around here. But, a lot have been in prison before. There is a lot of drugs and such. And, a lot live just terrible lives that they have nothing to lose by jacking you to see if you have some spare coin" said Manny.

"And, heaven forbid if you got raped by wondering around by yourself. You'll be safe with me. People will just think I am protecting my woman" said Manny.

"The economy is bad. If you look like anything or have anything...Well, don't worry about it. We'll get through together" said Manny.

"I'm just glad you are here. I haven't had any kind of family around me for years. You are becoming a 'sweet niece' to me. You made me feel a little better about life" said Manny.

"You need me. I haven't been needed by anyone for years except for this 'dumb job' which I am grateful to have. I get a small wage and this free apartment. But, it's not anything like the 'talent agent' life I thought I was going to have here that Brian thinks I'm living" said Manny.

"Well, let's eat supper so that I can get to bed early to go to that bus stop you are talking about" said Amanda.

"I have some beef stew meat; a bag of frozen mixed vegetables; and an onion. It looks like we have the makings of homemade beef stew" said Manny.

"Great. I'll set the table for us while you get that cooked for us" said Amanda with her stomach growling. She really loved food: the tastes; the colors; the smells; the textures; and how it made you feel good. She loved everything about it. And on top of it, she was hungry.

"I've written down the recipe in my recipe box. It's one of my favorites as it is" said Manny pulling out the recipe from the box before cooking. It said:

## BEEF STEW

## Ingredients

1 pound of beef stew meat
1 tablespoon of cooking oil
1 medium onion chopped
1 bag of frozen mixed vegetables
Add water (enough to cover ingredients)

## Directions

In a frying pan, put the cooking oil on low heat. Then, put in the beef stew meat and onion cooking the meat until browned on all sides and the onions until they are translucent. Then, with a slitted spoon lift out the ingredients into a large pot. In another pot, pour in the bag of frozen mixed vegetables. Cover with boiling water in the pot until cooked. Then, drain the vegetables and mix them with the meat and onion together. Cook on low to medium heat until the vegetables are soft and thoroughly cooked covering ingredients with water. Serve in a soup bowl for each serving.

So, this is what Manny did to cook his first meal with his new family member, his dear sweet Amanda. He was glad that he even knew how to cook something as great as homemade beef stew for him to share with her.

Manny was also happy to just have someone to eat with for a change. He always ate alone mostly in front of the TV for company. He would have been afraid to invite anyone in the apartment. He couldn't afford to jeopardize his job over it. If some rough neck made scenes, even if they seemed nice enough on the surface, it would be the end of the "paradise existence" he had. He couldn't afford to risk it thought Manny.

He hoped that Amanda would make it somehow and never forget her Uncle Manny here. He was dependent on her even if it seemed the other way around. He secretly thanked God for bringing her here to him. "Thank you. Thank you. Thank you Jesus" said Manny softly under his breath to God about now that God brought Amanda, a small ray of sunshine, in his otherwise "dumb life" in Manny's opinion.

"Let's go into the living room until our food is ready. It's nice to have company for a change. I don't usually see anyone unless they are moving in or vacating. Sometimes, I don't see anyone for months. And, there is the deposit slot for people to drop off their money order to pay their rent. They aren't allowed to pay by check or cash. I stay busy all the time at this job collecting rent every month; answering the phone, and calling back messages from voice mail. I just have to keep the place going to keep the job" said Manny.

"Understood. I don't want to jeopardize it in any way" said Amanda.

"Everything is cool. Just lay low. We'll get through. I've left a message or two to the man upstairs meaning Jesus to help us through. I haven't prayed for years. I gave up. I thought God didn't love me anymore. So, I didn't want to pray until now" said Manny.

"I understand" said Amanda feeling guilty about being upset with God her own self. But, how can you live without God? She didn't know thought Amanda.


Amanda and Uncle Manny sat in the kitchen together like real family who knew each other for years. Amanda was happy to have Manny but, sad about her life and his for right now. Tomorrow she would at least have a job which Manny helped her to get.

Amanda gave her uncle a hug goodnight before going to her bedroom. She closed the door and called her father. She heard her dad pick up the phone. "Amanda, what's wrong?" said Tom.

"Nothing. I am staying at the talent agent's apartment for now is all. He is helping me is all" said Amanda hoping that was an OK thing to say trying not to upset her father.

"Good. I'm glad things are turning out well for you there. I worry about you being so far away from home" said Tom.

"I'm OK for now. I would tell you if I wasn't. We just ate homemade beef stew for supper. Well, I have to call Leo so that he doesn't worry about me. I got a new P. O. Box here to get mail here. Manny, my boss' cousin, helped me to do that. I'll mail you the address so that you have it. OK?" said Amanda.

"OK" said Tom.

"I love you, dad" said Amanda.

"I love you too, Amanda. I'll give your love to your mom for you" said Tom.

"Please do. Goodnight, dad. I'll call you tomorrow so that you don't worry" said Amanda.

She told the same thing to Leo. She told him to look in the mail for his P. O. Box address she would send to him so that he had a mailing address for her. And, if he needed anything to call her dad, Tom.

"Promise" said Leo.

"I love you, Leo" said Amanda.

"I love you too dear Amanda" said Leo.

"Well, goodnight. I'll call you tomorrow" said Amanda.

"Goodnight" said Leo just before hanging up. Well, she got through that one OK. Thank God. She didn't want them to worry. She had enough of her own worries here to deal with.

She wanted to stop over sometime tomorrow to Mike and Tom's so that they wouldn't worry about her. Mike had been so good to her. It was only right to let him know she was alright. He had no way to know where she was at much less OK. But, for now she had better get to bed. Tomorrow was another day.

It was a bright sunny day, the day Amanda was hired into the call center. She later learned the weather was always hot and sunny except for the winter time when some days were downright chilly that went through her bones. But, her main job was to protect herself from the heat.

Amanda called up Manny around 11 AM for him to come get her from the bus stop.

"I'm here. And, I've been hired just like you said" said Amanda.

"Good. I'll come get you. I'll be there in about 10 minutes. Don't go anywhere so I don't freak out" said Manny.

"I won't. I'll stay put" said Amanda.

"Manny showed up like clockwork. Do you mind if on the way home we stop by the hotel I stayed at? I want the cab driver who brought me to you for free to know that I am OK and with you so that he doesn't worry. He was very nice. He thought that I reminded him of his daughter who had died" said Amanda.

"You can stay outside while I run in. I'll only be a minute" said Amanda.

"OK. I have to hurry back to the job" said Manny.

"I know. I'll be quick about it. And, it is kind of on the way home" said Amanda.

Amanda walked into the lobby. Mike was talking to his brother, Tom.

"Mike" said Amanda.

Mike put his arms around Amanda. How's it going, Amanda?" said Mike. "Good and bad. It turned out that my boss' cousin isn't a big time talent agent. So, he can't help me with any music career. He thought that he was going to have that job but, it didn't happen for him. He just wanted to save face with his folks. So, he never told them" said Amanda.

"But on the bright side he works as an apartment manager and has a second bedroom that he is letting me use until I get on my feet and all. And, I just got hired today at a call center. So, I at least have a job. I just didn't want you to worry about me since you were so nice to me and all" said Amanda.

"Well congratulations, kid on the apartment and the job. Tough break about the music career" said Mike.

"But, that's Vegas for you. You never know when a career could come up right around the corner to you that you will love or who you will meet, either. There are all types here. Nothing like it" said Mike.

"Well, I'd better go. My talent agent is waiting for me outside. He has been good to me. Like real family as best he can" said Amanda.

"Good to hear. Here is my business card, if you ever need your personal cab service to help you out. You sure remind me of my own daughter, Sierra" said Mike.

"I'm honored. I'll stop by from time to time" said Amanda.

"I will like that" said Mike.

Amanda left the lobby feeling good about herself. She told Manny what happened. She didn't want him to walk into the lobby. She didn't want him to feel embarrassed about his failure as a talent agent. Bad enough he had to go through it. It was even bad she had to go through it. Tomorrow was another day.

Work was reading a script over and over again. But, it was clean work. People stayed away from her for the most part. Most were potheads anyway looking for a quick fix in life. A little cash for drugs in between their stay in prison. They seemed to never get out. Nor did they seem to want to since they loved their drugs so much.

Manny advised that she stay away from them, too. "You are only there for the job. You have Uncle Manny to talk to who won't get you hooked on that" said Manny.

"I love you. You are so good to me. I'd probably go 'crazy' without you" said Amanda.

"I love you, too. Just like you are my own. Come on, let's go home. I have frozen pizza for us tonight for supper" said Manny.

"Love my Uncle Manny" said Amanda.

"I know kid. But, we have to get through with our walk from the bus stop. So, then we can throw our pizza in the oven" said Manny. Amanda held his hand as they walked together as he told her to do.

She was grateful for the job and her apartment with Manny. She was keeping a good front going with her family in Indiana. Better not tell the family right now. Maybe something would happen to give her this music career anyway so that she would never have to tell them. Or, she could tell them after things were more behind them. She didn't want anyone to unnecessarily suffer because of her "dumb life" right now.

After about a month of working at the call center, Manny was waiting for her at the bus stop after work. "What's up?" said Amanda looking worried.

"Nothing. I just found you an apartment. I'm not trying to get rid of you or anything like that. But, it is only $200 a month with utilities included. You have to take it. It's a find. Rent usually runs way more than that in this part of the country. The apartments I rent out that are 'dumps' are more than this" said Manny.

"The landlady owns the shop downstairs. She didn't know what to do with the upstairs because she didn't want anyone rowdy since she lives next door. She owns the building. So, she can do what she wants. She was using it for storage for extra boxes from the store. All she asks in return is if you can help her out once in awhile during the Holiday season when she is extra busy selling holiday gowns and accessories" said Manny.

"It's just if anything happens to me, heaven forbid, you won't have any place to go. I won't have it. The bedroom is still yours. You can stay overnight on Fridays and Saturdays so that you get to see me regularly. But, you have to get on your own. You won't find cheaper or nicer. And, it's on the bus line to work and where I'm at" said Manny.

"I took the liberty of signing a 3 month lease for you. I hope that is OK. But, I had to snatch it up for you. With a little cleaning, it should be alright. It has furniture in it already even though it hasn't been used for years that way" said Manny.

"You are so good to me" said Amanda kissing Manny on the cheek.

"I know. But, my little sweet niece has to have a place of her own. I don't want you to leave ever. But, what kind of life is that in the end? You have to start pulling it together. I have to believe you will be OK. You can take the bus from work right to the door of the dress shop. And, I'll come get you as usual there Friday night so that you can stay with me on the weekends. OK, sweetie?" said Manny.

"So, when do I see the place?" said Amanda.

"Right now. I have the key. We can clean up the place together on the weekends when the office is closed at the apartment until you are fully moved in. You can invite me over sometimes for a change" said Manny.

"I love you, Uncle Manny. But, I am going to miss you so much" said Amanda.

"I love you, too. But, I have to know my Amanda is going to have a good enough place to stay if anything happens to me" said Manny.

"I don't want anything bad to happen to you. I couldn't bear it especially after Ralph and all" said Amanda holding his hand tightly waiting for the bus to arrive to take her to her apartment.

She loved the idea of having her own apartment. And, yet, she hated it, too. She still called her parents and Leo every evening. But, life was here now. She appreciated still the love of her parents and Leo—and everyone she loved in Indiana. But, she was busy shaping together a life here. She wasn't ready to go back home defeated. She just couldn't.

And, she wasn't ready to leave Manny by himself. He was a changed man since they met. You could tell that he wasn't the same person. He no longer wore gray torn undershirts for one thing. And, he wouldn't dream of going outdoors without his hair combed and all. He needed her.

And, it turns out that Mike needed her, too. She was like a daughter to him. He never got over losing his own daughter to cancer at such a young age. He showered Amanda with love. She knew that he would help at the apartment if she asked. She wanted to invite Mike and Tom, his brother to the apartment.

Amanda opened the door to the apartment. It was at the front of the store with large windows overlooking the street. The furniture had white dusty sheets over them. The cupboards still had pots, pans, and dishes in it. The landlady said that she could use anything that was there in the apartment. Amanda was grateful.

The landlady wanted the extra money and the free Holiday help that was dependable. She didn't want to live with rowdies to have to deal with.

Manny and Amanda spent the weekend cleaning up the place. It had one bedroom; a living room; a kitchen; a bathroom; and a dining room that could double as a second bedroom. Amanda told Manny that she would like a day bed in there that would double as a couch and bed so that he could stay overnight.

He told her that he would get one for her because he definitely wanted to stay over sometimes. Anything to be close to his newly-found family. He loved Amanda so much. She was like the daughter that he never had. He secretly thought that he would die literally if anything bad ever happened to her.

His world revolved around her. He didn't ever want it to be different than that. She changed his life for the better! She was "his" Amanda. And, he was "her" dear sweet Uncle Manny" as she called him.

# Chapter 15

Amanda quickly washed the dishes in the morning. She almost never let there be unwashed dishes in the sink or uncovered food. They had to be in containers. Manny's apartment wasn't like that anymore. She didn't want to attract bugs. She hated roaches. The warm climate seemed to attract all kinds of critters like that she thought. Plus, people tended to live in such close quarters overall in this part of the country thought Amanda.

So far, this apartment was bug-free. And, Manny saw a lot less of them since Amanda came over to clean his apartment. She wanted Manny to be as healthy as he could. She didn't like the idea of roaches crawling over his food. He no longer kept an open garbage can either. Neither did she.

But, she had to make her way to the bus stop for work right now. How she hated the work. She would spend all day alone since she lived alone now. And then, she would take off for work to spend the rest of her time mostly alone since she worked in a cubicle by herself and stayed mostly to herself at work since it seemed so rough to her compared to what she was used to being around. Manny never knew how much she loathed the job that he helped her to get as much as she did. She always kept on her "happy face" about it. She didn't want to break his heart. Where would she go anyway if this was the best there was? Still, she secretly longed for better.

The bus stop was right across the street from where Manny took his bus home except it was going in the opposite direction. The good news is that she got dropped off from work right across the street from the work place.

But, as she neared the work place today, she got a gnawing feeling she wanted out. But, where? And, when? She hated these people she worked with. They were so mean and rough. Most had been in prison before. Most were on drugs of some sort. They were heavy smokers. They were loose with each other. They swore constantly. And, they stole from each other.

She had to keep her purse pressed up against her back to keep it from being lifted even to get a drink of water or go to the bathroom. She couldn't even bring a sweater in the air conditioned office because if she took it off for even a minute, somebody would try to take it from her. She wouldn't be able to afford a new one. And, the one she wore, her parents had shipped it to her as a gift. She couldn't afford to lose that. It was irreplaceable. She could keep it in a closet in the apartment. It would stay safe alright. But, then she would be freezing.

"Well, here we go" said Amanda as she opened the door to her work place. People here never rested on ceremony. She wasn't to say hello. They didn't want a hello back. It was understood.

Those who smoked cigarettes and marijuana smoked behind the building until it was time to start the work day which was the majority of the co-workers. They liked to huddle together. She didn't smoke. She couldn't afford to get hooked on any of it even if offered it for free.

"Thanks. I appreciate the offer. But, I can't afford it. My parents would kill me if I did this" said Amanda.

"Alright, suit yourself" said a tall dark man in his 20s smoking a joint right out in the open at work. Everyone did it. So, he didn't care...They got their munchies from the small grocery store next door to the work place. It had chips and pop and all kinds of convenience foods. Most ate from there. Amanda took her lunch to save money.

She couldn't afford to eat out all the time even from this small grocery store. These co-workers could because they fenced stolen property on the side, and sold drugs to whoever wanted it. It was a side living for them.

Amanda just wanted a decent paying job at this point to work at. The co-workers thought that she was "a wallflower who was just plain ol' not cool" because she didn't have intercourse with them. She was offered more than once. "My parents would kill me if I did" said Amanda more than once.

She was tempted to smoke a joint or to give in to sex with them just to "shut them up"...and to get along. "What would it hurt?" she often heard them say. But, Amanda was afraid—really afraid.

She just wanted her paycheck and to go home. Her apartment life was more her speed. She didn't know if she was just "oddball" here in this city or what. This was her first job here.

OK. Another day thought Amanda. "If I get through the day, its another notch under my belt. I will go home to the peace and quiet of my apartment" said Amanda. And soon, Manny will be once again snoring away as he always did in his spare bedroom.

Just then, a black man with long black braids sat down next to her in the cubicle. "I'm Stephano. This is my first day here. This isn't my real job. I am here for just a little extra green" said Stephano.

"Well, happy to meet you, Stephano" said Amanda shaking his hand.

"Yes, I am into tree and weed as my real living. You know what I mean?" said Stephano leaning toward her to say it softly in her ear.

"Well, Stephano. Thank you. But, I live in an apartment. So, I can't buy any trees or anything like that. And, my landlady takes care of the weeding. What there is of it" said Amanda.

Stephano looked puzzled at Amanda. His brother was sitting in the seat behind him in the aisle. He frowned and clenched his fists walking toward Amanda.

"Amanda, meet my brother Gangster. Gangster, meet Amanda. It's cool bro. She's cool. She thinks that we're in the landscaping business" said Stephano. Both, Gangster and Stephano laughed together. Amanda didn't understand the deal.

"Amanda, we sell drugs all hush hush, of course. Don't tell anyone because if you do, we'll have to kill you. It's nothing personal. We just don't want to go to jail. It's what we do for a little extra green. But, you're cool" said Stephano.

"I'm cool" said Amanda.

"Just don't hang around Gangster. He's not as nice as me. I'm a pussycat" said Stephano flashing a gold tooth in the front of his mouth as he smiled at Amanda.

"So, why is your brother called Gangster?" said Amanda.

"Because he kills people for money or when anyone messes with him or his homies" said Stephano.

"What's a homie?" said Amanda.

"His boys. You know. I like you but, you are so not cool. But, I like you" said Stephano.

"We had better get back to work before the boss fires us for talking" said Amanda bugging her eyes out in the cubicle where she worked. More than what she thinks she wants to know. Still, she felt more like an insider all the same. She wondered if Stephano would protect her here since he was friendly enough. She didn't know what she needed protection from but, she felt afraid a lot of the time.

Stephano put his fingers across his lips to indicate, he was going to be quiet from now on. He laughed softly and went to work.

Just then, a male co-worker came in huffing. He was wearing a shirt and underpants. His usual jeans were missing and his shoes. He drove a bike to work. He locked it in the bike stand outside.

"Where's your pants, young man?" said the boss to this man named Ernie. "I was mugged and raped on the way to work. My attacker took my clothes and my wallet" said Ernie who was a slender man about 5 feet tall who probably was in his 20s.

"I have a spare set of trunks you can borrow from my gym bag. Well, sit down. Get to work" said the boss. So, he did. Amanda's eyes just bugged out in her cubicle.

"God" said Amanda softly as she tried to keep her mind on her work. She needed her paycheck.

Lunch came soon enough. Amanda ate her P&J sandwich and a can of diet pop in her cubicle. She brought it from home. She saw that she had a good 15 minutes left of her lunch hour. She walked outside for some fresh air. Just then, one of the male co-workers named Jeff with his buddy who drove by were lifting cases of pop from the grocery store next to work.

"I'll kill you if you tell anyone. The pay is too low. We have to survive. You understand me?" said Jeff to Amanda.

Amanda nodded. Her body just shook in fear. It was lunch time. The store was packed with co-workers buying lunch. She was glad lunch time was over. She retreated to her cubicle. The bosses prided in keeping down the rowdies. One sign that they were doing good was to keep people in their place by having them sit quietly in their cubicle while the boss did a head count.

"Half a day to go. Half a day to go" said Amanda softly to herself. These people that she worked at were likeable enough but, they "scared the you know what out of her." She didn't think that she could take it anymore. But, where could she go? Probably just stay here thought Amanda. What else?

She was afraid to look at Jeff in the face the rest of the day. The same applied to Gangster. She wasn't sure how safe Stephano was at this point. But, he was the only "port in the storm" at this point. Her eyes just bugged out in her cubicle, the rest of the work shift. She stayed put during her 10 minute break in the afternoon. She couldn't afford anymore encounters today.

Amanda bolted out of work. She made it just in time for the bus to take off. She was grateful not to have to hang around at the bus stop longer than necessary. She didn't want to be solicited for sex which happened before.

Sitting in her seat on the bus, she longed to sit on her balcony porch of her apartment. Her landlady was in the next apartment. There was nobody else there. She never brought people there. Only gowns to alter that kept her busy. Amanda sometimes helped her carry them up the stairs. They were just gorgeous. All custom made. "Maybe someday, you can have one of these gowns, my dear" said Emily trying to be kind.

She hoped so. She would like that since they were so beautiful that they made her cry just to look at them. But, these gowns were for the upper crust for some special occasions.

Amanda's mind turned to her co-worker, Steve, who had his shorts down to his knees on the bus. A female co-worker named Felicia had her back to him holding onto the rail of her seat with her pants down, also. She was leaning forward. He was thrusting his hard-on into her hard. She was moaning with each thrust. That is how Amanda noticed them in the first place.

Amanda put her hand to her face to cover the side of her face. She didn't want to look at Steve and Felicia right now. The other passengers looked on stone-faced. Probably afraid thought Amanda. The bus driver just moved down quickly down the road with what seemed to be no attention to these two.

"Thanks" said Steve to Felicia as he pulled up his shorts.

"No. Thank you" said Felicia as she lit up a joint that Steve handed her for doing this for him.

Just then, Steve sat next to Amanda.

"Hi" said Steve to Amanda.

"Hi" said Amanda looking frightened.

"Don't worry about that" said Steve waving at Felicia. And, Felicia waving back.

"Alright" said Amanda. At this point, Amanda would say anything. She wanted off the bus about now.

"One hand washes the other around here. That's how it works" said Steve.

Amanda looked out the window the rest of the way home. She was disgusted with this day even if this was "typical" to these people. She wanted out. She hoped Steve didn't see her cry as she wiped her tears in the reflection of the bus window.

She hoped he just thought she was looking at the scenery of casino after casino as they drove past. After all, this is what people traveled even from foreign countries to see.

But, she was glad to be in the safety of her apartment again. And, the same aloneness that she loathed in the morning, she loved right this moment. No one around to bother her. Tomorrow was another day. For now, she could rest on her balcony porch barefoot with a cup of hot tea to rest.

She loved here compared to where she came from: her work. But, she didn't know anymore quite where she belonged or fit in. And, she didn't want to tell Mike what happened today at work. He would just show up there to talk sense to these people.

"Right.  He could get killed" said Amanda.

And, Manny, it might kill him if he knew the goings on there. He didn't want him to know anything that was happening there. As far as he knew it was a quiet safe place for a young woman to work.

"Since he loved her like his own, let him think that way for now" said Amanda under her breath.

Gulping down her tea, she went to talk to her landlady. She knocked on Emily's apartment door seconds later.

"Yes. How can I help you?" said Emily opening the door to Amanda.

"I've been thinking about buying a used car so that I can drive it back and forth to work instead of going on the bus. I was wondering if I can park in front of the shop at night. I'll be gone by the time the shop is open during the week. And, I can park down the street on the weekends.

"Why not use the garage in the backyard? The car will be safer there" said Emily. Emily walked down the steps of the apartment. Amanda obediently followed her through the backyard toward the freestanding garage at the back of the yard. Emily opened the garage door that was inside the backyard. There sat a black car that looked really beautiful but, older. She presumed it belonged to Emily.

"If I park my car here, where will you put yours?" said Amanda.

"My dear girl. This car belonged to my husband, Henry. I don't drive at all. This was his car. It is just sitting here collecting dust. If you want it, it's yours" said Emily.

"Come up to the apartment. I'll turn over the car title to you. You'll have to get insurance and plates. But, it's yours. It's the least I can do for Manny. He was always there for me. If you don't want to take the bus anymore, I'm going to see you don't" said Emily walking back to the apartment. She signed the title and handed it to Amanda.

"I don't know how I will even thank you" said Amanda.

"Just take care of it good. It belonged to Henry. Now dear, don't cry. God smiled on you today is all. You had better go because I've got a 'special order' on these gowns for a very posh wedding to get done by the end of the week" said

Emily handing Amanda the keys to her new car as she closed the door.

Amanda returned to her apartment stunned. She really liked Emily. She was so kind and good. I have to get plates and car insurance to drive my new car thought Amanda. The only person that Amanda knew in town that had wheels was Mike. She had better call him to help. Amanda got voice mail.

"Hey, Mike. It's Amanda. Call me when you can. I got myself a used car so I don't have to take the bus anymore. But, I need to get plates and car insurance before I drive it. I work the day shift so, I need your help. Call me" said Amanda.

Amanda sat on the balcony porch with another hot tea sipping slowly. The car will help alleviate some of the "hell" she was living through. No more bus once she got going.

An hour later, Mike called. "How can I help? I got your message" said Mike.

"Will you please meet me in the back of work so that my co-workers don't see a cab there and think that's how I get to work. I get out at 4 PM. I need to get my plates tomorrow for the car" said Amanda.

"OK. I'll be there. I'll bring a screwdriver. I'll put your new plates on the car for you" said Mike.

"Thanks, Mike, I love you" said Amanda.

"I love you, too. I'll see you tomorrow" said Mike.

"OK. See you then" said Amanda.

Amanda felt a little better about life as it was. She was able to microwave a TV dinner before turning in for bed.

Thank you God for everything. I'm exhausted God as you know since you are God. What a day! Please remember my needs God. Amen.

And, with that Amanda went to sleep looking forward to seeing Mike tomorrow. But, in the morning she still had to take the "dumb" bus.

Amanda waited for Mike after work. He showed up with his cab right on time. He waited on her to get her plates for her car.

"Now, take me to your car so that I can put on the plates for you" said Mike.

"It's at the apartment. And thanks," said Amanda.

So, they drove behind the apartment. Amanda opened up the door to the garage that faced the alley. "Wow! It's a dandy. Really pretty. And, in good shape, it appears" said Mike.

"How did you get it?" said Mike.

"Emily, the landlady gave it to me. It belonged to her husband, Henry that died. She doesn't drive. So, it was just sitting here collecting dust. And, she said that I could have it. Just take care of it good because it belonged to her husband, Henry" said Amanda.

"Well, you are a lucky girl. Let me put the new plates on for you. And, you'll be on your way" said Mike. Soon, the new plates were on the car. Then, Amanda said: "I will still have to take the bus until I get car insurance to be able to drive it."

"No you don't. I'm putting you on my car insurance. I'll list you as my daughter. I'll have to call my insurance agent tonight. You should be good to go. Just show me your title and drivers' license so that I can jot down any information I might need to give to my insurance agent" said Mike.

Amanda reached into her glove box to get her title and in her purse to get her drivers' license for Mike. Mike jotted down some information from each. Amanda hugged Mike. And, then he took off for work in his cab.

Amanda was grateful Mike loved her. Where would she be without him?

Tomorrow would be her first day driving in her new car even if it was old. It was new to her. That's what mattered.

"I see that you have new wheels" said a handsome man named Mark. He was a co-worker.

"Yes. I just got it" said Amanda.

"You mind dropping me off to my house on the way. I hate the bus" said Mark.

"No. I don't mind. But, I had better get to work. You know, the bosses say no talking on shift" said Amanda.

"Right. I'll see you after work then" said Mark pointing a finger with a gun shape with his finger.

"OK" said Amanda. It was only a ride.

Mark got a ride everyday now. And, everyday he wanted sex. "Come on, Amanda. You know that you want it" said Mark as he put his hands on her bosom. And, he put her hands in his pants to feel his genitals. And, he put his tongue inside her mouth.

The motor was always off on the car. She was sitting in the front seat of the car. She felt used.

"I have to go" said Amanda.

"I'll take only a minute. I need you" said Mark. He came around to the driver's side to open the car door. He grabbed her by the hand. He closed the door.

Every day the same. He pulled off his clothes to reveal what he had. He put her hands on it so that she could feel how hard he was and how much he wanted her.

He made her undress in front of him. He grabbed her hand. He laid her on the bed. And, he worked his way from her mouth to her nipples to between her legs with his tongue and mouth to make her come. Then, he put himself inside of her thrusting harder and harder.

"Now, you can go" said Mark handing her clothes back to her.

"Thanks" said Amanda.

"And, thanks for the ride. I appreciate it. I'll see you tomorrow" said Mark. He opened the front door to his house. He tapped her with his hand on her bottom. He then kissed her on the lips while he was still naked.

And next she knew she was driving home in her car to her apartment. Was this supposed to be the rest of her life this way? thought Amanda. Mark was a very handsome man but, she thought he was taking advantage of her. Her emotions were messed up. Her thoughts went to Ralph. She hadn't a boyfriend since Ralph died. She felt vulnerable. Probably Mark sensed it. The sex was good but...

Amanda didn't sleep well that night. Nothing seemed to rest well with her. She wasn't sure that she looked forward to being alone with Mark again.

And, she didn't want to tell him that, either. What to do?

As she drove close to work, she noticed several police cars sitting behind the building. She heard the boss tell another boss that they were looking for Gangster and his brother, Stephano. They were both wanted for murder of a gang member. "Drug related" they said. Everyone at work was especially quiet for some reason.

Gangster and his brother came out from the restroom just in time for the shift to start. Amanda had already impressed on Stephano that he had to be in his cubicle on time or risk being fired.

Just then, two cops came in through the door. They eyed Gangster. He spun around shooting one of the officers. He laid on the ground bleeding everywhere. People screamed. People were running around everywhere.

The second officer returned the fire hitting Gangster in the shoulder. Blood was running down his arm onto the carpet. When Stephano saw this, he pulled out a gun and returned fire to the remaining cop.

Stephano screamed to Amanda to "get down." She jumped off her work chair. She went on her haunches so as to not get hit by the bullets.

Just then, an unfamiliar face came next to her. "I know that it's a funny way to meet, but, I'm new here. This is my first day. My name is Frank. It appears that we have to get out of here. Fast" said Frank.

"You're right on that" said Amanda.

Frank was on his haunches, too like Amanda. Frank grabbed her hand. They stooped down until they got to the bosses' office. Frank opened the window. "Come on. We're going through the window. It's the only way. There is only one door in this office out of here. And, its blocked by the cops" said Frank.

"OK" said Amanda. Frank crawled out first. He pulled Amanda through the window with his two arms to safety.

"Bus or car?" said Frank.

"Car" said Amanda.

"Can we get to it safely" said Frank.

"I think so" said Amanda.

"Then, let's go" said Frank as he held her hand until they got to the car. She nervously opened her door and sat down. She opened the door to the passenger side. He sat down. They sped away.

"By the way, I don't know where we are driving? We probably both lost our job today. Where do you live?" said Amanda.

"For right now, I'm in a pricey overnight hotel. I want to vacate when I can. All my things are there" said Frank.

"Well, since you saved my life, I owe you one. Let's get your things. You can stay with me for a few days until we both get a new job and you get a place more better to stay. I have a spare bedroom at my apartment" said Amanda.

"Thanks" said Frank as he gave directions to his hotel. Amanda waited in the parking lot until Frank came out carrying a duffle bag and a guitar case.

"OK. It's a guitar. My dad insisted that I bring it with me. You don't mind, do you?" said Frank.

"How can I mind when you saved my life?" said Amanda.

Once in the apartment, Amanda called up her work place to leave a message. It said: "Yes, my name is Amanda Miller. I am calling to quit my job there. I'm sorry but, I could have gotten killed there today. Please mail me my check. You have my address. You can't expect me to ever come back there. But, thank you for the employment." Amanda hung up. She didn't want them to think that she wasn't polite or appreciated the employment despite what happened.

"Is it OK if I use your mailing address since I don't have one of my own?" said Frank.

"Sure" said Amanda.

Frank called on his cell phone. "Yes, my name is Frank Lucas. I just got hired today. I am calling to tell you that I quit. I could have got killed today at work. Please mail my check to Amanda Miller's mailing address. I don't want to come back there. And, thank you for hiring me" said Frank. Frank hung up the phone.

"Let me show you your room" said Amanda.

"I really appreciate it. I won't stay long" said Frank.

"I know. Just until you get a new job and a place to stay" said Amanda. Amanda hoped that he would be settled into a new job and place to stay before Manny showed up like he usually did on Friday.

She hoped that Stephano was OK. She would never know. She liked him despite all. He had tried to save her.

Frank and Amanda watched the evening news and read the evening newspaper. No mention of the incident at work. "Pretty typical in Las Vegas. There is so much going on here of all sorts since there are so many people here of all kinds" said Frank.

"Well, let's just forget about it for now. I can make us supper if you don't mind leftover chicken and mashed potatoes" said Amanda.

"Anything" said Frank.

"OK. Well, why don't you rest up on the porch while I heat us up that. There has been so much going on today, we didn't even get lunch, yet. We'll eat on the porch where it is cooler" said Amanda.

"Wonderful" said Frank worrying about how his life was going to go after this.

Later in the week, Amanda got a paycheck for the entire week even though she only clocked in for Monday. And, Frank got paid for the entire day's work even though he was only there for part of the day.

"They were nice. They just had problems is all" said Frank.

"Our paychecks will come in handy until we get a new job" said Amanda.

Frank nodded. He had a temporary home and food for now. He was grateful for what he had for now.

Both cashed their checks at the corner bank. Amanda and Frank went in half for a pizza at the pizzeria down the block. They needed the time to get to know each other. They talked and talked. They became good friends. From that point on, they went in on half for everything.

Amanda appreciated the help and company. Frank appreciated having a place to stay and a friend.

# Chapter 16

A week came and went. Frank and Amanda looked for work alright. But they were afraid to go back to work at the same kind of work that they had because of what happened.

Frank revealed to Amanda that he had come to Las Vegas, NV for a music career. "Me too" said Amanda pulling out her guitar from the closet.

Frank began fingering his guitar on the living room couch that his father gave him for a gift. She sat next to him doing the same.

"Well. We sure do make sweet music together, darlin'" said Frank. He was born and raised on a farm with southern ways. So, he had the southern drawl to go with it.

"We sure do" said Amanda.

"And, I love your singing voice darlin'" said Frank.

"I love yours, too. But it's not helping us to not have a job. We have to get a job too. We are lucky for now because normally Uncle Manny stays over on the weekends and stays in the spare bedroom where you are staying. But, he had to work this weekend. He has been putting in a lot of long hours lately. I haven't even told him about losing the job yet—or you" said Amanda.

"Have you squared it away with the landlady about my staying here for an extended stay?" said Frank.

"Yes. I stopped into the shop. She knows what happened at the job and all. She doesn't want you living in the streets. As long as we don't do pot and be rowdy, she's cool with it" said Amanda.

"She just wants her rent, I think. And, she thinks that she is doing Uncle Manny a favor by letting me stay here" said Amanda.

"OK. Cool" said Frank. Frank looked a little edgy.

"Anything else?" said Amanda sensing that he had something to say.

"Well, now that you mention it darlin', I do have something to ask you. I hope that you don't mind. And, please don't take it in the wrong way" said Frank.

"OK" said Amanda looking anxious about all of this.

"You know that we get along well. Right?" said Frank.

"This is true" said Amanda.

"And, I love being with you. I think that you love being with me" said Frank.

"This is true, too. And?" said Amanda.

"Well, we are already here in the apartment together. You don't have a boyfriend. I don't have a girlfriend. And, I was wondering if we could try a relationship" said Frank looking down.

"Well, I appreciate the offer, but, I'm a little gun shy because I was engaged once to be married to a very nice man that I loved very much. And, he loved me very much. And, he died suddenly" said Amanda.

"That's in part, how I got here to Las Vegas to get away from it all. And, I was supposed to be a big star by now having a 'big-time' talent agent in town. But, it turns out that he didn't have the connections or the job. But, we became good family together. He took me in like I am doing you. I am talking about Manny" said Amanda.

"And, you are never to repeat to him what I said because I don't want him to lose face and all. He is a good man" said Amanda.

"I understand, darlin'. So, there is no hope for us" said Frank.

"I didn't say that there wasn't any hope. I only said that I am afraid, right now. My emotions aren't really put together that well" said Amanda.

"Oh" said Frank looking down.

"Well, don't be so sad about it. Bad enough I have to go through the suffering much less you. Here, let me give you a hug, anyway" said Amanda.

Frank accepted his hug. Amanda was sitting on the living room couch. She showed no sign of leaving his arms. Finally, she looked up at him. He put his lips on hers—and kissed her. And, they kissed—and kissed again.

Amanda smiled. "I feel happy" said Amanda.

"Good" said Frank. He kissed her lips again first putting his lips on hers. Then, he pushed his tongue gently into her mouth making her long for him more. He kissed her neck and opened her blouse to kiss her bosom. He bit her nipples gently through her bra. He unclasped her bra to reveal her nipples. He kissed them until she moaned in desire. Then, he pulled at her slacks. She pulled them down and off to reveal her bush in front of him. He kissed her gently between the legs until she came.

Then, he stood up. "Come on." Frank said taking her to the bedroom. He undressed in front of her revealing his erection. He laid on top of her pushing himself inside her between her legs. She accepted the length of him inside of her as he thrust deeper and deeper into her with thrust after thrust until he came.

They lay in bed together holding each other. "Do that to me again, I'm probably going to fall in love with you. I am happy" said Amanda.

"I am too" said Frank.

"So when?" said Amanda.

"When? Give a guy time to recover. I will make love to you again—and again darlin'. I promise, darlin'!" said Frank.

"Well, as long as you promise. I have a hard time with anyone leaving me that I love" said Amanda.

"Did you say that you love me, darlin'?" said Frank.

"I guess I did. I love you, Frank" said Amanda startled at her emotions.

"I love you too" said Frank.

"Well, fancy that I'm in love" said Amanda.

"Me too, darlin.' Me too" said Frank putting his arms around her into the night.


Frank seemed to wake up in the morning with new resolve. He was no longer the resident of the spare bedroom. As far as he was concerned, he was Amanda's husband though he wasn't ready to propose with no job and all.

They shared a bedroom together. And, they loved each other. That is all that Frank needed to know.

Frank was already up at 7 AM. He made breakfast for himself and Amanda. He made dry cereal and milk; orange juice; buttered toast with strawberry jam; and fresh coffee. "It's nothing like you make, but, I had to get a newspaper while you were sleeping. So, we can look at the want ads together. I think this add I circled looks interesting" said Frank.

Amanda read the ad out loud: "Male and female singers wanted in upscale restaurant to work as servers. Pays hourly plus tips for a good singer with a good personality. Starts immediately" said Amanda.

"Well. What do you say? Huh?" said Frank smiling.

"If we get this job, we'll have to work our tails off" said Amanda.

"Yes. But, it's a music job. And, it's in Las Vegas. Its Vegas, baby! Anything can happen. It could be our big chance for a music career" said Frank.

"OK. Enough selling me. We're going to apply for this job together. And, we are getting hired together" said Amanda.

"That's the attitude, darlin'" said Frank.

"Look. There's a sundog in the sky. It's an omen" said Frank.

"What's that?" said Amanda.

"It's a sign from God. It's a miniature rainbow. It's been raining all night. I didn't sleep well worrying about getting a job. I prayed a lot, darlin'" said Frank.

Amanda just smiled at Frank. God had blest her twice. First with Ralph. Now, with Frank. She was truly happy.

"Well, we had better get dressed. We need to be the first ones there, so we can impress the 'hell' out of our new boss" said Frank.

He jumped into the shower. Amanda joined him. He longed to make love to her right then. "You are making me hot, darlin'. Tonight, when we get back, I will make love to you again" said Frank.

"You promise" said Amanda.

"I promise" said Frank kissing her lips while he stood dripping wet in the shower. He grabbed a bath towel from the rack to dry her off. She grabbed a bath towel from the rack to dry him off.

They went to the closet to find their best casual dress clothes for the job interview. Amanda and Frank headed for the car to get to their new place of work. They both really wanted this job really bad.

"We did it. We did it" said Amanda after she left the restaurant.

"I know. I was there. We're hired. We will be working the evening shift only which is understandable since that's when most people dine" said Frank.

"Aren't you excited?" said Amanda.

"Very. It's going to be a new life for both of us" said Frank.

"I'm so excited about it" said Amanda smiling.

"We'll sleep and make love by day. And, we'll work at our music career at night" said Amanda.

"Sounds like a plan" said Amanda.

"We had better go home right now" said Frank.

"What for? The day is young. It's still morning" said Amanda.

"I know but, I made a promise that I intend to keep" said Frank.

"Oh. So, you are ready to make love again to me" said Amanda.

"I've been ready since the shower this morning. You looked so hot then" said Frank.

"Then, let's go home" said Amanda enjoying every minute with Frank.

Frank put soft music on in the bedroom while he stripped in front of Amanda. Then, he undressed her. They lay in the bed together warming each other's body.

Then, Amanda lay on her back. Frank took the cue. He began kissing her lips pressing his tongue inside her mouth. He rubbed her gently between the legs. He heard her moan.

He was aroused. He began kissing her between the legs. Her hands were on the back of his head as she coaxed him on. She grabbed his genitals and gently kissed them. Then, he thrust himself gently down her throat rocking back and forth. She moaned with desire.

He moved himself between her legs and pushed himself inside of her again. Amanda arched her back indicating she had come. With a final thrust, he came laying on top of her nibbling at her nipples.

"You liked" said Frank.

"I liked it" said Amanda.

"Good darlin'" said Frank. They kissed and embraced as Amanda fell asleep. She was exhausted from the job interview. She was happy about it, but, it took a lot out of her.

Amanda and Frank worked at a joyful cabaret. It was all "make jolly." One big smile after another.

"I think that my jaw is going to break from smiling" said Amanda at work as she passed by Frank with a tray of beer.

"I know. But, think of the tips. We are making twice of what we made at the call center" said Frank.

"OK. OK. And, you look so cute in your green pants; white shirt; and red & green arm garter" said Amanda.

"And, you look cute too in your white blouse; fish net stockings; and red and green hooped skirt" said Frank.

"OK. So, we are both two cuties together" said Amanda.

"So, let's go out there. And, let's show them what showmanship is all about, darlin'" said Frank.

Manny was very surprised to see Amanda with another guy after her relationship with Ralph ending with his dying. But, Frank seemed like a "heck of a guy" thought Manny. And, he did want to see Amanda happy. He was all enthusiasm.

In the end, he was a welcome member to the family since he seemed to be so loyal to Amanda. That's what mattered to Manny.

Manny still came on the weekends to stay in his spare bedroom. Life was easier for Amanda since she split the rent together with Frank.

"Amanda" said Manny one Saturday after Manny sent Frank out to the store for him to buy some ice cream which was Amanda's favorite dessert.

"What is it?" said Amanda looking concerned and taking her Uncle Manny's hand.

"You know when sometimes I couldn't come on the weekends because I had to work overtime" said Manny.

"Yes, I do. And, I missed you too" said Amanda.

"Well, the reason that I have been working like this is because I am considering quitting the job. I haven't been feeling real well. I went to the doctor. He said I had a mild heart attack. Stress is the cause of it. He wants me to live an easier life" said Manny.

"I owe the company I have worked for all these years. They have been good to me. They gave me a wage when nobody else would. And, they gave me a place to stay with that free apartment" said Manny.

"Alright. We can live with this. As long as you are alright" said Amanda.

"I am alright. But, I don't know where to go? I am glad enough to take early retirement. I am really worried" said Manny.

"Well, worry no more. You'll have to move in here with me. That's all there is to it. I can't have you anywhere else. I could barely stand you being in that apartment without me. But, you insisted that I come here" said Amanda.

"Are you sure?" said Manny.

"I am sure that I want you here with me. I wouldn't want it any other way. You took care of me. Now, I can take care of you" said Amanda.

"OK" said Manny.

"OK. That's settled" said Amanda.

"You don't think that Frank will mind" said Manny.

"Don't worry about it. Frank loves you. You love him. Don't you?" said Amanda.

"Yes. Absolutely. He seems like a 'heck of a guy'" said Manny. "He is" said Amanda.

"You love him" said Manny.

"I love him" said Amanda.

"Then, I love him, too" said Manny.

Just then, Frank walked in the door. "Ice cream everyone" said Frank. Amanda got out 3 bowls and 3 spoons.

"By the way, Frank. Manny is moving in with us. He's had a mild heart attack. So, the doctor recommended a less stressful life. He is quitting his job at the apartment and taking early retirement" said Amanda.

"Wonderful" said Frank.

"Wonderful. That's all that you've got to say" said Amanda.

"Yes. We all love Manny. Manny loves us" said Frank shrugging his shoulders.

"OK. Then, we had better eat our ice cream before it melts" said Amanda.

"I told you, Frank is a 'heck of a guy' " said Manny kissing Frank on the forehead.

"Quit. You're embarrassing me" said Frank. Amanda laughed. Manny smiled.

The next day, Amanda woke up Frank to get some of Manny's belongings from the apartment since he had to be out of there by the end of the month. A new apartment manager was taking over then.

Manny was a happy man. He would never have to live alone or without his Amanda again.

Frank and Amanda did spectacularly well at the restaurant. In fact, they sang their hearts out until the crowd applauded. The problem was jealous eyes especially one Benjamin Jordan who fancied himself the "star" of the restaurant.

"Hey big shot. How would you like me to beat the stuffing out of you? This was my restaurant before you came along" said Ben pressing his chest up against Frank pushing his body back.

"Hey. No fighting" said the boss separating the two men.

"You both are suspended for 2 weeks" said Julian, the owner of the place.

"But, I didn't do anything. It was Ben who started the fight" said Frank defending himself.

"I'm sorry. But, I can't have fighting here. We'll lose customers. They expect a happy time here—not a fistfight. Since I don't know who did what, you both have to be punished. I'm sorry," said Julian.

"But, maybe after two weeks off from work with no pay, you'll learn—both of you to get along. Clock out—before I change my mind by being so generous" said Julian.

Just then, Amanda passed by seeing Frank looking down. "What happened?" said Amanda.

"Ben is jealous of the tips I've been getting at singing here. He thinks that he is getting less tips because of it. He tried to beat me up. Julian saw it. He suspended me from the job for two weeks without pay. He told me to clock out immediately" said Frank.

"We sing together as a team here. So, I'm probably suspended for two weeks, too" said Amanda.

"I'm sorry, darlin'. I didn't mean for this to happen. We're doing so well, too" said Frank hugging Amanda.

"I had better let Julian know that I'm clocking out with you. He will understand" said Amanda.

They both walked out of there with their heads held high. They had loving loyal fans there thought Amanda. They would be missed.

Money was tight for the next two weeks without the paycheck and the tips. Frank decided to drag Amanda to a karaoke contest in a local bar. Frank managed to drag her to the stage to sing from the prompter with the lyrics standing in front of the microphone. The purse was $500.

"I knew it. I knew it, darlin'" said Frank.

"We needed the $500 from my winnings from the karaoke contest to see us through until we are back to work. But, how did you know that I would win?" said Amanda.

"I just knew it. You have a beautiful voice. You have a beautiful personality. You are beautiful. What, are they blind?" said Frank.

"Thanks, sweetheart. You made me a happy woman today" said Amanda.

"Let's go to bed. I need to keep my promise to you" said Frank.

"So you do" said Amanda.

This time, Amanda climbed on top of Frank. She was determined to make love to him instead of the other way around after all he did to keep this family together.

She kissed his lips. She gently pushed her tongue down his throat. Her lips moved from his head to his genitals. After kissing and caressing them, she sat on top of him allowing himself to thrust inside of her as she rocked back and forth until he came.

Then, she rested in his arms. "You liked it" said Amanda.

"I liked it, darlin'" said Frank.

"I love you so much" said Amanda kissing his cheek and hugging him under the comforter.

"I love you too, darlin'" said Frank.

Soon, they were fast asleep. The 2 weeks passed by quickly as they spent the time together in each other's arms and making love together. And Amanda appreciated the extra time at home with Manny as well that she wouldn't of had if she was at work like she usually was.

By the time Frank and Amanda returned to work, Ben had quit the job. Two weeks was too long to be out of work is why. He was miserable without a paycheck is why.

"Welcome back. The customers missed you both. You were a favorite. Now go out there, and sing your hearts out as you usually do" said Julian. He extended his hand warmly to both Frank and Amanda.

"He's a nice man" said Amanda leaving the office. "This is true. But, I don't want us to suffer from anymore time off of work like this again. We suffered without our paychecks, too" said Frank.

"This is true" said Amanda putting on her best smile. She was happy to be back to her old job.

"And, what is your singing pleasure tonight?" said Amanda to the customers sitting at her booth where she was working. Amanda pulled big tips from her job—and so did Frank. They both longed to sing. And, the customers could sense the love in it.

Amanda slept in on Saturday. Frank knew that she wasn't feeling well. She tossed and turned during the night.

"Amanda, I'm driving you to the doctor. No worries. It's just a checkup" said Frank.

"OK" said Amanda. Amanda told Manny who made his own breakfast of dry cereal and milk until she got back to the apartment to cook that Frank was taking her to the doctor's for a checkup.

"No worries" said Amanda.

"OK, I love you" said Manny hugging Amanda goodbye.

Amanda came out of the doctor's office looking pale. Frank took her hand as they walked to the car.

Amanda began crying as Frank turned on the car motor.

"So, what did the doctor say?" said Frank.

"He said that I am pregnant. I am probably 2 or 3 months along. It probably is Ralph's baby" said Amanda putting her head on his shoulder.

"So, what is so terrible about that?" said Frank.

"You probably don't want to marry me with another man's baby in my belly" said Amanda crying.

Frank sighed. "Amanda, will you marry me?" said Frank. "Yes" said Amanda, just amazed that Frank still wanted her.

"OK. Then, let's go tell Manny the good news" said Frank.

"I love you, Frank" said Amanda.

"I love you, too" said Frank as they drove away to the apartment.

"Manny will be happy" said Amanda half way there.

"I know that he will. And, I'm going to be a dad" said Frank smiling.

God how I love this man thought Amanda. I love you too Ralph, my dear husband in heaven thought Amanda.

Amanda would have to call her parents and Leo—and all her friends back home with the "good news" about the baby and her new husband, Frank. They would be so happy for her and her new family. Surprised since they thought that she was only here for a singing career but, God worked His miracle in her.

# Chapter 17

Amanda's hands shook as she dialed the phone to her dad's cell phone. He would know that something was up because she never called him in the middle of the day. This was in the shank of the work day. He probably was out in the farm field working or in the barn. Rarely was he indoors in the farm house during the day except in the winter time when it was snowing.

Amanda could tell that her father had picked up his cell phone to answer the ring. "Hi, dad. It's Amanda" said Amanda.

"Hi, Amanda" said Tom.

"Well, I'm calling to tell you some news. I hope that you take it in the right way" said Amanda.

"I'll try but, I can't promise anything until I hear what you have to say. I am your dad, you know" said Tom.

"I know that you're my dad. That's why I'm calling you. I need your support more than ever before" said Amanda.

"Now, you're scaring me" said Tom.

"Dad, I have to tell you this. I went to the doctor the other day because I wasn't feeling well. He said that I am pregnant. He said that I am probably 2 to 3 months along. Dad, it's Ralph's baby. Dad? Did you understand what I am saying?" said Amanda.

"So, when are you coming home? You have to come home so that me and your mother can help you during this pregnancy. And, we would like to be around to help you raise this kid. We don't want you to have to do this yourself " said Tom.

"Dad. I love you for saying what you have said. But, there is more. I met a man. His name is Frank, Dad. I never thought this would happen to me after Ralph" said Amanda.

"But, he knows about the baby. I almost thought that I was going to lose him when he found out about the baby. But, he wants to marry me and be the father to this baby. I think that you will like him" said Amanda.

"Well, that is a lot to lay on your ol' dad. But, I'm happy about the baby and this man named Frank" said Tom.

"Thank God. I want everyone to love each other like family. It's important to me" said Amanda.

"I understand. We will want to have the wedding here. And, we will want to have some kind of wedding and baby shower here, too. I will tell your mother. You will have to give me some idea of when you'll be coming home first" said Tom.

"I don't know about dates yet since everything happened so quickly" said Amanda.

"So, when will I be meeting my future son-in-law?" said Tom.

"I don't know yet. But, he is standing right here if you want to say hello to him. Here" said Amanda giving the phone to Frank.

"Hello. This is Frank" said Frank.

"Hello, son. I hear that you are planning on marrying my daughter, Amanda. And, you have a baby on the way" said Tom.

"Yes, sir" said Frank.

"You can call me dad or Tom since we are going to be family and all" said Tom.

"Thank you, dad" said Frank with Amanda smiling in the background.

"Well, take care of Amanda and the baby. I already told Amanda that we will have the wedding here and have a wedding and baby shower of some kind here, too. I will have to tell Carolyn. Carolyn is Amanda's mother. She will be thrilled. Do you know if it's a girl or boy, yet?" said Tom.

"No. Not yet" said Frank.

"Well, put Amanda back on the phone" said Tom.

Frank handed Amanda the phone again. "Amanda, I want you to consider moving back to Indiana with that baby and your new husband there. We need you home more than ever to help raise that baby of yours" said Tom.

"This family has been through too much with Ralph passing like he did—and, Tommy being gone for such a long time" said Tom. Amanda could hear her father crying on the phone. Her father never cried.

"I will try. We'll have to stay here for awhile. And, then I will let you know. OK, dad?" said Amanda.

"OK" said Tom brightening up.

"I love you, dad" said Amanda.

"I love you, too. But, let me get off the phone to tell your mother the news. OK?" said Tom.

"OK" said Amanda hanging up the phone.

"Your dad seems nice" said Frank.

"He is. He took the news of the baby and you quite well considering it was so unexpected. Well, I have to call Leo and everybody else with the news. I haven't even gotten around to telling dad about Uncle Manny or Mike or anything. They just think that I'm a big star and all here in Las Vegas. I didn't tell them anything different so that they wouldn't worry about me" said Amanda.

"Of course. But, you are a star to me, Amanda" said Frank.

"Thank you. I appreciate that" said Amanda hugging Frank.

"Everybody needs to know about our wedding and the baby that is close to you. I'm going to have to do the same thing with my folks and all, darlin'" said Frank.

"My dad wants us to move back permanently to Indiana. We have to consider it if we think it would be best for the baby—and us. It certainly would be best for my parents and Leo. But, I can't leave Manny behind. He would have to come with us. And, I don't know what to do about Mike, yet. He is very attached to me like his own daughter" said Amanda.

"Well, we have some time to make plans. It's early in your pregnancy" said Frank.

"That's true. Well, let me get these calls behind me. I'm sure that you need to do the same with your parents. They will have to come to the wedding. And, you probably have some others that you want to invite" said Amanda.

"I do" said Frank holding his cell phone in his hand getting ready to dial.

Amanda planned a special meal for Manny. It was raining outside heavy which was rare for Las Vegas. But, it was a good time to eat indoors at the kitchen table together. And, the oven being on would only take any chill out of the air. Amanda knew Manny's favorite food: pizza. It was Frank's favorite as well. So, Amanda decided to make her own pizza. She brought out her recipe:

HOMEMADE PIZZA

## Ingredients

Frozen pizza dough
Pizza spice
Tomato paste
Pepperoni slices
Mozzarella cheese, shredded

## Directions

Preheat oven at 375 degrees for 10 minutes. Put one slice of frozen pizza dough on an aluminum tray to pre-bake according to directions on package or until lightly browned. Remove from oven. Using a spoon, spread a light to medium layer of tomato paste over the surface of the pizza dough. Then, sprinkle over it, pizza spice for taste. Then, sprinkle the cheese on top of this as much as you like. Then, on top of this, lay pepperoni slices that touch each other over the entire surface of the pizza. Put in the oven until the cheese is entirely melted and the pepperoni is hot to the touch. Take out of the oven. Cut into slices which is usually 6 to 8 slices. Serve hot.

Amanda put the slices of hot pizza in the middle of the kitchen table for everyone to serve themselves. Frank was busy eating while his food was still hot. He knew Amanda and he had a lot of things to take care of now with maintaining their home life—and the wedding—and the baby coming and all.

"This is delicious. It's my favorite thing to eat" said Manny.

"I know. I made it on purpose for you. I have something to tell you. I don't know everything that is going to happen" said Amanda.

"But, you remember when I was sick recently and went to the doctor. It turns out that I wasn't sick exactly. The doctor said that I am pregnant. Probably 2 to 3 months along. Ralph is the father. I told my folks tonight. They took it well. Frank and I are going to get married and raise the baby together" said Amanda.

"Well, congratulations. This is good news indeed" said Manny hugging Amanda and Frank.

"Wait. There is more. My parents want me to move back home permanently to Indiana to raise the baby there and to bring Frank, too. They want us to have the wedding in Indiana. And, they plan a shower there with all my friends and family there" said Amanda.

"I am going to really miss you, Amanda. But, you have to do what's best for you and your new family" said Manny with a tear rolling down his left cheek.

"This is true. But, if I go, I'm not leaving you here by yourself. You'll have to come with us. You'll be living with Frank and me and the baby. OK?" said Amanda.

"OK. I don't care where I go as long as I am with you" said Uncle Manny wiping his tear from his cheek.

"We've got things to do. And, we have plans to make. We don't have everything set. But, I thought that you have a right to know since it's your life, too" said Amanda.

"Thanks. I love you, too" said Manny.

"I love you, too. You will always be my Uncle Manny" said Amanda kissing his cheek. Manny smiled.

"Let me run down the hall to tell Emily the news. OK?" said Manny.

"OK" said Amanda.

Manny left the apartment. A few minutes later, Emily came bursting in the door. "Darling, congratulations. I heard the good news. I told Manny that I will provide the wedding dress for you and all the accessories from my own shop. It's on me: for the wedding party" said Emily hugging Amanda.

"This is so generous of you" said Amanda feeling so grateful. Frank stood behind her smiling.

"Anything for Manny's dear Amanda" said Emily hugging Amanda again.

"Again, thank you so much" said Amanda kissing Emily on the cheek.

"You will have to come for a fitting. I will make you a special dress just for you. It will be beautiful just like you" said Emily squeezing Amanda's hand.

"I'm sure that it will. I will look forward to it" said Amanda.

"We are having the wedding in Indiana with my parents. That's what they want. You are invited to the wedding, of course. I don't know the dates yet" said Amanda.

Emily put her hands on her cheeks. "I haven't been on a trip in years—not since before my sweet Henry passed on. I will be there darling. Just let me know when" said Emily.

"I will. And, congratulations on the baby, too. Auntie Emily wants to kiss the baby's cheeks all over and hug the little angel" said Emily.

"I am sure that the baby will love you. I know it will" said Amanda.

"Thank you, darling. You are so dear" said Emily grabbing a tissue to dry the corner of her eye. Manny showed Emily to the door. He was pleased with his friend, Emily and what she was doing for Amanda.

After he closed the door, he turned to Amanda and said: "Well?"

"It's just fantastic. Just fantastic. I'm going to have the most beautiful wedding on earth. And, I will have a sweet doting auntie for the baby to boot" said Amanda.

"Well, you deserve it" said Manny.

"I love you, Uncle Manny" said Amanda.

"I love you, too" said Manny hugging each other.

Manny went to the porch to take in the evening air. He loved looking at the single tree that stood in front of the shop and the balcony porch. Life at his old apartment manager job seemed far behind him. He had a true family now with Amanda and Frank and the baby. He was a happy man.

Mike took the news well about Amanda and Frank and the baby. He wanted to be the dad to the new family. Tom wanted to be called "uncle" when the baby was born. Amanda invited both to the wedding in Indiana. She told them that she didn't have the dates yet. She didn't want to tell them that she might move back permanently to Indiana because she didn't want to break their heart. And, she didn't know for sure if she was going yet.

"Better to spare them from unnecessary grief" said Amanda. Frank agreed.

"They are dear people" said Frank. Amanda nodded as she sat back in the chair at the hotel where Tom worked. She had brought Frank with her for support and to introduce him to Mike.

Tom joined them for dinner. "I hope that you don't mind but, I'm famished. And, they have such great food" said Tom.

"Of course not" said Amanda.

"Well, things went pretty well. Don't you think so?" said Amanda as she headed for the car with Frank. Frank nodded holding Amanda's hand as they walked.

Frank decided that Amanda and he should work at the restaurant for a month or so at least to save up the money for the baby and other expenses such as if they were moving. Amanda agreed. She wasn't showing yet and probably wouldn't for awhile under the hoop skirt she was wearing.

"That skirt would make a great square dance skirt, you know" said Frank.

"Yes, it would" said Amanda.

When Frank got paid on Friday, he took Amanda to the jeweler's to purchase an engagement ring and their wedding bands. Amanda chose—matching wedding bands. They were made of gold. The engagement ring matched the wedding bands. It had three imbedded diamonds.

"It's a symbol of you, me, and the baby because there will be three of us in the family" said Frank.

"I love it" said Amanda kissing Frank in front of the jeweler.

"Don't mind me. I see this all the time" said the jeweler putting his hands up.

"Amanda, I want you to wear your engagement ring now. You are an engaged woman" said Frank taking the ring out of the box. Amanda, for the first time, tried to remove her engagement ring from Ralph. She couldn't. Her fingers must have swelled.

"That's OK. Leave it on. It's only right since he is the father of our baby, you know" said Frank.

Frank slipped the 3 diamond ring on her left wedding ring finger. "It's beautiful" said Amanda.

"Just like you. Come on. Let's go home" said Frank smiling as they made their way toward the car.

Amanda sat through many fittings of her custom made wedding dress. "It has to be loose enough at the waist to accommodate the baby no matter how large you are then and still be fashionable yet" said Emily.

"Yes" said Amanda standing in front of Emily wearing the wedding dress that was filled with straight pins at this point while Emily was still designing it.

"Don't worry. It will be beautiful when we are done. It always is. I will need the dimensions of everyone in the wedding party including the men. I will take care of everything. OK?" said Emily.

"OK" said Amanda still smiling.

"That will be it for today. Let me sew this. And, you can re-try it on then. And then, we'll select together the sequins and the beading. OK?" said Emily kissing Amanda's cheek and touching the other with her hand.

"OK" said Amanda as she slipped out of the dress and wrapped herself in a robe as she headed down the hall to her apartment.

Amanda made a list of those in her wedding party for Emily for the wedding since she was designing the clothing:

1. Amanda and Frank
2. Carolyn and Tom, her parents
3. Uncle Manny
4. Brian Goldman, her old boss
5. Mike and Tom
6. Jerry (the "flower girl—bridesmaid")
7. Sarah, her bridesmaid and her husband, John
8. Leo
9. John, the farm hand (the ring bearer)
10. Frank's parents
11. Emily

Two days later: Amanda sat with Emily at her dining room table. She handed her the list of those in the wedding party. "Everything must be matching but, flexible to fit all possible needs. Yes?" said Emily.

"Yes" said Amanda.

Emily looked at her list of people in the wedding party. "I see that there are eleven possible men. I will need the measurements of what they wear for a long-sleeved shirt is all. They can rent a tuxedo. But, their shirts will at least be matching. And, I see besides yourself that there are possibly 4 women in your wedding party. I will need their measurements around the waist and the bosom is all. Now, get that for me as soon as you can. OK?" said Emily.

"OK" said Amanda. Amanda hugged Emily goodbye and headed for the apartment to write to her family and friends so that they would send her back their measurements for the wedding ASAP.

Mike held a shower at the hotel for Amanda and Frank. Tom, Mike's brother, invited the staff to come. The room was packed. It was a catered affair planned by Tom who was excited about the wedding and the baby. He had passed around a list of what people might buy for gifts and circulated it around the hotel so there wouldn't be duplicate gifts.

"It's a combination baby—wedding shower. Great idea. Isn't it?" said Tom as the gifts piled up on the long linen table against the wall.

"I really appreciate this" said Amanda hugging Tom. Tom hugged back and smiled.

"This food didn't cost me a dime. I have a friend who I've given so many free rides in my cab over the years who owns a catering company. It's free advertising for him every time he gets his name out here. He owes me. That's how things work around here. Tom, my brother, was a big help on selection of the food. Everybody seems to be enjoying themselves" said Mike.

"Yes, they do. I so appreciate this Mike" said Amanda.

"Well, I love you like my own daughter" said Mike squeezing her hand.


"Well, it's good that we have the car to bring home our shower gifts. We will need to send out thank you cards for each gift after we open them up at home. Manny will be surprised how many presents we have. People were really generous" said Frank.

"Mike and Tom know how to put on a good show for the guests. They appreciated the invite and the chance to wish us well. They did it for Mike and Tom because they were good friends with them. We'll need these gifts for ourselves and the baby" said Amanda.

"Mike and Tom are really nice people" said Frank. "Yes, they are. I really love them" said Amanda as they drove closer and closer to the apartment.

Frank carried up the gifts with Amanda up the stairs to the apartment. They stacked them on the dresser in the bedroom next to the desk. On the desk sat a stack of wedding invitations already with postage stamps on them.

"Once we know the date of our wedding and where it is taking place, we can send out our wedding invitations and put them in the mail" said Amanda.

Frank put his arms around Amanda. He was standing behind her. He put his hand on her belly. "I look forward to our marriage and our baby, darlin'" said Frank.

"Me, too" said Amanda putting her hand on his.

"Let's show Manny our gifts in the morning when we open them" said Frank.

Frank grabbed Amanda's hand softly. He walked with her to the porch to look at the stars together as they both loved to do. Amanda loved resting her head on his shoulder while he rested and reflected on life.

He will be such a good husband and father thought Amanda. And, while she still missed Ralph dearly, she knew she had a special and dear man to be her husband and father to her baby. "Thank you, God. I hope you are seeing all of this from heaven, Ralph. I still love you, you know. And, I love 'my' Frank, too" said Amanda softly. She had never called him hers before. It felt good. She closed her eyes falling asleep as Frank sat in the glider with her on that starry night.

Amanda kissed Manny's cheek when she got in the door. Why don't you two sit on the porch for a while. I'll bring out supper. I need to write something that is wedding related to someone I am inviting to the wedding. I'll be out in a minute.

Amanda sat at the desk in her bedroom:

Dear Brian,

I have news about your cousin, Manny Coleman that I want to share with you. And, I have news about me.

First of all, I want to thank you for trying to help me with my music career and introducing me to Manny. But, Manny didn't want to tell you himself. He didn't want you to think bad of him. But, he isn't a big talent agent at all. He worked here as an apartment manager instead. He tried for that job but, this is what he ended up with. And, he didn't want to tell you at all.

But, he is a good man. And when he found out that you sent me, he invited me into his home. He let me stay in his spare bedroom for free until I got on my feet. And, he helped me get a job.

Manny is living with me now. He suffered a mild heart attack and after many years of working there, had to quit that job. Manny has been good to me through thick and thin. And, I love him as family now. I found out recently that I'm pregnant. It is Ralph's baby. Too bad in many ways that Ralph passed away without knowing.

But, I fell in love here with a good man named Frank—even though I never thought I would love anyone again. He knows about the baby. He had asked me before I knew about the baby to marry him. I am engaged to him now.

My parents want the wedding in Indiana. Manny will be there. I want you there too. Please be nice to Manny. He loves you. That's all he talked about when I met him. All he talked about was how much he loved you and his childhood with him. You mean the world to him.

We have no dates for the wedding set yet. I will send you an invitation, when I do. Sarah already knows about the wedding and all. I called her. She and her husband will be at the wedding.

I am still living in Las Vegas, NV. My parents want us to move back there. If I do, Manny will be living with me. He is a permanent family member as far as I'm concerned. He was always there for me. I should be there for him.

Well, I'll be seeing you in Indiana soon for the wedding. I will let you know the plans as I know it.

Love,<br>Amanda Miller

Amanda addressed the envelope to Brian Sullivan. She put a stamp on the envelope. She slipped it into her purse. She didn't want Manny to see it. And, then she went to the kitchen to see what she was making for supper.

# Chapter 18

Amanda and Frank decided on an autumn wedding in September since the family farm was especially beautiful with the autumn harvest of the crops in the field. The shimmering leaves of the trees looked like jewels that were orange, red, yellow, and brown in color. The weather was warm enough to hold the reception outdoors.

Amanda's parents planned a big shindig of a wedding with all of their farmer friends and the family. Her mother did all the cooking and had to know ahead of time how many guests to expect that she would know the number of plates to have and how much food to make. Once Amanda and Frank knew the date of their wedding, the arrangements were made at the Catholic Church Amanda attended when she was a kid. And, once that was set, Amanda and Frank sent out invitations for their wedding.

It took a good 2 weeks to pack up their belongings from the apartment. Amanda and Frank decided to pack up the car instead of flying. That way, they would have the car with them. And, they didn't want any of their shower gifts to get broke by shipping them. And, with Uncle Manny's health the way it was they didn't want to risk it. Also, with Amanda's pregnancy getting toward the end, she didn't want to risk it traveling by plane if there was any chance at all that she would have a miscarriage or get sick in flight.

Amanda came to realize how precious this baby was. It was her only chance to have Ralph's baby. He wanted kids. There would be no other chance since he had died. It was what she had that was part of him that expressed to her their marital love together—even though they never got to marry. It was their intention that held them together—until his sudden death.

Amanda thought that she would be especially doting on Frank since she wanted this to never happen again. "You never know when you will have your last day with your husband" said Amanda softly under her breath. She thanked God everyday for bringing Frank into her life. She wouldn't have wanted to raise this child without a father. Frank would be a good father and husband. She could feel it in her bones.

Amanda looked forward to her wedding day. Amanda traveled to Indiana with all the gowns and accessories that Emily custom made for the wedding plus the men's custom made matching shirts. They certainly were an expression of love by Emily for Manny and herself. And, it showed the skilled needlework of Emily as she labored late in the night doing the needlework on the gowns and the collars of the men's shirts so that they matched and looked beautiful together. She also had made Amanda's wedding veil as well.

Amanda's dress was made to accommodate for the fact that she was pregnant. There were many layers of veils that began just below the bosom and ended at the ankle. Emily didn't want anything to fit snugly around the waist. The bosom was the centerpiece of the gown with the beading hand sewn into rosettes with very pale green sequins in the background of the flowers that almost looked white. The wedding veil had a circle shape that went around the head like a halo with similar beading to the gown. In the back was a veil that trailed down to her ankles that was edged in white-beaded rosettes and very pale green sequins that looked like the leaves to the flowers.

The other gowns in the wedding party were designed with the same pattern of white beaded rosettes and very pale green sequins to look like leaves to the flowers to match the wedding gown. The men's shirts that Emily designed also had hand sewed beaded white rosettes and very pale green sequins that looked like leaves of the flowers as well all hand sewn into the collars to match beautifully with the gowns. Emily was well known for her beautiful gowns and such she made. You could see that her work was a labor of love. She was an artist of cloth, beads, and sequins thought Amanda. Amanda's eyes sparkled from happiness as she saw her wedding going so beautifully for her special day.

Amanda rolled up to the farm house. She didn't know how she ever tore herself away from it or this part of the country. It was where she was born. It was one of her big loves: Indiana.

There the farmhouse stood where she was raised all white with a wraparound porch for sitting during warm summer days. Upstairs, she could see the window where her bedroom was where she slept as a kid. Behind it, was the apple orchard. To the left of the house, was the barn all bright red with white trim—which was the traditional colors for a barn in this part of the country.

In front of the barn and to the left of it stood the cornfields getting ready to be harvested. Behind the house was the family vegetable garden which was the tradition of farm families here. And, next to that was the family's garage for the car.

Memories poured back into her mind as she drove up to her childhood home with her newly acquired family from Las Vegas. Her parents had never met Frank or Uncle Manny. She wanted everyone to just love each other as much as she did.

Tom and Carolyn heard the car as it approached the driveway. They were familiar with the sounds that passed by the nearby roads since so few cars passed by at all since it was so rural. Tom and Carolyn ran out of the house to hug Amanda, their daughter and to be introduced to their future son-in-law. They had heard so much about Frank. And they were anxious to meet Uncle Manny who had done so much good for their daughter's life in Las Vegas. They were grateful to him in their absence of how he watched over her.

"So this is Frank" said Tom as he shook his hand. Carolyn came forward to hug him. "Welcome to the family" said Carolyn.

"Thank you so much" said Frank smiling.

"And, you must be Uncle Manny. We don't know how to ever thank you for being so good to our daughter, Amanda. We've heard so much about you" said Tom smiling while he shook his hand. Carolyn came forward to hug him. "Welcome to the family" said Carolyn.

"Thank you so much" said Manny smiling.

Neither of Amanda's parents had been to Las Vegas, NV. In fact, they never stepped foot out of Indiana except for the shores of Lake Michigan where Indiana and Michigan meet. Even so, they knew enough about life to understand that Manny protected their only daughter. They got news from Amanda that he took her in when she first got there with very little money in her pocket to survive. They appreciated that fact.

"Well, I love her like my own" said Manny.

Amanda interrupted. "Mom. Dad. The back of the car and the trunk are filled with our things. We have all our clothing. And, the back seat is stacked with gifts from our shower that Mike and Tom put on for us as I told you about. Also, our wedding outfits that Emily custom designed for the wedding party are sitting in the back seat in boxes. We need to bring them in. I don't want them sitting in the car in the hot sun like that" said Amanda.

"Of course" said Carolyn. And, everyone began grabbing the things in the car and carried them up the stairs to the house. Everything had been carefully packed in boxes for easy travel. The boxes were stacked in the living room for now. "Well, that's done" said Tom.

"Please, thank Emily for the car and all this beautiful clothing for the wedding" said Carolyn.

"You'll be able to thank her yourself. She'll be at the wedding. She is running the dress shop that is under the apartment where I had an apartment. Her apartment is next door. She owns the building" said Amanda.

"She will be taking a flight later to the wedding. I told her that she can stay here on the farm after the wedding. She will be taking a cab from the airport to here" said Amanda.

"Of course, Amanda. We have plenty of extra room in the farmhouse here for guests. We welcome her" said Carolyn.

"And, Tom and Mike—? When are they coming? I want to meet them" said Tom.

"Of course. They will be arriving just before the wedding. They will take a flight here. Tom works in a hotel there near the Strip as a bellhop. His brother, Mike, works as a cab driver at the hotel. There is a lot of tourist trade there. He gets good tips there. They will take a cab here from the airport. I told them both that they can stay here" said Amanda.

"We will look forward to meeting them" said Carolyn sincerely. She loved people and would look forward to having plenty of house guests to visit. Usually, the farm only had the farmhands and dad for company.

"We are going to stay overnight here. Then, tomorrow, we are heading for the feed store so that Frank and Uncle Manny meet Leo. We'll spend the day. And, we'll be back to spend the night tomorrow" said Amanda.

"OK" said Carolyn. Everybody was sitting in the living room by now.

Everyone was anxious to get their "howdies" in with each other thought Amanda. So, the sooner that was done the better.

Amanda woke early. She had promised Leo that she would be at the feed store for breakfast and spend the day with him.

Amanda pulled into the back of the store with the car. Frank talked on the way about perhaps extending the single car garage into a two-car garage to accommodate Amanda's car since he was handy that way. Ralph's car was still in the garage as he left it.

Leo came running out from the back of the store to hug Amanda.

"Amanda, I was beginning to think I would never see you again. It's been lonely here without you" said Leo with a tear running down his cheek.

"Leo. I could never leave you. You are Ralph's only cousin. You are so dear to me. You were there when I needed you to help me run the store" said Amanda kissing Leo on the cheek.

Frank and Uncle Manny looked on.

"Where's my manners? Frank, this is Leo, Ralph's cousin" said Amanda.

Frank extended his hand to shake Leo's hand. "It's so nice to finally meet you" said Leo.

"Likewise" said Frank.

"And, Uncle Manny, this is Leo, Ralph's only cousin" said Amanda.

"It's so nice to finally meet you" said Leo. Uncle Manny hugged Leo. Amanda smiled.

Amanda looked around the backyard. The tomato bushes stood in silver hoops heavy with bright red and green tomatoes. The 4 by 4 garden had carrot and onion tops and beet greens waving in the wind ready to harvest. Also, green peppers hung from bushes looking like they were ripe.

"I see that you put straw under the vegetables to keep the soil from getting too dry and to keep the weeds out. Everything looks well kept including the St. Mary's garden that Ralph so loved" said Amanda. She leaned down to put her nose inside a pink rose blossom to smell.

"Yes, I came out here every day to sit in the garden by St. Mary like Ralph must have done to pray. And, I bring in the ripe vegetables, too from the garden. We have a few green tomatoes now getting ripe on the window sill upstairs in the kitchen. The garden has kept me busy and so has running the feed store while you were gone" said Leo.

"Well, I'm so grateful for all your help" said Amanda.

"We're family" said Leo.

"Well, let's go in. I want to give Frank and Uncle Manny a tour of the place" said Amanda.

She went through the closed feed store which was also sold hardware. Amanda showed Frank and Uncle Manny what they sold here. Then, they headed upstairs which was the most important to Amanda since she planned to live here with her family.

The wedding dress was still on the hook of the bedroom door that was to be for when she married Ralph as she had left it. "I didn't want to touch anything in the bedroom of yours and Ralph" said Leo.

"It's fine" said Amanda.

Then Amanda said to Uncle Manny and Frank: "This will be our bedroom. And, we can put the baby's crib in here with us for awhile. Leo's bedroom is next to ours. Down here next to Leo's is where Manny's bedroom will be. Ralph used it as an office. We'll put the storage cabinets downstairs in the storage room. And, we'll ask dad to help convert the living room into partly the baby's bedroom when the baby gets older. The room is huge so that we won't miss dividing it in half. And, there are two doors to this room. So, it won't be too hard to make it into 2 rooms. I want everyone to be living on one floor as one family. I kind of had it planned out in my mind before we came here. Everyone happy?" said Amanda.

"It seems we are. But, how about that breakfast? I've heard so much about it on the way here" said Frank.

Leo escorted everyone to the kitchen. Leo already had the table set for his guests. He was happy to have family live with him. He wasn't as handy as Amanda at the stove. But, he insisted on cooking up pork sausage links; scrambled eggs; and toast with strawberry jam for his guests. He managed to brew a strong tasting cup of coffee. He poured orange juice in everyone's juice glass.

"This is beautiful" said Amanda to Leo as he put breakfast on the table.

"Thank you Amanda," said Leo.

Then Frank said: "Let's say grace before we eat." He bowed his head and said:

Heavenly Father, thank you for this beautiful breakfast that Leo made for us this morning. And, thank you for this new family of ours. We thank you, heavenly Father, for each family member here including our baby. And, we thank you for this home and the wonderful store downstairs to help keep this roof over our head. We thank you for our blessings and for many years to come. Amen.


"Thank you for that beautiful prayer. I love you" said Amanda.

"I love you, too darlin'" said Frank.

"Well, let's dig in before everything gets cold" said Uncle Manny. He loved to eat. This new family sat together long after breakfast over a cup of coffee getting to know each other. Then, Amanda's new family, just before sunset, including Leo, headed back to the farm to take in the wedding festivities.

Mike and Tom arrived first to the farm by cab. The neighbors from the farms must have noticed a big yellow cab kicking up dust on the road as it traveled down miles and miles of farm fields to where Amanda was. Those friendly with the Millers over the years, would be coming to the farm for the festivities anyway and were invited to the church for the wedding.

Amanda ran out of the farm house to greet the cab. "You're here. You're actually here" said Amanda hugging first Mike, and then Tom. Tom,

Amanda's father, came out of the house to grab the suitcases.

"Come inside. I'll introduce you to my parents" said Amanda.

"Some spread you have here" said Mike looking around as he climbed the stairs to the farmhouse.

"Yes, it's quite a handful. A lot of work running a farm. But, it's been in the family for years. I grew up here" said Amanda walking up the steps to the farm house with Tom, Mike's brother already at the top of the steps waiting for his brother, Mike.

Mike and Tom were here a few days earlier than expected. It turns out that Tom took a leave of absence from work. He had developed a heel spur in one of his feet from working too many double shifts at the hotel.

And, Mike had put the cab in "dry dock" as he called it until he returned back to his job. They were here for the wedding and some R&R.

Carolyn was delighted to meet both Mike and Tom since they were so kind and nice thought Carolyn.

"Good folk" she called them to Amanda's delight to hear this from her mother.

Mike and Tom took to taking long walks at night with Amanda's dad. They sat on the porch outdoors enjoying the still warm autumn air. Frank and Amanda retired upstairs to Amanda's childhood bedroom. Leo slept in Tommy's old bedroom upstairs with Uncle Manny using the roll-away bed.

One such evening, Mike and Tom mentioned to Tom, Amanda's father, how much they enjoyed their stay here. "I hate to even leave. My brother feels the same. This is the life. The life we had is OK. It did good by us and all. But, to live and work on a real farm is something else. I can see a lot of love in the farm fields you tend. They are immaculately groomed and so is this farmhouse. What a farm!" said Mike.

"The corn is about to harvest and so are the apples. It's something else. I could live here forever.—So could Tom, my brother. The fresh air alone" said Mike.

Tom sat in his usual rocker by the front door as the 2 men sat on the top of the steps looking at Tom. Finally, he spoke. "You two can stay here on the farm until the end of time if you like it so much here. We've got plenty of room. We need the help" said Tom.

"I couldn't impose on you. We wouldn't want to uproot ourselves just to find out that we are in the way. And, you were just being polite. But, we appreciate...truly the offer. And, we love you for it.

We'll just go back home after the wedding like we planned" said Mike.

"I thought you said you liked it here. In fact, I thought that you said you loved it here and never wanted to leave" said Tom.

"I do love it here. And, my brother Tom loves it here too. But, we're not family so we can't intrude. But, we thank you all the same" said Mike.

"If the issue is that you're not family, we'll take care of that right quick. My only son has run off to the military. He has been gone for years now. Probably had his fill of the farm. I have only one loyal farm hand that lives in the attic upstairs bedroom. He has for years. I need strong sons who will help me run this farm. I am tired of begging farmhands to help me out. If you are willing to live here to make this your home, I am willing to adopt you both as my sons that will live and work on this farm. My wife could only bless me with one son. What do you say? Deal?" said Tom looking straight into Mike and Tom's eyes with all sincerely he could muster.

"What do you say?" said Tom looking longingly into Mike's eyes.

Mike looked at his brother Tom's face. Then, he stood up directly in front of Tom, Amanda's father. He put out his hand to shake it. "Deal" said Mike.

Then, Tom, Mike's brother stood up in front of Tom, Amanda's father to put out his hand to shake it. "Deal" said Tom.

"Welcome to the family, sons. We'll tell Amanda tomorrow in the morning. I think that she will be pleased. I'll call my attorney tomorrow so that we can do this formal-like" said Tom hugging his new sons. He was a happy man.

The three men decided to go to their bedroom to retire for the night. They wanted to "Thank God" for their new family.

In the morning, Tom told his daughter the news about Mike and Tom. "Dad, you have made me so happy bringing Mike and Tom into the family" said Amanda.

"Simmer down, Amanda" said Tom.

"I can't. I can't believe it. This makes me so happy" said Amanda.

Tom hugged his daughter, Amanda. "We are going to adopt Mike and Tom as my sons today. They will live here permanently on the farm like family and help out on the farm" said Tom.

"You know what, dad? I want to bring Leo and Uncle Manny, too, so that they are adopted into the family so that they always have a home either at the feed store or the farm. And, please adopt

John, the farmhand as your son, too. He has no family but, us. OK?" pleaded Amanda.

"OK. Bring them along. I love a large family" said Tom.

And so they did. Everyone signed the official paperwork in the attorney's office making them legally members of the Miller family. Everyone hugged. And, they smiled together. Amanda was elated. She didn't want to leave any of her loved ones behind.

It was a happy day for the Miller family. Carolyn was so pleased. She would have the large family that she always dreamed of having.


Dad and his sons came by the feed store to help carry down the file cabinets upstairs from Ralph's old office to the storage room downstairs. He laid down a new carpet on the floor. Tom and Mike helped Amanda's father, Tom to carry up a bed and dresser for the room that they brought from the farm that they didn't need for Uncle Manny's room. Now, he had his new bedroom even though he was staying overnight on the farm until after the wedding.

Manny was pleased to have his own bedroom. And, outside his window was a beautiful tree with autumn leaves for him to look at while resting. He loved trees. He would ask Amanda for a nice rocking chair to sit by the window for hours looking at "his" tree. Just beautiful he thought.

Before leaving, Amanda's father headed for the living room. "The room is huge. Big enough to be a great room" said Tom.

"I know. And, it has 2 door openings. I want to convert half this room into the baby's bedroom" said Amanda.

Tom looked at the peeling wallpaper. "We'll get rid of this old wallpaper while you are at the farm. We'll paint the walls. We don't want you breathing in paint fumes while you are pregnant," said Tom.

"Thanks, dad" said Amanda hugging her father.

He began peeling away the wallpaper with his hand. It was peeling off by itself. Under it was a sliding door on both sides of the wall. Amanda knew about the sliding door from Ralph. He lifted the carpet.

"Well, I'll be. There is a track for these doors on the floor. The carpet had hid this. We can pull these doors shut to divide this room in half. That's why this room had 2 doors. When we are through, the baby's bedroom will be beautiful. My sons will help me" said Tom beaming. Mike and Tom were getting used to the sound of that—and feeling so happy about it.

"I'm so grateful things are turning out all the way around. I will stay on the farm until you are through painting. And, Leo can stay overnight until the painting is done so that he doesn't have to be smelling any paint fumes either until everything is aired out and dried" said Amanda.

Amanda locked up the feed store and took off with her family to the farm. Before leaving, she put a sign on the front door: "Closed for a wedding." She liked the sign. It pleased her to look at it. Frank saw it and just smiled. He loved his little Amanda so much.

The next day, with Tom, Amanda's father and Mike and Tom, Mike's brother, working on the great room, the baby's bedroom was getting completed. Mostly, Tom stayed on the farm while his 2 sons stripped off the old wallpaper. He had the farm to run. The 2 men stripped off the old wallpaper; washed and primed the walls; and then painted it. It took several applications that had to dry in between layers. Finally, the old carpet was stripped revealing a wood floor, which polished up to a beautiful shiny surface. Just beautiful, they thought!

The next day, Amanda decided with Frank to go to an obstetrician. "We need a doctor to deliver the baby" said Amanda.

"Good idea" said Tom, Amanda's father.

So, Frank and her took off for the doctor. The doctor ran tests on Amanda. He told her what her due date was. He also let her know the news: It's a girl! Amanda and Frank were thrilled.

As they drove home, they talked together. "We have to have a name for the baby" said Frank.

"I know. I want to name the baby 'Angel' if that's OK with you. I believe in my heart that it's a special baby. So, it should have a special name. Angel seems the most perfect name for this little girl of ours" said Amanda.

Frank was driving these days. She was starting to get big. "I love the name" said Frank.

"Good. We'll have to tell dad and mom when we get home" said Amanda.

Amanda come running up the stairs with Frank as soon as she got home to her parents to tell her parents about her visit to the doctor's office. "It's a girl. We are going to name her 'Angel' " said Amanda with Frank smiling as she spoke.

"What great news! Don't you agree?" said Carolyn as she hugged her husband, Tom.

"Yes, we are truly blessed. And, we are going to be grandparents for the very first time" said Tom hugging his wife Carolyn back. Then, Carolyn and her husband, Tom hugged Amanda and Frank. They were a happy family.

The news of the baby girl, Angel was also told to Mike and his brother Tom to their delight of hearing this. The next day, they went to Angel's bedroom to paint the walls pastel pink since Amanda was having a girl. Then, Mike and Tom hand painted together over that an angel on the wall to represent the name Amanda chose for the baby: Angel.

Tom drove Amanda to the apartment to show her the baby's room once the paint dried. Everyone agreed that it was beautiful. She opened the door to a 9x12 bedroom where the angel loomed over it with a white flowing gown and gold tipped wings that sparkled with metallic flecks.

"I can't believe how beautiful this room is. Angel will love this her grandpa and her two uncles Mike and Tom made for her. Just love it" said Amanda hugging her father. She looked forward at the farm what would take place at her shower.

The guests raved about Carolyn's cooking "You should write a cookbook. You should sell your jellies and juice in stores. It's so good" said guests at Amanda's baby-wedding shower. Carolyn just nodded smiling. Tom was standing next to her helping her serve her guests.

"No. You really should write a cookbook and sell your juice and jellies in stores. The people love it. You'll make a lot of money that will help the farm. I will help you in any way I can" said Frank.

And that started Carolyn's career as a cookbook writer and best seller in all the major book stores. She became a local celebrity in her own right that people stopped in the supermarket for help to make their own recipes.

And, it began the start of the Miller Farm Food Company. The local supermarkets were more than willing to sell what juice got bottled in the local factory under their label. They also sold their apple jelly as well. It brought extra income to the family which delighted Tom which was always his preoccupation to get as much income from the farm as he could.

Now, on the opposite side of the serving table was another similar table for the gifts the guests brought for Amanda and Frank and the baby. What Amanda needed was registered at the local department store. Brian bought Amanda a crib that could be converted later into a youth bed. Sarah and John bought Amanda a matching dresser for the baby. Emily bought a rocking chair for Amanda to rock the baby.

And so forth and so on.

Most of the basics for housekeeping were already there in the apartment since Ralph had the apartment already furnished before she had met him. The only thing that she knew that she needed was a new set of plates and glasses; bedding; and towels plus some wash cloths for the bathroom since her family had expanded in size recently. These things her guests generously saw that she got as wedding gifts.

The wedding ceremony was set for the morning at the Catholic Church. Emily also was part of the wedding party for the wedding. She had designed her own dress to match the others in the wedding party.

The day was sunny when Amanda and Frank as well as her guests arrived for the wedding. Amanda wanted it to be a special day for her. Mike and his brother, Tom was to be on both ends of her veil carrying it to the altar. Uncle Manny and Leo were to be the attendants who saw the guests to their seats. Manny was on one side of the aisle. Leo was on the other side of the aisle. John, who lived on the farm, carried the wedding rings down the aisle on a satin pillow. Then Sarah, the bridesmaid, followed John down the aisle, holding a bouquet of flowers matching Amanda's bouquet. Jerry was the "flower girl/bridesmaid" throwing white rose petals on the white sheet banner that lay over the carpet from the door to the altar. Also, Jerry wore a gold pin on his lapel that said: "Bridesmaid" and wore a sequin-beaded scarf that matched Sarah's dress, that was waiting for him at the church. Emily sat in the front pew, enjoying her special role as aunt to Amanda's baby and "dear" family member. And, Amanda's mother and father gave her away at the altar. They stood side by side. Amanda had been through so much to finally get married that she wanted both of them there at the altar with her.

Amanda didn't forget Ralph when she said "I do" to her husband. Her hand touched her belly. She thought of her love for Ralph as she committed herself to Frank. Frank understood that she loved Ralph to the end of her life—and even in heaven if she could see him there. Ralph would always be the father of her little girl. But, so would Frank, her husband.

She vowed to love him for the rest of her life as her husband and in heaven if God allowed her too as well. Frank understood this. He was a good man. He would be a good husband and father to her baby.

Frank said "I do." And, John handed to their Catholic priest the couples' wedding rings for them to place on each others' wedding ring fingers as they said their wedding vows to each other.

Then, Amanda and Frank kissed each other in front of the wedding guests. They were now man and wife. Photographs flashed from guests and the photographer that Brian had paid for the newlyweds. He also paid for most of the wedding that Emily hadn't provided. He was a much loved family member.

Amanda and Frank headed out the back of the door of the church. The guests followed grabbing a handful of bird seed to throw at the newly wedded couple from the two silver bowls at the end of the church to wish them well.

The wedding car was driven by a limo driver provided by Brian. The rest of the guests followed including the Catholic priest who was invited to the reception. He liked good food and "make jolly" at such a happy event as this like everyone else. He was a welcome guest.

The tables and chairs from the shower were still in place from the shower the day before. Carolyn and Tom escorted the guests to their seats at the table. The reception was held outdoors on the Miller Farm in the barn that was all scrubbed for the occasion. It was a favorite place for this kind of thing on the farm because of the ample room it offered.

Mike and Tom, his brother carried out the food for the guests from the kitchen. There were two baked hams with baked pineapple and maraschino cherries on it. There was hot rolls and butter. There were two bowls of Carolyn's farm apples for the guests. There were also two freshly baked sweet potato casseroles. Carolyn looked at her recipe.

## SWEET POTATO CASSEROLE

### Ingredients

Six to eight sweet potatoes (since potatoes vary in size, use as many as needed)
Three tablespoons of butter
Whole or skim milk (add ½ cup at a time or as needed)
One maraschino cherry as a garnish
Cinnamon as a garnish

### Directions

Bake potatoes at 375 degrees in aluminum foil. Wrap individually. Bake potatoes for 1½ hours or until potatoes can easily be pierced with a fork. When this happens, turn off the oven. Put the potatoes on a plate. Get out a knife since you will be removing the potato skins of the potatoes by peeling off the skins with the knife and cutting off the ends off of each potato until what is left is the inside of the sweet potato only. This has to be done when hot from the oven since the skin of sweet potatoes tends to cling tightly to the sweet potato when cool. So, it is easier to do this while the potatoes are hot! Once done, mash the potatoes with a potato masher or fork into each other in the mixing bowl. Add small pieces of butter at a time since the butter will melt that way from the heat of the potatoes. Use as much butter as needed to add sweetness to the sweet potatoes but, use sparingly by adding a little bit at a time to determine this. Now, using an electric mixer, pour in milk into all of the ingredients in the mixing bowl using a little bit of milk at a time so that the thickness of the mixture is as close as can be to what you see with mashed potatoes using white potatoes! Once this is done, you can coat the sides of the casserole dish with a non-stick cooking spray before putting in the ingredients to keep it from sticking to the sides of the dish. Once done, pour the sweet potato mixture into the casserole dish. Now, garnish the sweet potato mixture with cinnamon and place a maraschino cherry in the middle of the casserole as a garnish. And, then place the lid of the casserole dish to keep the casserole warm. Note: Can double the recipe if making two sweet potato casseroles by using twice the ingredients and two casserole dishes instead of one! Can wrap the casserole dish in a clean towel to keep the ingredients warm until ready to serve. Serve while warm.

Also, white baked potatoes covered with foil sat in a silver serving bowl. Brian had a three-tiered wedding cake with white roses and pastel green leaves shipped to the farm. It sat in the center of the table. It said "Congratulations Amanda and Frank." Brian insisted on being seated next to his cousin Manny so that he could let his dear cousin know how much he really loved him which just delighted Amanda to no end. And, she could just see the happiness in her Uncle Manny's eyes which meant so much to her to reunite these two.

Now, Brian supplied the band that played soft love songs in the background. The bride was asked at the reception to have the first dance with her husband, Frank. The guests followed. They danced for hours with everyone laughing, dancing and hugging each other.

Frank put the traditional garter on Amanda's leg which was the tradition with the band playing which to Amanda was supposed to be a sign that she was "sexy." She hoped that she was sexy and remained sexy to Frank forever because forever was how long she wanted this marriage to last with Frank.

Amanda threw out the wedding bouquet to the wedding guests. The Roman Catholic priest caught it inadvertently. "Thanks, Amanda. I'll put this bouquet on the altar at the church. I am sure that the Virgin Mary will love it" said Father Mike. Amanda smiled. She was embarrassed.

"I didn't mean to do that" said Amanda looking at Frank.

"He knows that. But, he loved the bouquet anyway. Better it goes to the Virgin Mary than anyone else anyway" said Frank.

"I love you husband" said Amanda kissing Frank. The guests applauded.

Frank put his hand around his wife's waist. He whispered: "Your dad is driving Leo to the feed store tomorrow morning. He will watch the store for a week. Uncle Manny will stay on the farm. We are going on a honeymoon for a week up north along the shoreline of Lake Michigan. It's late in the season being autumn so I got a great rate on a cottage on the beach for you and me" said Frank.

Amanda and Frank stood by their car Emily had given as a gift. Their suitcase was packed in the back seat. Amanda and Frank kissed her parents cheeks goodbyes. She also kissed Frank's mom and dad goodbye also. So did Frank. She was so glad that they could make the wedding. She knew that she would love them with her whole heart as family to her. They were excited about the baby coming as well.

"Goodbye everyone. We are on our way to our honeymoon. We love you" said Amanda and Frank waving and throwing kisses to everyone as they drove off.

Then, they drove off to Lake Michigan while their wedding guests stayed still at the farm celebrating. "I can't wait to begin our honeymoon. It will be so romantic to spend the week in a cottage on the beach" said Amanda.

"I agree. It should be very secluded this time of year" said Frank as he drove closer and closer to Lake Michigan.

"I love you, husband" said Amanda.

"I love you, too, wife" said Frank.

Amanda thought that a great beginning to her married life. At last, she was a married lady. She put her hand on her belly as Frank drove reminding herself of the baby growing inside of her. "Thank you God" said Amanda softly as she smiled. She was a happy woman.

# Chapter 19

The Christmas tree in the apartment looked especially beautiful to Amanda this year. She had a dinner and gift exchange to go to Christmas day at the farm with her parents and her family there. But, this first Christmas of her daughter, Angel was being spent in her apartment this morning with her husband, Frank.

"You'll have to help Angel open her Christmas presents this year daddy since your little girl isn't even a year old yet" said Amanda kissing Frank.

"More than glad to do that darlin'" said Frank. Leo and Uncle Manny were also there anxious to open their Christmas gifts as well.

"My first Christmas present is meant to be a big surprise to you since it is our first Christmas together. So close your eyes" said Frank.

When Amanda opened her eyes, what was sitting on her lap was a brown colored classical guitar with a red bow on it. It was encased in a black guitar case. "Wow" said Amanda kissing Frank again.

"OK. So, close your eyes now" said Amanda. He did.

Amanda laid her gift on Frank's lap. It was a brown colored acoustical guitar. It had a red bow on it. It was encased in a black guitar case.

"Wow" said Frank kissing Amanda as a thank you to his wife.

Now, Amanda handed Frank one of Angel's Christmas presents. "She is too young yet to know what this is. But, we'll save it for her all the same. But, you can open it up for her now since you are her daddy" said Amanda.

Frank opened up the box to find a children's book called "Angel." "It's a story about a little girl named Angel whose daddy went to heaven. And, mommy met a daddy who was on earth after that to take care of Angel and her mommy who loves her. The proceeds goes to the Ralph Tomlinson Foundation to help orphaned children" said Amanda.

"We will keep this safe on the bookcase until she is old enough to appreciate this" said Frank kissing Amanda.

Amanda handed Frank another box. Frank opened a typed manuscript with the title: "Amanda Goes to Las Vegas."

"I see you finally wrote it" said Frank.

"Yes. It's a book about our life in Las Vegas, NV and here in Indiana. I thought that people would like to know what happened. I want to have it sold in book stores and made into a movie" said Amanda.

"I see that you took my advice with the title of your book: 'Amanda Goes to Las Vegas.' I can see it now in movie theaters everywhere" said Frank. He put his hand in front of him going from left to right indicating what a marquee might read.

"I surely hope that God hears my prayers on this" said Amanda.

"I am sure that he does darlin'" said Frank.

They passed out the rest of the presents to each other and Leo and Uncle Manny. Angel sat in her playpen looking on as her parents showed her clothing and toys bought for her. Leo and Uncle Manny got new clothing for Christmas from Amanda and Frank which they loved getting. They were happy that God blessed them so.

Amanda and Frank spent the rest of the day playing the guitar for each other. They were deeply in love. And, Leo and Uncle Manny were deeply in love with the idea that Amanda and Frank were deeply in love. They were a happy family this Christmas morning—their very first Christmas together.

Frank and Amanda was planning on attending the church bazaar. Tom liked it when his daughter helped out at the church. They are having a bazaar to raise money for the church. Amanda agreed to make the chili to sell by the bowl.

"So how do you plan to make enough chili for at least 100 church goers at the bazaar?" said Frank.

"Well, look at the chili recipe with me" said Amanda.

## CHILI

Ingredients

1 green pepper, chopped.
1 can of tomato pieces (add more if needed for more tomato taste)
1 tablespoon of chili powder (add more for spicier flavor)
1 can of kidney beans (can use 2 cans of beans also)
1-1½ pounds of ground hamburger, cooked
1 yellow onion, minced
1 large can of tomato juice

## Directions

Cook the hamburger, onions, and green pepper together in skillet until hamburger is browned. Stir frequently. Drain and put ingredients in large soup pot. Pour in can of kidney beans including sauce and the can of tomato pieces. Stir ingredients together. Pour tomato juice in enough to cover ingredients and how liquidly you want the chili. Stir together. Pour in one tablespoon of chili powder. Stir together. Cover the pot. Cook over low heat until warm enough to serve. Serves 4.

"So, if this serves 4 people then, I will divide 100 people by 4 servings so that I just need 25 times more of this recipe such as 25 green peppers and 25 yellow onions. And so on and so forth. Correct?" said Amanda.

"Correct" said Frank.

"It's for a good cause. It's my dad's birth church and all. Can we bring some of our CD's that we made in Las Vegas to sell? It's for a fundraiser for the church. And, they are just sitting here in the back of the closet collecting dust as it is. The church can sell them at the bazaar to help out the church" said Amanda.

"Sure. You're going to let me help you with all of this. Correct?" said Frank.

"That's the plan. You know that I always need you" said Amanda kissing Frank's cheek. Frank patted her hand as she spoke.

The crowds were everywhere at the church bazaar. Frank was surprised as to how many people came to the gathering. The minister was pleased. Tom was pleased to help the Reverend that he loved so. Carolyn came along to help.

The bowls of chili with a can of pop and oyster crackers with extra chili powder at the picnic tables sold for $5 a bowl. The chili went fast. So did the CD's that Amanda brought with her to help out the church bazaar. The CD's sold like hot cakes at $15 each. Amanda brought 50 of them that was sitting in the back of the closet in the apartment for nearly a year now.

Amanda's father was pleased with her contribution to help his church that was dear to him. He wasn't one to tell her so. But, it mattered to him.

Amanda and Frank had been busy running back and forth between the feed store and the farm keeping everything going. They loved it. All this love and family fit them well.

The baby, Angel was growing into a charming little toddler who liked to hang on her daddy. Amanda didn't mind that she was a "daddy's girl." In fact, she wouldn't have had it any other way considering what happened to Ralph and her.

"You realize that we made for the Reverend $750 at the church bazaar from selling our CD's that were just sitting in the back of the closet for a year plus the money from selling our chili that sold like hot cakes, also. That was mom's recipe, by the way" said Amanda.

"We did good for the Lord today" said Frank hugging Amanda.

It was starting to become dusk. Amanda and Frank wanted to get back home to the baby. They grabbed their pots and ladle to take home with them. Amanda and Frank hugged Tom and Carolyn goodbye. They wished the Reverend well at his church bazaar.

"We hope that we helped" said Frank to the Reverend as he headed to the car.

Some weeks later, Brian called Amanda on the phone. "You've got to hear this. Some DJ in Indianapolis got his hands on your CD. He is playing it for people driving in to work in the morning. They love it. They can't get enough of it, I want you to know. You are a star. People want you to perform. Calls are coming into the radio station wanting to know more about these two bright stars: Amanda Miller and Frank Lucas. Tell Frank. I'll talk to you again, soon" said Brian.

Amanda was stunned. Somebody from the church bazaar must have given it to the DJ.

Sure enough the DJ tracked Amanda and Frank down. They were invited to the radio station to talk live to the audience. People loved them. "They were an overnight success" said the DJ to the audience on the radio.

The CD's were selling in the stores. People were requesting them. A casino owner called in while Amanda and Frank were at the microphone in the studio. "Will you come to my casino on the Strip in Las Vegas to perform?" said the man.

"We sure will" said Amanda.

"And, thank you, sir" said Frank.

"They just got an invite to perform at the world famous Strip in Las Vegas. Don't you just love this couple? Singing stars and married to each other with a daughter named, Angel. Let's hope that we hear a lot more from them" said to DJ to the audience.

The DJ shook both their hands and thanked them for graciously coming to the studio.

"We should be thanking him, the DJ. He is giving us our music career back" said Frank to Amanda.

"Yes. Isn't God wonderful?" said Amanda.

"He sure is" said Frank holding Amanda's hand to the car. They hurried home to the baby who was with Leo and Uncle Manny.

Emily let Amanda and her new family stay in her old apartment when she and Frank came to perform on the world famous Strip in Las Vegas, NV. Emily hadn't the heart to re-rent the place after Manny had lived there. Emily gave Amanda a dress from the shop to wear at the concert hall. It was for "good luck."

Amanda just looked at it stunned. It was silver, glittery, and long.

"It's my dream dress. I dreamt about it. The very same one" said Amanda to Emily.

"That's how God works, my dear" said Emily patting Amanda's hand.

The front row seats of the concert hall were reserved for Amanda's family: Dad; mom; Uncle Manny; Leo; Jerry; Sarah and John; Brian; John; Emily; Tom and Mike; and their daughter Angel.

Frank was on stage with his wife, Amanda. They stood in front of the microphone.

"Howdy, I am Amanda Miller" said Amanda. The crowd roared. Frank was wearing jeans and a cowboy hat and cowboy boots which were his favorite things to wear. He came to the microphone. "And, I'm Frank Lucas" said Frank. The crowd roared.

"We came to perform for you lovely people. We can hardly believe that we are here but, the

Lord put it in someone's heart for us to be here. We used to live here trying to have a music career. We went back home leaving our music behind us to get married and have a baby. And, just because I wanted to help my dad at a church bazaar by selling my CD's that were sitting in the back of the closet for nearly a year that we recorded here, somebody gave it to a DJ in Indianapolis, IN. Can you believe it?" said Amanda. The crowd roared. The stood up applauding and whistling.

"So we'd better get to work and play some of the songs you've been waiting for" said Frank.

The crowd sat down. The lights to the concert hall dimmed. Everyone was quiet for Amanda and Frank. They were a happy couple performing together. Song after song, the crowd applauded. These were all original songs that Amanda and Frank created. The crowd loved it.

After a standing ovation from the crowd, Amanda said: "Let me introduce you to my daughter, Angel. She is our pride and joy. I wrote a book about Angel and her biological father, Ralph Tomlinson who never met his daughter. He passed away before his daughter was born. My husband Frank is now Angel's daddy. Please. Please. Buy the book for your children and grandchildren. It will mean so much to us. The proceeds of each book sold will go to the Ralph Tomlinson Foundation in honor of Angel's father and to help orphaned children everywhere" said Amanda.

And, my book about my life and my experiences in Las Vegas: "Amanda Goes to Las Vegas" is being sold in all major book stores as well. We hope that you will buy a copy of that for others as well as for yourself. We surely would appreciate it" said Amanda.

"Now, that we have our plugs in, I just want to tell you how grateful we are that you have invited us into your hearts with your love for our music. It means so much to Frank and myself. We just love you for it. And, you are in our hearts as well because we came here to Las Vegas with only one home in our hearts which is where we came from. And, we came back to Las Vegas who invited us 'home' as well. So, now we have two homes. We love you, Las Vegas" said Amanda. The crowds stood up and applauded.

"We hope that you will invite us back often" said Frank waving at the crowd.

"We truly do" said Amanda at the microphone holding Angel in her arms. The lights dimmed. The curtain went down.

Emily returned back to the dress shop. The rest of the family took a flight back to Indiana to resume their usual life.

Sitting on the porch of the farm house after dinner with the entire family there with him, Tom thought about all the good Amanda had done for his life; the family; and the family farm. He had a nice large family of sons to help him run the farm thanks to her. He paid off the mortgage on the farm thanks to the money she gave him from her music career. She gave him Leo and Uncle Manny for the family who were just swell. And, she gave him and his wife a wonderful son-in-law, Frank and a beautiful granddaughter, Angel. I'm really proud of her thought Amanda's father for all she did.

"Amanda, I'm proud of you daughter" said Tom in front of everyone.

"Hearing this from her dad, Amanda's eyes widened. She struggled her whole life trying to get her father to love her as much as a son. He always suffered because Tommy, his only son had left the family farm. He meant the world to him.

Amanda goes berserk. She grabs her hair by both hands. It begins to rain. She runs out in it in the driveway. "My dad is proud of me. Did you hear that world? My dad is proud of me" said Amanda.

Carolyn stands up smiling at her daughter. This is a proud moment for Amanda. She is so happy for her—and the family. She raised a good daughter who brought the family together.

As the sun was setting and thoughts turned to going indoors, everyone noticed a car coming down the road which was rare on this road since it was so rural. It was coming closer and closer to the farm. "I wonder who this could be?" said Tom. Everyone else remained seated.

Just then, the car pulled in down the long driveway to the farmhouse and stopped in front of the farm house. Tom craned his head to see who it was. Out of the car came a man and a pregnant woman.

"My God. It's Tommy" said Tom running down the stairs to greet his only son. He threw his arms around Tommy longingly to hold his child once again to him.

"Dad, I've come home" said Tommy.

"My God. You've returned home to me" said Tom with a tear rolling down his cheek. Carolyn ran down the stairs after Tom to hold her only son in her arms once again, also.

Tommy introduced everyone to his pregnant wife. "My wife, Anne is about to deliver a baby boy very soon" said Tommy.

"My son is going to be a dad" said Tom to everyone. Everyone smiled and hugged each other.

Now, the family was truly reunited. Everyone has finally come home for good to the Miller Farm.

And, life was the way Tom dreamed it was supposed to be. He considered himself blessed.

# About the Author

Nancy Dick is a graduate from Ball State University, in Indiana, with a degree in writing: journalism. And, she has a Bachelors and Masters degree in sociology from BSU as well. She also has a degree in art from Thomas Edison State College in New Jersey, just outside of New York City. She has also been in the publication *Powerlines* of Reverend Robert Schuller. She graduated from high school from a parochial school: Nativity of Our Lord in Michigan. Any religious reference in this book would come from that time and experience. Likewise, she has been an avid gardener since childhood which gave her a wide range of experience with the life of nature and gardening to reference this in this book: Amanda Goes to Las Vegas. She spent many years living in or near farming communities in Indiana where the popular yellow and green John Deere tractor dotted the landscape as farmers there plowed their farm fields.

www.ingramcontent.com/pod-product-compliance
Lightning Source LLC
Chambersburg PA
CBHW030652120726
47905CB00001B/183